VALIANT JOURNEY

John (Jack) Callahan

AuthorHouse™
1663 Liberty Drive
Bloomington, IN 47403
www.authorhouse.com
Phone: 1 (800) 839-8640

Published by AuthorHouse   11/12/2015

ISBN: 978-1-5049-6104-2 (sc)
ISBN: 978-1-5049-6102-8 (hc)
ISBN: 978-1-5049-6103-5 (e)

Library of Congress Control Number: 2015918599

Print information available on the last page.

Any people depicted in stock imagery provided by Thinkstock are models,
and such images are being used for illustrative purposes only.
Certain stock imagery © Thinkstock.

This book is printed on acid-free paper.

Because of the dynamic nature of the Internet, any web addresses or links contained in
this book may have changed since publication and may no longer be valid. The views
expressed in this work are solely those of the author and do not necessarily reflect the
views of the publisher, and the publisher hereby disclaims any responsibility for them.

ALSO BY JOHN (JACK) CALLAHAN

* * * * *

MY SLICE OF LIFE

SUCCESS IN MOTION

LOCKER #12

THEO LOVES ME

THE GENERAL IS MISSING

EMILY

THE PRINCETON CONNECTION

* * * * *

Dedicated with love....
To my wife, sons, and extended family

1

The door to the operating room burst open. Two nurses entered the hallway with Brian Mercer on a gurney. The five-hour brain operation was complete. His brother Cliff and sister Marianne waited anxiously in the lounge for the surgeon to appear.

Forty-eight hours earlier, Brian, their elder brother, was in a car accident on his way home from a birthday celebration. This was his third operation in the last twenty-four hours. Cliff questioned whether Brian was going to survive this marathon of operations, while Marianne prayed he would be able to resume the work he loved to do. Brian's recent years as a lead scientist at the Livermore Laboratories, doing secretive work for the Government, separated him from his close-knit family. His birthday was the first time they had seen in him in a month or two.

The 2:00 am emergency call two nights earlier brought Cliff and Marianne to the San Jose General hospital. It all occurred on the evening Brian celebrated his 32nd birthday with all the members of his family. The party broke up early, but Brian stayed to reminisce his childhood days with his aging father.

Cliff paced back and forth. Marianne sat and prayed while waiting for a report from the operating surgeon on how well the surgery went.

A tall, dark skinned surgeon, dressed in his sweat-soaked green operating garb, approached them, and in broken English voiced, "I'm Doctor Ulsheeh. I understand you are the patient's brother and sister. Things went well considering the massive brain injury Brian suffered in the accident. For now, I'm not sure if I was able to do enough to restore him to the life he previously lived, or if he will be the same person he was before the accident. Let's wait and see— only time will dictate the final results. It will take 24 to 48 hours for the swelling to recede, and then we'll know more about how his recovery will go. I wish the news was better, but this was an extensive surgery. Sometimes a patient with injuries similar to Brian's has an unpredictable future, but that said, he is young and strong, which is in his favor for him to recover well. Whether the damage to his brain persists I can't predict. A portion of his skull was removed in an earlier operation, leaving his brain exposed to allow for the swelling. If everything goes as expected, then in twenty days or so, I'll replace it; however, if complications occur, I'll need to operate again. There is only so much I can do at this time. I would say hope and prayer would be in order. He should sleep for twenty-four hours, and I suggest you get some sleep too."

The doctor turned and left. Cliff handed his sister a handkerchief. Moments of silence followed while Marianne wiped the tears from her eyes.

"Sis, that doctor really cares about Brian, doesn't he?"

"Cliff, let's go into the chapel and say a few prayers for him. It wouldn't hurt, you know. That doctor hasn't been in this country very long, because he doesn't speak very good English. He must be from one of those Middle-Eastern countries."

"That shouldn't make any difference, should it? He appears to care a lot about Brian's recovery. It's more important to have a surgical doctor interested in his recovery, than one who is in it only for the money."

"I guess so, but a lot of doctors these days are foreigners, wouldn't you say? Ted would never go to one of them. I'm surprised he is a brain surgeon. I wonder if he got his education in this country."

"Sis, that's Ted for you. Your husband is ultra-opinionated. He wouldn't cross the street if a car was within two blocks of him."

"I don't know why you dislike Ted so. You're always making dissenting remarks about him."

"Sis, we have more to worry about than the doctor's nationality. I'll check with the nurses about his history if that concerns you so much. Our worry needs to be for Brian's recovery. He's been through a lot the last few days, and we don't know how this accident will affect his future. Let's leave now, and come back in the morning like the doctor suggested. Brian isn't aware we've been here been all of this time. It's best if we don't tell Dad about Brian's operations until we have some news about his progress."

Cliff gave one last look into Brian's room. Everything had settled down and he was peacefully asleep.

His sister was anxious about the foreign surgeon. Cliff considered it unimportant, but to satisfy her concern he visited the nurses' station to inquire about the doctor's history.

Everything the nurses said was favorable about his skills as a surgeon. He had been the chief surgeon for a number of years, and the nurses had a high regard for his surgical skills. He took his sister home and crashed himself. It had been a sleepless two days of waiting, coffee drinking, and praying for Brian's recovery— now it was up to Brian to recover and return to his previous life.

When Cliff arrived at the hospital the next morning he looked into the intensive ward window to see if Brian had awakened from his coma yet. Brian was in the same position he was the night before. Nothing had change—*disheartening*— he concluded.

He rushed to the nurses' station. Stored up questions about Brian's recovery flew at every nurse on duty. He rushed from nurse to nurse without an answer. He wanted answers—immediate answers, but the nurses turned their backs on his demanding voice. A strong hand grasped his shoulder from behind. He turned around to face a young doctor.

"That's no way to get the answers you want!"

"I'm a bit overwrought. Sorry. You're right. I shouldn't take out my frustrations on them. There appears to be no change in my brother's condition. I'm fearful for his life. Doctor Ulsheeh said he should be awake by now."

"I'm sure Doctor Ulsheeh didn't assure you of that! He probably said, 'it would be 24 to 48 hours,' and it's only been about fifteen hours. Each patient responds differently to surgery. I looked in on Brian moments ago, checked his vitals, and he is doing well. You'll have to learn to be patient and control your temper if you want to get along with the staff. I'm Doctor Marsh, and you're— Cliff Mercer— the patient's brother, aren't you? We know each other, don't we?"

"I'm Cliff Mercer, but Doctor Marsh I don't recall meeting you before."

"You don't, huh? We went to high school together. I was your understudy in 'The Maiden wore Tights.' Believe it or not, I still remember the lines. We both got A's in the class, but our performance wasn't the best, was it?"

"Oh, I remember now. I was pretty bad, wasn't I? I try to forget memories when my ego was bigger than my ability to act. At the time acting was my ambition, but it didn't happen. Instead I went to law school to become a lawyer, and by the looks of it, you went to medical school to become a doctor. Interesting, huh?"

"I think memories of our high school days are worth keeping. Since then it has been work, work, work."

"I'm sorry for creating such a fuss with the nurses. It's totally unlike me to do something so out of place. For now, my brother Brian financially supports my elderly father, and he is the brother my sister and I both look up to for guidance. He's a great brother, very smart, and he works as a lead scientist at the Livermore Laboratories. If he doesn't completely recover it would devastate our family, and my life would not be the same without him. We are two years apart and a lot of people think of us as twins. I don't know how I could survive if he didn't completely recover and return to the work he loves so much."

"I understand. I witness these tragedies every day. I chose medicine because I can make a difference in peoples' lives. Rest assured, I will take extra good care of him. I'm here from morning till night, and we have a good staff that will watch over him day and night."

"Thanks, I appreciate your help and reassurance. Have you been here long?"

"A little over six months. I'm in my fourth year of medical school at the university. Professor Ludwig sent me here for further training by Doctor Ulsheeh. I want to become a brain surgeon just like Doctor Ulsheeh. He is one of the best surgeons in the western United States."

Cliff inquired about seeing Doctor Ulsheeh, but the nurses were too busy tending other patients to answer his questions about the doctor's arrival time. Cliff paced the hallway, his anger increasing with each step. He ended up in the cafeteria where he sat down to nurse a cup of coffee and allow his nerves a minute to rest. This was all new to him, although his mother had spent time in the hospital before she passed. He called the Highway Patrol to see if they had determined the cause for Brian's accident.

"Sergeant, I'm calling about Brian Mercer's accident on Interstate 76 near Jamache road three nights ago. The Sergeant on duty said he would get back to me, but I haven't heard anything."

"Let me see what I can find. This will take a couple of minutes, and you'll need to be patient… Aw, here it is. Let me read this one page file to you. 'A single car accident was reported by cell phone at 12:08am. The caller didn't reveal his name. He saw a pair of headlights shining up into the sky from the ravine just south of Jamache Road, and he thought it might be an accident. He did not go down to view the car. Car 127 arrived at the scene at 12:18am. An ambulance arrived minutes later and the driver was extracted from the car in an unconscious condition. There were no other occupants in the car.' That's all that's in the file. Do you know the name of the sergeant you spoke with?"

"No, I don't."

"Just a second. I'm scrolling through my computer. Sometimes I can find something posted by the investigating officer or the officer removing the vehicle from the scene of the accident. I believe I have found something. We don't have many accidents at that particular section of the road. Here is report 1721, filed by the officer on the scene when the vehicle was removed from the ravine. I'll read it to you, but you'll have to speak with the investigating officer if you want any more information."

"It appears the car turned over a number of times before it came to rest at the bottom of the ravine. The skid marks indicate the subject's car was hit quite aggressively on the driver's side, causing the vehicle to leave the pavement. Heavy skid marks measuring eight feet plus indicate the subject's car was deliberately pushed off the pavement into the ravine. There were traces of a blue vehicle on the front left fender and the side of the vehicle.' That's all the report covers."

"What investigations are ongoing, like what, and who caused the accident? Did the other car leave the scene? My brother was a very careful driver. He races cars for a hobby, and I would assume he could control his car even if someone struck him from the side. It said in the report you read he was deliberately forced off the road?"

"I can't speculate for you. The investigation hasn't gone that far. It takes time to investigate hit and run accidents. This case is in the open file, which means an investigation is ongoing."

"Is there someone I could talk to about this?"

"Give me your cell number, and I'll have someone call you."

Frustrated with how everything was progressing, Cliff left for his office in town to deal with his legal affairs that had gone unanswered for the last several days.

His cell vibrated. It was Marianne. "Cliff, I was going over to Peggy's house on Merrimac Avenue this morning, and as I went by the Mosque on Clairemont Drive I saw several Arab-looking men coming out of the Mosque. They were all dressed in Arab garb. I took a double take when I recognized Doctor Ulsheeh among them. I took a number of pictures of them. Shall I send them to you?"

"No, hell no. It doesn't mean a thing. Are you sure it was him?"

"I'm dead sure, it was him all right! I'll send them to you. I called Ted and he is upset about the whole thing. Ted and I don't like it. That doctor could be one of those terrorists, like the ones that did the 9/11 thing."

"Sis, what could he possibly do to harm Brian? He saved his life. Don't you know that? He's entitled to follow his religious beliefs just like you and I are allowed. They dress in those outfits when they pray at the Mosque. Sis, I'm busy. I can't be bothered with your nonsensical suspicions right now."

"Just thought you would want to know. Anyway, Ted thinks he is an outright terrorist like the rest of those Moslems at that Mosque. Ted says the FBI arrested several of them because they were part of the 9/11 planning. Remember we discussed which country Doctor Ulsheeh came from originally. He could be from Pakistan, Iran, or Syria or someplace like that. You don't think he could be a transplanted terrorist like the ones that did the 9/11 thing, do you?"

"Sis, your imagination is working overtime, and Ted is an alarmist. You are curious about his heritage, that's all. Doctor Ulsheeh has been at the hospital for a number of years and is well thought of by the nurses. Sis, I'm buried in work here. Could you come in to answer my phone for a day or two? I could really use your help."

"Cliff, you know how Ted feels about my working. He wants me to stay home with the kids. Just call Anne, she would be glad to help you out. She told me she likes being close to you."

"You're a matchmaker, aren't you? Right now I don't have any romantic vibes in this tired body. Forget it, I'll get a temp for a week or so. Go visit with your friend and forget about the doctor and his Arab grab for the time being, and tell Ted to keep his opinions about our family affairs to himself."

"There you go again. Ted is part of our family whether you like it or not."

Cliff snapped his cell shut. He didn't want to argue with his sister. His law practice had suffered considerably in just a few days. His one-man office had been to his liking for several years, and only lately had he felt overburdened with the additional cases he recently accepted. He called to get a temporary secretary, and thought about a possible merger with another attorney in town. He needed a full time secretary or office manager, but his one-man office didn't warrant the expense. It was his lifetime ambition to build a business of his own, and the thought of seeking a partner needed further nurturing.

2

A late night trip to the hospital proved to be futile. Brian was still in a coma. *He should have been awake many hours ago,* Cliff muttered to himself. The on-duty nurses said it was best if he stayed in the coma until morning when the doctor could evaluate his condition.

Disappointed, he felt like throwing his computer against the wall to vent his anger over Brian's lack of improvement. *Stupid thought,* he knew, but Brian's continuing coma lingered in his mind. He sat next to Brian and said a prayer, but somehow it made him feel uncomfortable. He hadn't prayed in over three years, and it was when he took his state exam to become an attorney. In the last couple of days Marianne had prayed enough for both of them. Brian was not recovering like Cliff expected, and it appeared there was nothing he could do about it.

Cliff's mind strayed into the past. Brian was such a good guy. In high school and college he was the top quarterback for two seasons. He was always on the dean's list throughout his scholastic career, and most of all he was popular with the girls. He tried to emulate his brother's achievements, but he could never reach his level no matter how hard he tried. After Brian's graduation from Stanford, a brief stint at MIT, and a year getting his Doctorate at University of California at Berkeley, he finished his schooling. Brian had prepared himself well for a rocket launch into a lucrative career. With his schooling behind him he was chosen to become a lead scientist at the Livermore Lab in a matter of months, which was unheard of in the past. He became the lead scientist on their laser projects, a specialty that challenged him to achieve.

So why would something this devastating happen to him, especially when he was at the peak of his career? The door opened and in walked in Doctor Ulsheeh. He sat next to Cliff.

"Cliff, I'm surprised to see you here so late. I'm making my final rounds before heading home for the evening, and I wanted to check on Brian. I've had a busy day. It seems there is no end to these automobile accidents. Brian hasn't come out of his coma yet, which indicates his brain swelling is slow to subside. Believe me, it may be for the best. I see Doctor Marsh prescribed a sedative for him two hours ago. The coma will allow his entire body to recover from the trauma he's been through. When the brain is disturbed like Brian's has been, it takes a toll on the entire body. I carefully examined his brain tissue, and when I finished cleaning all of the ruptures in his brain I was sure I got them all. After finishing, I made a secondary examination to verify my findings. In my opinion he should recover completely."

"That's all good news. My brother and I are close, and it would be extremely difficult for my family and me if Brian doesn't completely recover."

"I hear that a lot. Family is important, I agree. I need to leave.

Doctor Marsh is closely monitoring Brian's condition during the day, and the night nurses have my instructions to call me if any setbacks in his condition should occur. Believe me, he is being well cared for both day and night. It is my opinion Brian is a strong man, and he should survive this ordeal without a setback."

"Thank you Doctor, your assurances are welcome, but I'm still angry about the whole situation. Brian has worked so hard to achieve what he has accomplished, and you say he may not be able to continue his work."

"Being angry won't help him or you. I didn't say he wouldn't completely recover and lead a normal life; I was merely preparing you for the worst scenario just in case he doesn't. Twenty years ago he wouldn't have survived this accident, but with all of the new techniques available we are able to treat our patients in a way they can go back to their regular life without a handicap. I can't predict how each patient will respond. The body is rather complicated, and doctors like myself don't always have the answers on how a patient will recover."

"Believe me Doctor, I'm not complaining about your talents, or questioning your ability to help him, but Brian has worked so hard for the last fifteen years, I meant it wasn't fair. He and I are very close, and most people think of us as being twins. We think and do things alike."

"I understand your concern. Go home and rest yourself. We will take good care of your brother. I'll instruct the nurses to get in touch with you if there is any change in his condition."

Doctor Ulsheeh's assurance gave Cliff hope for his brother's recovery. He crossed the dark parking lot on his way to his car and thought about calling his sister, but it was late, and Ted wouldn't like her receiving calls so late. He also thought about the caring doctor and his assurance that Brian would recover and be able to continue his work.

Cliff slept well that night. Brian's accident had disrupted the entire family's life. The doctor's kind words put his worry to rest. He rose early and went to the office. It would be a good time to get caught up on his work. A little after eight o'clock a Highway Patrolman entered his office.

"Cliff, we've made some progress on your brother's accident. Our investigation revealed he was forced off the road by a blue SUV. Judging by the damage to the left side of his vehicle he was hit several times, with each time moving him closer to the ravine. From that determination—I've concluded he was purposely driven off the road. The paint scrapings indicate he was struck a number of times before being driven off the road. We have identified the make and model of the hit and run vehicle, and have put out an all-points bulletin on it. Perhaps we'll get a lead or so in the next few days. The hit and run cases always increase the length of our investigations, but we generally get the person responsible. Be patient—it takes time."

"Well, I'm pleased you are making progress on how he was driven off the road. Brian is a careful driver, and I can't understand why he would allow anyone to push him off the road."

"The skid marks and damage to the side of his car indicate he was hit rather hard and pushed off the pavement. We are seeing more and more of these kinds of accidents. Sometimes it begins with road rage over nothing and escalates into something this severe. I've concluded it was a hit and run case, possibly caused by a group of drunken fools in a stolen vehicle. I hear Brian was a high-caliber scientist and a good man. I am anxious to talk with him about the accident. I would appreciate if you would let me know when Brian is well enough for my interview. Perhaps he could shed some light on what happened. We finished checking his car for clues so you can get it released from impound whenever you want. Here is the authorization number, and my card to call me."

The officer left and Cliff leaned back in his chair, sighed, and put his head in his open hands. Perhaps they would find who ran Brian off the road, and possibly find a good reason for all that had happened. This whole event had been difficult for him and his family to accept. Since Brian was promoted to be the leading scientist on a laser project he had little time for family. Neither Cliff nor Brian were married, and it become his job to take charge of Brian's legal affairs while Brian was totally consumed with his work at the Lab. He knew little about Brian's work because he worked on secretive projects that he would never discuss. He arranged to have Brian's damaged car towed to a storage facility and planned to check on it at a later date. He'd made some progress on his own work schedule, and didn't feel as pressured as before. His two court appearances had been delayed, which cleared his calendar for the present.

Cliff left for the hospital, where he planned to camp out until his brother awoke from his extended coma. As he made his way down the hallway to Brian's room he saw a man standing by Brian's door. He started to go in, but the man stopped him from entering.

"What is this?" Cliff demanded. His irritation running at octane levels since Brian's accident.

The man drew a badge from his coat pocket and showed it to him.

"Don't approach me with an attitude. I'm an FBI Special Agent. I can't allow you to go in."

"He's my brother. I demand you allow me to see him."

"Shelf the attitude. Identify yourself, and then I'll decide if you can visit or not."

Cliff showed the FBI agent his driver's license. "What going on? Has something happened to my brother I need to know about?"

"Look through the window if you wish, and maybe I can get clearance for you to enter in an hour or so."

Cliff looked in and saw a woman sitting next to Brian's bed. It appeared Brian was awake. He left to call his sister Marianne to ask her to meet him at the hospital.

"Cliff, I'm not coming down there unless you tell me what's wrong. I can tell from your voice something is wrong. Is Brian worse? Tell me, what's wrong."

"Sis, don't ask, I'm not in the mood. Brian is awake, and I wanted you here so we could see him together. Please come, I need you with me."

"Okay, I'll be there in about an hour. Ted won't be happy about it, but I'll handle that part."

Cliff called his secretary for messages.

"The Highway Patrol called several times, and he wanted you to call him ASAP. Something important has come up. He said you have his number."

Cliff called the Highway Patrol, and asked for officer Brannigan.

"Cliff, why didn't you tell me your brother was such an important person?"

"You knew he was a scientist."

"Yes, I know, there are a lot of scientists in this area, but he must really be an important one to get the FBI involved. The FBI was here a while back and took my complete file and they are looking for the car that ran Brian off the road. Furthermore, they told me to shut down my search and they would take over the investigation. Do you know what's going on?"

"No, I don't. The FBI wouldn't allow me to see Brian this morning. I'm puzzled about all of this too."

"I wanted you to know that I'm completely off the case. You'll have to go through the FBI from now on if you want any further information. I understand they will be in touch with you."

Cliff went to the cafeteria. Maybe a cup of strong coffee would settle his nerves. *This is an alarming turn of events,* he muttered. As an attorney he'd handled many criminal cases, but the FBI or any Federal Agency were never involved. Ideas churned swiftly through his mind as he attempted to understand why all of this was happening. An excited Marianne showed up just as he was finishing his second cup of coffee.

"Cliff, there is a man at Brian's door, and he stopped me from going in to see Brian!"

"Sis, I know. Sit. I'll tell you what I know."

Cliff explained the call he received from the Highway Patrol about the FBI taking over Brian's accident investigation.

The FBI agent who wouldn't allow Cliff into Brian's room approached them. Cliff introduced his sister. He told them they would be allowed to visit Brian for an hour each day, but an FBI person would need to record their conversation.

"I don't understand what is going on here. Why have you taken over like this?" Marianne snapped.

"You needn't know what's going on. Just follow my instructions, and we'll get along just fine. My name is Philip Moore. I am attached to the FBI office in the San Francisco region. Your brother has been working on a number of highly classified governmental projects for the last three years. His superiors are concerned that he might inadvertently disclose delicate information about the projects he was heavily engaged in. It is important for our department to make a report to the Livermore Lab on his condition, record any visitors he may have, and monitor all conversations he has with anyone. You have been cleared to visit if you wish. I'll accompany you, and monitor your conversation with him on your visit."

As Cliff and Marianne approached Brian's bed he turned his head and looked at them. His stare was one Cliff hadn't seen before. They waited for him to speak, but he didn't. Cliff wasn't sure if Brian recognized them, or if he was playing one of his practical jokes on them. After all, he had always been a prankster with his younger siblings.

"Brian, we've been here since the accident. It's your brother and sister."

Brian stared at them without saying anything. Cliff looked at Marianne, wanting her to say something to him, but she didn't. It was clear Brian didn't recognize them, or...

Distraught, they both left the room without saying another word. Marianne began crying and Cliff told her to quit.

"Cliff, what shall we do?"

"Hell, I don't know. Wait a minute! I'll call Doctor Ulsheeh to see what he thinks about what just happened."

Cliff was unable to get in touch with the doctor and he searched the hallway for Doctor Marsh. He was making his rounds and didn't have time for Cliff. His cell vibrated. It was a close attorney friend.

"Cliff, what's going on? I had a visit from the FBI inquiring about you and your background. I told him you were a lousy football player, and you couldn't play golf worth a damn."

"Be serious for a change. What did they ask you about me?"

"Well, they asked what kind of clients you have recently defended, who were your closest friends, and what organizations or clubs you belonged to. They didn't ask whom you were sleeping with lately."

"Damn it! Be serious. It must have something to do with Brian being in the hospital. Someone is afraid he will talk about his work. He has been working on some ultra-secret projects lately. Thanks for letting me know."

"You bet. Are you free to play golf this week or next?"

"No way, I'm up to my neck in work and going to the hospital. I'll talk to you later in the week. Thanks for letting me know about the FBI."

Cliff laid down his cell and thought for a moment. He hadn't been this uptight since his pre-college days when studies were his whole world. His attorney work was stimulating and required every bit of his attention, but now, with Brian being hurt, Cliff's whole world had turned upside down.

Cliff leaned back in his chair, with the FBI's entry into his and Brian's life weighing heavily on his mind. In the past, he had reasoned his way through normal business problems, but this intrusion by a Federal Agency was something he hadn't dealt with before, and something he didn't understand. In a matter of days his life had become a living hell.

3

Cliff's secretary came in from the outer office to tell him an FBI agent was in the waiting room.

"Okay, send him in."

"It's not a him, it's a her."

"A her? What will they think of next? Our Federal Government is always making changes, aren't they?"

Cliff paused to enjoy his private joke. His secretary, obviously annoyed with her boss, repeated her statement dripping with sarcasm.

"Lighten up, will you? Life is not all gloom and doom. If you are going to work here, the least you can do is enjoy my jokes whether they are funny to you or not. Send her in."

She turned sharply and left. Cliff leaned back in his chair, not pleased with the exchange with his temp, and waited to meet this woman FBI agent.

A petite woman in her early thirties appeared in the doorway. Cliff rose to greet her. She stood before him displaying a badge in one hand and a cell phone in the other. She was dressed in a dark blue blazer and slacks. Her hair was rolled into a tight bun and placed securely on the back of her neck. She wore no lipstick or makeup of any kind. Her face portrayed no emotion.

"My name is Special Agent Salture. I overheard your remark, and I'm not pleased with it. Women have been agents in the FBI for decades now. Here are my credentials."

"Well hello, I didn't mean any harm with my remarks, believe me. My family was raised in a jokester exchange. We learned to dish it out and we learned how to take it too. Since Brian's accident I haven't been myself."

Without acknowledging Cliff's apology, she asked if she could sit down.

"Of course. Forgive my manners. You're the first woman FBI person I've met."

"You're not forgiven. Believe me, I'm not an oddity. There are several thousand women agents presently in our service. I'm a regular agent for the FBI and I have been so for several years. I prefer to be respected like any male FBI agent. I have been assigned to head up Brian's Mercer's case to make sure he doesn't inadvertently transfer any vital information about his Livermore Laboratories project. We are aware Doctor Ulsheeh has operated on him several times since his accident. The doctor has been on our radar for some time because of his association with known persons with terrorist leanings. We've been informed by Brian's superiors he is quite reliable, but since the accident happened he may have lost his sense of responsibility especially during his multiple operations and recovery times. I understand you and your brother are very close, and that's why I am here."

"Sounds like you are on top of the case already. It was you talking with Brian when I looked through the door at the hospital. Please, don't be offended by my remark, I meant no harm. It's a family tradition to joke with each other when things aren't going well."

"There is a time and place for humor, and this is neither the time nor the place for it."

"You're all business, aren't you?

"Get serious, will you? This assignment is most important to me, and in the coming weeks I will need your complete cooperation."

"I'll reshuffle the deck, wipe the smile from my face, and get serious like you want me to do. As brothers, Brian and I are very close. You can rest assured Brian would never discuss his work with me, and I'm sure he wouldn't give any information to other people.

He is a person of impeccable integrity, and he would never cross that line. Besides, he is a patriot beyond belief. You have nothing to worry about."

"The FBI doesn't chase worry. You're saying next to the Pope, he's infallible. If he's human he is not infallible. We operate on known facts, and proceed from there. Since Brian has been in an uncontrolled, unstable, and unfamiliar surroundings since his accident, he may have inadvertently given or transferred information concerning the project he was working on. We are currently monitoring all of his medications, conversations, and visitors. I will caution you not to disclose any information on the subject we discuss today or you will be arrested and charged with obstruction and taken down to the Federal lockup. Do you clearly understand what I am telling you?"

"Does that mean twenty years in the slammer and you throw the key away? No offense meant, but you sling those threats around rather loosely, don't you? Lighten up a little. We're both levelheaded, intelligent people in a discussion about my brother's accident. I'm as trustworthy as a newly minted penny, and if you don't believe it, ask me. Kidding aside, I'll cooperate with you. I'm on your side. Can't we use first names?"

"Enough foreplay! Can your sales speech. I've heard it many times on my past assignments. Just address me as Agent Salture—that will be fine with me."

"You're as rigid as a cut of oak wood. You should be out fighting crime instead of housekeeping my brother. You know, chasing the bad guys that would harm our country. This couldn't be a case of life or death, and I can't fully understand why the FBI is so interested in my brother. He merely had a car accident. He is the most stable person on this earth. Something like this could happen to anyone some time in a lifetime. I am an attorney, and I fully understand the necessary precautions that need to be observed, but to come into my office and threaten me with arrest if I don't explicitly follow your orders to the letter is absurd. I want to make it clear to you that I understand my rights as a citizen of the United States of America, and I don't like being treated like a criminal."

Agent Salture laughed. "Spoken like a newly graduate from law school. Keep in mind —I'm also a lawyer, and I always operate within the guidelines of the law, and I meant every word I said."

"Wow! I didn't know agents laughed, doesn't that beat all?"

"Enough of that kind of talk. This is a serious assignment for me. I notice you have been recording our entire conversation since I entered. Does that mean you don't trust me as much as I trust you?"

"Oh! You noticed, did you? You're more observant than I have given you credit for. It's just one of those things attorneys do."

"I know. I was one before I got my badge. All agents must get their law degree before they are considered for employment. Shut the recorder off now, erase our conversation, and then we'll continue. Otherwise, we'll finish our conversation downtown."

"There you go again, throwing that threat around. You take your work rather seriously, don't you? I'll turn it off and erase it now. Let's continue, shall we?"

"I appreciate your cooperation. The FBI has become actively involved with Brian's case for two reasons: Doctor Ulsheeh has been under our surveillance for a couple of years because of his association with fellow countrymen whom we've had on our watch list since 9/11. Also, three other scientists in this immediate area were involved in accidents similar to Brian's and were operated on by Doctor Ulsheeh within the last three years. Presently, we have nothing to go on concerning the doctor's operating practices or his involvement in any foul play; however, we are in the process of reexamining all of the facts. Our investigation is merely in a embryonic stage."

"It sounds to me like he is being profiled because he came from Iran. Could that be true?"

"No, it isn't. I've already shared as much as I can with you at this time."

"Curiosity has got me. Did the other three scientists live, and were they able to return to their previous positions?"

"I won't share any information beyond what I've already given you. I need you to wear a wire recorder each and every time you talk with Doctor Ulsheeh and with your brother. You have to be cautious about anything you say to Doctor Ulsheeh about your brother's work. And I needn't tell you not to speak with him about what I am asking you to do. Do you have any questions regarding my request?"

"I have no knowledge of my brother's work. He's as close-mouthed as a clam that just washed ashore."

"You have to add a little humor to everything you say, don't you?"

"I don't like to work in the dark. Can't you share more information with me?"

"No, I can't. Work with me, will you?"

"As long as anything you ask of me doesn't hurt my brother in any way, I'm willing to go along with you. I wouldn't want to get arrested and thrown in the Federal slammer with a lot of other people falsely charged with a crime found in the smallest of print of some obscure law."

"Enough with all of your fantasies. Take off your shirt and I will hook up this gadget, and you can visit your brother whenever you want without an agent accompanying you."

"Hey, that gadget is cold. Be careful. Besides, I'm sensitive."

"Grow up, will you! Hold still. Once this is on you'll only need to change the recorder in this little compartment every time you record something. Are you watching me?"

"I'm watching. Thank goodness, I couldn't go through this very often— a person of the opposite sex pawing me like you want more of me."

"Hold still, will you? If you would quit moving around, it would make it easier for me to finish. I'm almost done. Turn around so I can see if it's comfortable. It would be less difficult if you held still for me."

"You embarrassed me. I wasn't prepared for you handling me like a sack of potatoes. I hope no one knows I'm wearing this gadget. There is only one hitch with your plan. My sister will want to visit Brian when I'm not around. She has a will to get what she wants. It will be fun watching you two duke it out. Will she have to wear one of these gadgets too?"

"No, only you will be allowed to visit Brian without an agent present. Just tell her she can only visit him while you're together. You're a big boy— handle it. Is that a simple enough solution for you?"

"You're quick. Did you learn that in your teens or was it when you became an agent, or maybe you've always been like that?"

"Quit, will you? I don't appreciate you flamboyant trend of conversation. Frankly, I wish you would quit joking around. Agents are restricted from discussing our personal lives. Please don't ask questions like that in the future."

"Do you have a list of do's and don'ts I could use for the future? I don't want to end up in the slammer."

"This is getting tiresome for me. If you think you're funny, the answer is no, you are not."

"I'm getting educated in a hurry."

"Enough!"

"Got it. Give me a schedule when I can see Brian, and I'll contact my sister."

"Make your own arrangements, but make it plain to her that she can't see him without you being there with your recorder turned on. Keep your visits within a fifteen minute time limit because that is the length of the tape."

"This is all new for me. Does it record my heart beat too?"

"There you go again. Let's not take this assignment too lightly. Terrorists have been a thorn in our sides since 9/11. One more thing, I want to caution you that if you forget to turn on the recorder at the times I've requested, you will be arrested and charged."

"There you go again. Don't want to go down the road of being arrested by you. By arrested, you mean handcuffs, and thrown in the slammer without representation? I bruise easily, you know. I'll do what you ask, and will do my best not to foul up."

"Good— we're finally on the same page. Schedule your time when you want to see him, and I'll make the arrangements. Brian wouldn't talk to you on your recent visit because I instructed him not to recognize you or your sister."

"Unbelievable! Sis and I came out of that meeting believing he would never recover."

Cliff called Marianne and she agreed to meet him at the hospital. He turned on his wire, remembering the consequences of forgetting to turn it on. An inward smile erupted as he thought about his discussions with Agent Salture, and how she rejected his jests. They entered Brian's room together. Brian greeted them both.

"Hi guys. It's good to see you both. Marianne, give me a kiss right here on my cheek. Cliff, it's good to see you too. Give me a hug. I smell antiseptic, but I can't help it. Those nurses are continually doing something to me. I understand you two have been here for quite a spell since my accident. How long have I been in here?"

"Way too long. I'm beginning to think I'm a resident here too," Cliff responded.

Brian laughed. He appeared to be in good spirits, and shades of his old self were present. He asked about their Dad and the rest of the family, but he didn't want to talk about the accident. He joked about staying sober at the party and commented, 'I understand they gave me a blood test for alcohol and drugs, can you beat that?'

"Brian, I didn't know you were so important at the Lab. We couldn't come in to see you because an FBI agent stopped us at the door."

"I know, Agent Salture explained all of that to me. Just precautionary, I'm sure. She appears to be quite thorough. As she explained to me she is here to see to my safety. Frankly, I have never been so looked after in my life. You'd think I was a celebrity or something like it. My superiors are concerned I will discuss my work, but you know I couldn't do that. I know my work at the Lab is highly classified, and very important to our Defense Department. I'm sure their concerns are legitimate, and I agreed with Agent Salture to go along with all of her security concerns. When I pretended not to recognize you before, I was just following her instructions. You should have seen the look on your faces."

"As usual Bro, you were very convincing. You scared the hell out of both of us. I wanted to bring Dad in to see you, but I was afraid it would upset him too much. He said he kept you up late that night talking your leg off about Mom and the family. The accident has him terribly upset. I'll take your picture and tell him about our visit. He'll understand. Smile big for him."

"Dad and I needed that talk. Lately we've had some issues about my not being around the family enough. I explained to him I was in a critical stage of building my career just now, and things would change for the better in the near future. He was worried about passing on and we would be at odds with each other. I assured him I couldn't let that happen."

"I'm glad you and Dad had that talk. He hasn't been doing well lately, and when you are out of here, I suggest you spend some quality time with him. Sis and I should do the same. Since Mom passed Dad hasn't been the same."

Cliff, I'll make sure I do. I need to tell you something really important. This was no accident—that car deliberately ran me off the road. You know I'm a good driver, but I couldn't avoid being pushed off the road into that ravine. I felt my car roll over once, and I lost track of how many more times it rolled. Luckily I was wearing my seat belt."

"Let's not talk about that now. You need to concentrate on getting well and returning to your work."

"I'm beginning to think the Lab doesn't want me back. No one from there has come in to see me or even called since I came out of the coma. It's like they don't care about my recovery. I was right on the edge of a great breakthrough that would advance my whole project by leaps and bounds when all of this happened. I'm puzzled about my future there."

"Brian, your one and only concern should be about getting better, and those things will take care of themselves when they release you from the hospital. You'll have time for all that later."

Marianne didn't say anything. She just listened to Brian and Cliff talk. During her teens she relied on Brian to help her when she first entered high school, and it was during those years when they became so close. During the previous days of waiting, crying, and praying she never gave a thought to his not recovering and returning to the Lab to work. She asked him about the doctor's visits.

"He was in this morning. He wants to wait for a time before he replaces the piece of my skull he removed earlier. I must have taken a huge bump to the head, but I'm back to my normal self again, except, I do have those terrible blackout times and memory lapses that last and last. Sometimes they last for over an hour or so. They come on when I least expect them. I get a blinding headache, flashes like lightning throughout my head, and then the memory lapses. When I semi-recover I call the nurse and she gives me a medication. I think it is a sedative because I get real sleepy within a short time. It's worrisome, because I don't know if I can ever start back to work again if those spells continue. Something tells me I'll never be able to return to the Lab."

"Brian, don't worry about details like that. Just concentrate on getting out of here and back to work. We'll leave for now. The nurse said we could only stay for a few minutes. Keep getting well. We want you around for a long time."

Brian laughed. "Sure, so I can keep fooling you guys."

Marianne kissed him again. Brian was grinning as they departed the room. He appeared normal, but the blackout periods and memory lapses presented a major concern for Cliff.

"Cliff, I still don't understand why they have a guard on the door, and why the FBI is involved in all of this. Ted thinks Brian did something wrong, and they are going to arrest him as soon as he gets well enough. You heard him say he feels like he won't return to the Lab, didn't you? If he couldn't support Dad like he has been, it would be disastrous. Ted and I are stretched to the limit, and you're not flush either."

"Damn it, Sis. You and I know Brian. He's not capable of doing anything wrong. And Ted always has a negative slant on everything. I believe the Lab is just being cautious. I need to get back to my office for a couple of hours— my life, my work, are in tatters also. I'll keep you informed if something unusual happens with Brian. It would be best if you didn't share anything about Brian's problems with Ted or

Dad. Ted might try to stop you from visiting Brian. And Dad—we wouldn't be able to keep him out of the hospital."

"There you go again! I do what I well please. Ted doesn't run my life. We have enough to concern us about Brian's future without you picking on Ted. He is a good husband to me, and a good father to the children. It's you who has all of those negative thoughts about him. Brian's accident hasn't been good for my life either, but we are all Brian has because Dad is not going to be with us very long. We'll have to wait to see how all of this washes out."

Cliff returned to his office only to find Doctor Ulsheeh waiting for him. Questions about why he was waiting at his office flicked through his mind.

4

Cliff invited the doctor to his inner office and motioned for him to sit across from the desk.

"Why didn't you ask the secretary for a chair inside instead of sitting on the floor in the hallway?"

"I'm too troubled to be thinking straight. Cliff, this FBI presence in my affairs has greatly upset me, and it's interfering with my work as a surgeon. I have been an upstanding citizen ever since I came to this country, and I have no idea why the Federal authorities have targeted me. A number of my associates at the Mosque have complained they too are being followed and investigated by the FBI and Homeland Security. I need legal counsel, and I would appreciate it if you would represent me. After all, I did save your brother's life."

"Yes, you did, and I'm immensely grateful for what you have done for Brian, but I can't represent you. I am emotionally involved with you because of my brother's accident, and the FBI has contacted me, questioned me, and asked me to report any unusual happenings during Brian's recovery. My caseload is over-flowing, and I can't handle my present cases in the manner I must. I think it's best if I help you find you another attorney."

"Cliff, you know there are only two attorneys in town, and the other one handles only family affairs."

"I'm aware of that, but there are many fine attorneys in the immediate area. I could recommend one for you."

"I'm asking you to represent me. Your brother's wellbeing is in my hands. I feel as though we have developed a kinship. That should mean something to you."

"It does, and I'm grateful for what you have done for him, but I'm a one-man office, already completely over-booked, and it would be unethical for me to take you on as a client. I just can't do what you are asking of me."

"You owe me. I won't take no for an answer. I don't know why you're so wary about representing me. I was a foreigner, but I've earned my citizenship the hard way. I'm a citizen now."

"Well maybe I could do limited work for you. Is that satisfactory with you? Bear in mind I can't stop the FBI or any Federal Agency from checking into your past history, and I can't stop them from investigating your Mosque friends if that's what you want me to do, but I can protect your legal rights as a citizen of the United States. If you haven't done anything wrong, then you shouldn't have anything to worry about. Do you have any additional information to tell me at this time?"

"Because you asked, several of our former Mosque worshippers were involved in the attack on the twin towers on 9/11. It's a well-known fact, and my fellow Moslem friends are still being harassed for the evil they caused. Unfortunately those arrested worshipped at our Mosque—but all of that is in the past, but those agencies continue to park outside the wire fence to photograph and watch us when we leave the Mosque. Lately, my friends tell me there are inquiries about me at the hospital and around my neighborhood. Two of my neighbors recently moved because the FBI and Homeland Security were parking by their house to spy on me and my family. Everywhere I look I see one of their black SUV's. My whole neighborhood is upset with me because of their presence. My wife tells me the neighbors will no longer speak to her or our kids. I call that harassment by the FBI and Homeland Security. Their surveillance has increased tremendously during the past two years. Just because we practice the Moslem religion doesn't mean we are terrorists. I cannot give up my religion to satisfy them. If you look out your window you'll see a black SUV parked across the street. It is a Government car, probably the FBI. I feel threatened, and I want you to put a stop to it. I cannot continue my practice under such harassment."

"I understand your problem, but I'm not sure I can help you. I'm just a small town lawyer without much influence. Perhaps I could visit your Senator and Congressman and make a complaint for you. I would need to ask you for a retainer."

"Thank you, I was sure you would help me. I'm feeling better already. It's good talking with someone outside the Mosque who understands my problems. I'll drop off the retainer with your secretary. Keep me posted on your progress, will you?"

"I appreciate what you did for my brother, and I will do everything I can to help you. I will talk with the FBI and your Federal Representatives in Washington on your behalf to convey your concerns about their harassment of you and your friends."

"We're off to a good start and I look forward to you representing me with this affront to my character. I came to the United States to get away from heavy-handed government control. I am a United States citizen now, and I want my civil rights protected."

Doctor Ulsheeh left.

Another burden to deal with, sighed Cliff. *And what would Agent Salture make of all of this?* Cliff carefully perused the doctor's statements, and wondered how he could perform brain surgery with a troubled mind. In a way, the doctor had a likable personality, a good reputation as a surgeon, and should be above reproach, so why was the FBI and Homeland Security so interested in him? The question that remained in his mind was; what did all of this have to do with Brian and his surgery? Surely this brain surgeon hadn't broken the law. *So, what could it be? What could he possibly do to harm his brother? After all he had saved Brian's life.* Cliff's mind questioned. Freedom of religion in this country was a sacred right for all Americans and it included lawful immigrants. Doctor Ulsheeh had a right to pursue his own choice of religion. It was his right and privilege as a citizen, which he earned ten years previously. Marianne's suspicions came to mind, but her reasons were totally unfounded. Cliff believed the

Doctor was a credit to his profession. And now Cliff found himself in a precarious position—he was working for both the FBI and Doctor Ulsheeh. It was a conflict of interest for sure, and something he was sworn not to practice when he received his license to defend the law.

For him, life needed to move on regardless of the everyday burdens and recent problems he wasn't used to dealing with. He'd worked through tougher parts of his life in the past, and he'd learned to shake off those depressed feelings. Perhaps he was just exhausted from the recent events, and it reflected on his mental state of mind. Normally this was the month when he could kick back and spend time in the outdoors for a few days, but not this year. His thoughts turned to the hunting trips Brian and he and their father took throughout the years. Hunting season opened a week earlier, and he sorely missed the annual trips with his father and brother in search of a big buck. Two years ago he bagged an eight pointer. The memory of that success temporarily relieved his troubled mind. They were good times. The trips were good therapy, and the time spent in the wilderness always cleared his mind from the heavy schedule he kept as a single attorney. Since his Mother passed, his father had aged considerably, and he seldom left the house. He decided to take a walk to clear his head and to relieve his troubled mind.

He told his temp he would be back in an hour or so and left for the elevator. When he reached the first floor he realized he'd left his cell on his desktop, and he punched the button to return to his office. When he entered the outer office the temp and Agent Salture were studiously going through his clientele file.

"What the hell are you doing? You have no right! Am I under investigation, or what? If so, what am I being accused of?"

"Here's my search warrant. I understand you just took on Doctor Ulsheeh as a client. You agreed to record anything said between the doctor and you. May I have the recording?"

"The recording. Oh yeah, I didn't turn it on. Client privilege overrides any other statutes the Federal Government has invented. As an attorney I have to abide by my rules too."

"You're glib, but you're trying my patience. I'm getting tired of you constantly fighting me. Perhaps a trip to the Federal lockup would remind you to turn it on. I figured you were reasonably smart because you are an attorney, aren't you?"

"That's hitting below the belt. I have my reasons, okay?"

"Don't you realize you have a conflict of interest, or aren't you smart enough to realize that?"

Cliff didn't have a rebuttal because he knew he shouldn't have taken Doctor Ulsheeh on as a client, but he finally conjured up a rebuttal.

"If you and your bunch would quit violating Doctor Ulsheeh and his family's rights as a citizens of the United States they wouldn't need my services."

"Please be quiet. You're disturbing me while I search for the documents I'm looking for."

"I have no idea why you are searching my files. If you would tell me what you want to see, perhaps I could help you. I don't appreciate what you are doing. I represent clear-cut business people. I'm sure you won't find anything out of line in my files."

Agent Salture continued to rifle through Cliff's files regardless of Cliff's objections. As each minute passed Cliff's temperature rose to a boiling level.

"Your actions are approaching the harassment level. I have rights too, and I can't stand to have them trampled on."

"You're full of legal jargon today, aren't you?"

Agent Salture finished searching his clientele file. She handed him a receipt for two files she took with her and left. Still boiling from the search of his files, Cliff called the temp into his office.

"Your agency assured me that you were well qualified, reliable, and trustworthy for this job, but you allowed the FBI to search my files without my permission."

"Agent Salture showed me the search warrant. I had no other choice—I needed to immediately honor it."

"You could have delayed her when she handed you that search warrant. Do you have an excuse for that?"

"Not really. Do you have something to hide, or are you a difficult person to work for?"

"Perhaps I'm being difficult. This is my first encounter with federal law enforcement. Regardless of that, as a legal secretary you're expected to know ways to delay anything like this search from occurring. You could have stalled her until I returned. All the files were padlocked. You could have told her you didn't have the keys. You could have told her you just arrived today, and you weren't familiar with the files. Reason after reason, and yet you allowed the search to happen. I pay you to think, besides answer the phone, and handle the normal functions of my office. You're well paid for your services and you came highly recommended. You are expected to handle my affairs when I'm not in the office. Your fired, and I'm reporting your lack of proficiency to the agency that sent you here."

Without speaking the temp reached into her pocket and drew out a badge.

"You see, I am also with the FBI, another woman, and a well qualified Special Agent of the FBI. I'm sorry you returned so soon."

"You! An FBI agent—that's unbelievable. You were planted here by that scheming Agent Salture, weren't you? And you're sorry I returned so soon? You're saying I wouldn't have known my files were searched if I hadn't returned so soon? Can you tell me what I'm suspected of doing?"

"I'm not obliged to discuss this case with you. If you need further information you need to talk with Agent Salture. She is my superior."

"Pack your stuff and get the hell out of my office, and don't bother looking back. I will need my key. Surely you haven't made a duplicate, have you? Never mind, I'll have the locks changed for my office and files. Don't return—I don't want to see your face again."

Cliff called the temp agency and reported the incident. They apologized and offered to send over another secretary right away, but Cliff declined. He made arrangements to have the lock changed on his office door and the clientele file cabinets.

Genuinely pissed off, he strode briskly to the park to clear his mind. Things were fast escalating out of control, and he didn't have an answer for the latest series of bizarre events.

He stopped at a Starbucks to get his morning coffee and to make some calls. He called an attorney friend who agreed to meet him in a few minutes. He was bursting with anger and indecision.

While waiting, Cliff thought about his situation in general, and the uncontrollable circumstances that befell him. He couldn't just give in to the FBI with their every request and let them ride roughshod over him, but what alternatives were available? Maybe his attorney friend would have some answers for him. Neal Umber and he went to law school together, and they both set up separate offices in the same town with the thought of someday merging their businesses. In the meantime, Neal married, and he and his wife Debbie had started a family.

Cliff and Neal occasionally played golf, but no longer went out for a night of fun and laughter like they had before his friend got married. Neal was a tall, thin, handsome man, with slick back hair. He got along well with women, and for that reason, he built a specialized practice of representing women in divorce cases. Cliff chose to follow business law.

Cliff drummed his fingernails on the table as he waited impatiently for Neal to arrive. He looked constantly to the door for any sign of Neal. The past few days had disrupted his life and left him unsure and anxious about his immediate future. His practice had suffered for lack of attention, and the huge thought of being disbarred for representing two conflicting clients bothered him.

Neal said it would be a few minutes, but it had already been a half-hour. The coffee shop was busy and he moved to a quieter table in the back. Most of the patrons were noisy college kids who came in to have a cup of coffee and work on their studies, but it seemed they just wanted to converse with one another. Neal finally arrived and apologized for being late. Both attorneys ran on tight schedules. It was that way because they worked sixty-hour weeks just to make a living.

"Hello Cliff. Sorry for being late, but Debbie and I are having another baby, and it could be this very day. It's hard to juggle business and family at times like I'm now doing. So, what's up with you? You sounded miserable on the phone."

"Neal, my life is floundering. I have reached the bottom of the barrel. I need to share my troubles with someone, or I'll burst. Being we're so close, I chose to call you."

"Fire away, old buddy, I'm full-on listening."

Cliff related his story about Brian's accident, the FBI seeking his help, the brain surgeon asking him to represent him, and about returning to his office only to find the temp and the FBI agent going through his clientele files. He leaned back and asked Neal for suggestions.

"You need a shovel to dig a hole and jump into it. What the hell were you thinking?"

"Come on Neal, I need a solution to my problems, not your dry humor and criticism."

"You shouldn't have taken Doctor Ulsheeh on as a client."

"We both learned that on our second day in law school. I know what I did was wrong, but I had a good reason for doing it."

"Reasons—baloney! You could be disbarred for doing that. Are you desperate for money or something? You know the FBI arrested a number of those guys from that very Mosque after the 9/11 bombing. I've never known you to get into such a pickle."

"Neal, don't be critical with me. I don't need that! With Brian's accident all of this has come down hard on me, and I'm not sure what the FBI suspects me of doing? As each day passes I am totally consumed with these new intrusions in my life. Do you have any suggestions?"

"Suggestions—right the boat immediately. I'd call Doctor Ulsheeh and tell him you have conflicting clients, and you can no longer represent him, and then tell the FBI you are no longer representing him. Possibly work with the FBI and get them back on your side, and maybe they will ease up the pressure they have on you."

"That's all well and good, but the Doctor is still treating Brian, and if I get him angry he may take it out on him. That was the main reason I accepted his retainer. Maybe I could call the FBI agent and tell her I will discontinue my relationship with Doctor Ulsheeh as soon as he releases Brian from his care."

"Sounds like you solved your own problems. Listen, I've got to run. Debbie needs to go to the hospital. It's time for it to happen. I'm looking for a boy this time. Wish us luck."

"Neal thanks. It makes it easier to talk it out. Let's keep in touch. Oh, maybe I'll see you at the hospital, I'm there every evening."

Cliff returned to his office and called Agent Salture. He looked out of the window and saw a black SUV parked across the street. He couldn't concentrate on his work because of the distraction. This FBI aberration had taken its toll on him and his whole life. Agent Salture entered his office.

"I'm here, what do you want?"

"I owe you an explanation. I couldn't refuse taking a retainer from Doctor Ulsheeh because he is still treating my brother. Does that make sense to you?"

"In a way it sounds reasonable, but you could have been up front with me from the very beginning. All that said, I'm asking for a little cooperation from you instead of an, 'I know my rights' statement. I'm willing to overlook the conflicting interests, but I need you to be up front with me in the future."

"Good, I'm pleased we understand each other. Perhaps you could let me know what's going on with your investigation with the Doctor? The more I know, the more cooperative I can be."

"Oh! You're seeking an opportunity to learn more about my case. I'll be up front with you as much as I'm able. Silicon Valley is a hotbed of activity. The Livermore Laboratories, Stanford University, the University of California, and a number of tech industries are located here in Silicon Valley. The brightest of minds, and the very edge of our future lies right here in this immediate area. Foreigners are constantly trying to steal the secrets that embryo in this immediate area, and it is the FBI's job to prevent that from happening. In the last two years your brother is the fourth scientist in this area to be been run off the road. All four have suffered brain injuries, and have been operated on by Doctor Ulsheeh. His skills as a brain surgeon are unquestioned, but his association with suspect Middle Easterners is a major concern for us. Also, these multiple accidents have increased our suspicions that foul play is afoot. Brian's accident will give us another shot at nailing this Doctor. Somehow he is involved, but we don't know how deeply."

"I had no idea this was an ongoing investigation. I appreciate your sharing this information with me. You can rest assured I will not discuss anything you told me with anyone, and I will cooperate with you in the fullest. All I want to do is to get past my brother's accident, and get on with my normal life."

5

Agent Salture left, and Cliff sat alone with his thoughts. The reasons for the FBI's presence were now clear. It wasn't just his brother who was involved in an accident, but three other leading scientists from this very area were also involved in similar accidents. The FBI had centered their investigation on Doctor Ulsheeh because he had operated on all four scientists. After all, he was the leading brain surgeon in the area, and the only surgeon capable of operating on all four men. But how could the FBI suspect Doctor Ulsheeh of having anything to do with the accidents? He had an impeccable reputation, and was considered to be on top of his profession. Could it be because of his religion and his association with the men at the Mosque? And what could he possibly have done to the scientists during the operations to make the FBI suspicious of him? After all, his brother could have died if it hadn't been for Doctor Ulsheeh's skills as a brain surgeon. Agent Salture knew all of that, but she continued to believe he was somehow involved. It didn't make sense, unless the FBI was withholding information from him.

Cliff needed to clear his mind. He decided to take a drive in the country and relax for a day before starting work again. He called Anne, his long time companion, to ask if she would join him on a picnic. A change in the weather was approaching and he wanted to experience a good country day to allow his meandering mind to relax.

"Cliff, I don't hear from you for two weeks, and you call me at the last minute wanting me to drop everything to go for a ride and a picnic with you. What's the matter, couldn't you get Cheryl to go with you? I can't miss work like that. Do you want to get me fired?"

"Forget it. No reason to get all riled up. It was just a passing thought. For your information I didn't call Cheryl, so you needn't worry about that. I wanted to go with someone I could talk to about my recent experiences. I haven't seen you for a while and thought we could get together for an afternoon. Have a good day at work, and I'll see you when you have more time for me."

"That's downright crappy, and you know it. I've been waiting to hear from you for over a week. You never called, not even to say hello. Marianne and I talked several times and she told me what was going on with your brother and all. I'm sorry if you're hurting right now, but I can't do what you're asking. Cliff, I'm here for you, but not on this short notice."

Click. Cliff laid down his cell when Anne hung up without giving him a chance to respond to her accusations. Instead he decided to spend the day with his ailing father. When he arrived home he found his father still in bed.

"Dad, get up. I'll fix you a nice breakfast, and we can spend the day together."

He didn't respond to his urgings. Cliff pulled his covers off while pleading with him to get up. His father's stern look told him to back off. Since his mother's passing his father had spells of anger highlighted with periods of depression.

Cliff went into the kitchen and found dirty dishes piled high in the sink. Dad didn't know how to use the dishwasher and he relied on Marianne to clean them for him. He loaded the dishwasher and opened the refrigerator only to find it almost empty, so he went to the store for groceries. When he returned he found his father still in bed. Short tempered, Cliff called his sister.

"Marianne, I'm at home with Dad and he won't get up for me. I plan to spend the day with him. Could you come over and help me get him up?"

"Come on Cliff, you want me to drop everything I'm doing and come over to help you. I have a family to care for and I don't have any free time right now. Besides, Ted wouldn't like it."

"To hell with what Ted likes or dislikes. I need you here to help me with Dad. Something is terribly wrong here. He gets angry if I just touch the bed. I need your help. You have a way with him, and he will listen to you. I don't ask you for much. Please come over to get him out of bed. He'll listen to you."

"You'll owe me, big time. Okay, I'll be over there shortly. Lay out some clothes for him."

Cliff smiled inwardly. When his sister said, 'You'll owe me' she always found a way of getting paid back, and it was generally with a larger favor than he had received. It was like he handed her a blank check.

Marianne arrived and took charge just like Cliff knew she would. She had Dad up and dressed in less than a half-hour. Cliff fixed him a nice breakfast and laid the morning paper next to his plate like Mom used to do. His father looked at the plate and the paper beside it, looked at him, and smiled. Cliff's cell vibrated, but he ignored it. This was a significant moment for him. Dad hadn't smiled at him since Mom had passed.

Marianne stowed the dishes in the dishwasher and cleaned the kitchen before she left. She and Cliff had their differences, but when it came to family they were on the same page. Cliff took his father out to the cemetery. That's what he wanted to do. The day with his dad brought back memories of when his mother and father were young and when Brian, Marianne, and he were children. Of course, they had the normal family squabbles from time to time, but nothing serious ever occurred. That life was all in the past now. His mother's passing changed all of that. His Father's retirement hadn't gone well because they hadn't planned their future like they should have in their younger years. Brian had been supporting them financially for several years, but he didn't have much time to visit even when his Mom was so ill. Cliff and Marianne checked in with them daily in case something unusual happened that needed fixing.

Cliff returned to his apartment. It had been a good day— a day he would remember long after his father passed. They hadn't talked much, but the day together was well worthwhile. His father was aging rapidly, and Cliff knew it wouldn't be long before he lost him. He missed his mother, and thought of her at moments like today. He was trying to relax in an effort to get his mind back on business, but memories of his mother and father lingered. Since his mother passed the family was held together by a string. Father had lost all his desire to live.

As he unwound in his overstuffed chair, he gazed around his apartment, searching for a way to relax his overworked mind. His wandering eye caught something different. His eyes settled on the couch cushions. That was it—his fetish—the cushions were turned, exposing the zippers. They were flipped over exposing the cushion zippers. When he first moved into the apartment his mother called his attention to it. Since then, he always made sure they were in their right place and the zippers were hidden. The cleaning lady knew of his fetish about the couch cushions and she correctly arranged them before leaving the apartment.

Besides the cushions being turned over, it appeared the main couch cushions were also moved, and not pushed back into their proper place. His roving eye searched for other changes, but none were apparent. He put the cushions back in place while his mind searched for a reason. Gripped with curiosity, he went into the kitchen to look for other changes. Everything was in place as his wandering eyes searched for anything misplaced. He opened the refrigerator door— no change. He opened the freezer door— no change other than it was almost empty, as usual. Not finding anything different, he went into the bedroom and opened the closet. No change. He sat on the edge of the bed with his mind probing for reasons—or was it just his imagination? He opened the dresser drawers and found his underwear in disarray— not like he always carefully arranged them. He was meticulous about how he placed them in the drawer because his mother would occasionally comment on his personal habits when she visited the apartment. Since her passing he continued to follow her suggestions. Every time he refilled his dresser drawers he thought of her and her rigid rules for neatness. He carefully searched the other drawers. His clothes had all been searched. *For what*, he pondered. He shrugged his shoulders to ward off the feelings he was experiencing. He frantically remembered his gun next to the bed where he always kept it. He opened the drawer and sighed with relief. It was there, but when he examined more closely he noted the cartridge clip was missing. He sat on the edge of the bed to regroup his thoughts. This was something new to him. No one had ever searched his apartment before. *Someone was in my apartment and searched it. Was all of this my imagination, or what?* He queried aloud. He hadn't removed the clip from the gun for some time. Perhaps he'd been careless of late, and had done all of these changes himself. He thought about the FBI searching his flat, but quickly dismissed the idea—but what if they had? His mind searched for other reasons. He had nothing to hide, but someone thought he did.

His cell vibrated. "Cliff, it's Agent Salture. About two hours ago my associates observed two people from the Mosque entering the front door of your apartment building. We know they don't live there, and I thought they might have come to your apartment. Did they visit you?"

"They would have no reason to visit me, I don't know any of them."

Cliff was taken aback with Agent Salture's message. He breathed deeply while searching for an answer—then he blurted out.

"Someone's been in my apartment. I can't see they took anything, but someone's been here. Thanks for the heads up. I'll look into it a little further."

As he laid down his cell, his computer came to mind. Excitedly he ran down the hall to the bedroom. He hadn't thought about his computer before. It had privileged information on it that shouldn't and couldn't be shared with anyone. He quickly scanned through the various programs. He checked the conclusions he'd entered after Doctor Ulsheeh's first visit. They were there. He looked at his printer. It was on—something he would never do. His only clue was someone had left his computer and printer on. He always turned them off when he finished using them. It was a standard routine he carefully followed.

But why would the intruders search his apartment, use his computer and printer, and take the clip out of his handgun? He had nothing to hide. He couldn't think of a reason someone from the Mosque would search his apartment—unless Doctor Ulsheeh was behind this intrusion.

Nothing like this search of his apartment had ever happened to him during his years of practice. He had nothing to hide. Surely it wouldn't have anything to do with Brian's accident, or would it? What could the intruder be looking for? He searched for answers, but none came to mind. He sat in his recliner to think through his dilemma. There was a knock on the door. When he opened it, Doctor Ulsheeh was standing in front of him.

"Doctor Ulsheeh! How did you know where I live? Oh! I'm sorry, please come in."

"Your brother told me. I wanted to talk with you about him. Are you busy? I'm not intruding, am I? You look more than surprised to see me."

"I am surprised you knew where I live. Sorry. My day has been rather hectic, and I'm a little on edge. Please sit. May I get you something? A glass of water or something."

"I'll only be here for a few minutes. Brian appears to be making good progress, and I'll release him in another week or so. Has he confided anything about his work to you?"

"Why would you ask me about something like that?"

"Nothing, just curious, that's all. I did recall you mentioning several times how close you and Brian were growing up."

"We're still close. Not as close as we were before Brian started working at the Lab. Since he is involved in a number of secret governmental projects, he and I don't have much to talk about. He's never discussed his work with me. I find it strange you would ask me about that."

"Actually, the reason I asked may seem frivolous and unimportant to you, but during my time with him he kept repeating equations that didn't make sense to me. It has been bugging me for some time, and I wanted to discuss them with you. I thought you'd be able to help me solve this puzzle. I wrote them down, and thought about showing them to Brian, but decided it might embarrass him. I'd like to show you what I copied. He was talking about combining $H2C102$ and $H25202$. That would be a lethal combination and could cause an immediate explosion. Since you two are so close, I thought you could talk with him, and find out what he meant by quoting them in his sleep. You could also tell him he quoted a number of other equations. It might be embarrassing to him, but it wouldn't distress him as much as if I approached him about his loose tongue."

The doctor handed the written equations to Cliff. He glanced at them, and shook his head.

"I'm a lawyer, not a scientist. I don't understand all of this gibberish. I'm thoroughly surprised you'd write them down. Surely you knew he was delirious. I can't understand why you would do such a thing. Has the FBI asked you anything about this?"

"No, they're not aware I have these equations in my possession. You're my attorney and anything that's said here is kept here, isn't that so?"

"Yes, it is, but I can't do what you are asking. Your secret is safe with me. Are you aware a couple people from your Mosque entered my apartment and searched it? You wouldn't know anything about that, would you?"

"I'm troubled you would harbor such thoughts. I have my ethics too! My friends don't do that sort of thing. You are harboring evil thoughts about my friends and me. I am here for a single reason and that is to discuss these equations. You may not think so after our discussion, but I am possessed with equations— that's all. It is merely a way to take my mind off of the stressful profession I pursue. Equations are my hobby. Some people are obsessed with crosswords, some play bridge, some play golf or tennis, but I'm different, I gather equations. I work on them daily to take my mind off the stressful things I do."

"You made an unusual request of me. I don't like it at all."

"I am so sorry to have upset you so. You're making unusual facial expressions. Can't you accept my simple explanation? Equations are a hobby for me?

"I find your request most disturbing. Your actions are too troubling for me to understand. I know we are from different cultures and beliefs; however, I am deeply disturbed about what you are asking of me. Your reasons for not approaching Brian yourself I find to be inappropriate, and I am suspicious of your intentions."

"Hold on. You accepted my retainer. When you did that I understood we would work together to safely discharge Brian in the near future, and you would relieve the tension the Federal harassment has caused me."

"The misunderstandings are entirely on your part. I have drafted letters to your Congressional Representatives about your harassment concerns, and I have spoken with the FBI person in charge of Brian's case. Any action from either party will not happen overnight and may not occur in the near future, but you will receive a letter of apology written on Congressional letterhead along with a statement from the Federal Law Enforcement Departments describing the reasons for their vigilant surveillance of you and your activities. I have been very active with your account."

"I'm pleased. You've eased my mind about the actions you have taken. I appreciate everything you have done on my behalf. I apologize for being so quick tempered—it is not of my nature to do so. Perhaps I should be leaving now."

"Before you leave, I must remind you that I can't forget what you asked of me this afternoon. I'm your attorney, but your request to get this information from Brian is beyond the scope of our attorney-client bounds. You're asking me to do something bordering on irregularity, and outside my bounds as your attorney to do."

"I thought you and Brian were so close he would share this tiny bit of information with you, and it would not distress him. Believe me, I have only good intentions. I have brought your brother back from obvious death, and you are suspicious of me at every turn. If you don't have a mind to help me, forget it! You're my attorney and anything I say to you must be held in strict confidence."

"You needn't remind me of that! I am aware of my responsibilities as your attorney. We're done here, please leave."

Doctor Ulsheeh left. Cliff plumped himself into his recliner while deliberating his dilemma, and tried to make sense out of what happened with the doctor.

Just a hobby, I bet, Cliff declared loudly. He wanted to shout it, but restrained himself. Could he break the lawyer code and tell the FBI what he and the doctor discussed? The thought ran rampant through his mind. *The wire.* He'd inadvertently turned it on when the Doctor first entered. He could give it to the FBI agent and he wouldn't have to say a word. It wouldn't be entirely ethical, but what the hell, he concluded.

A knock on the door! He was taken aback. A second knock before he rose to answer it. He opened it.

"Ted, what's up? You haven't been here before, have you?"

"Marianne sent me to get you. She called, but you didn't answer your cell. It's your father. The ambulance took him to the hospital. I don't know what is wrong, but he has been taking a lot of Marianne's time lately."

"I'm sure you wouldn't understand. Did you ever have a mother and father?"

"That's a hell of a question. I'm not here to fight with you, but you didn't answer your cell, and Marianne needs you at the hospital. I got to go, the kids are in the car."

Ted turned and left without another word. Cliff, still holding the doorknob, leaned his head against the door. *What next*, he murmured. The door vibrated, and then he heard the knock. He opened the door. It was Agent Salture.

"What's the matter? You look like hell."

"I wasn't expecting you. This has been a pure hell day."

44

"You shake easily, don't you? I'm here to get the tape from your wire. Surely you turned it on when Doctor Ulsheeh was here, didn't you?"

"Help yourself. I can't voluntarily give it to you. Attorney client privilege, you know. You'll have to take it from me under protest."

"Don't be so dramatic. Unbutton your shirt."

"I can't give it up. You have to take it from me. Otherwise, I can't give it up."

"Grow up! No one is listening."

"If you want it, take it and leave. My father is in the hospital, and I must go."

Agent Salture took the tape, installed a new one and left. Cliff rushed to the hospital. He arrived at the Emergency Center and found Marianne in the waiting lounge.

"I called, and Dad didn't answer. Ted suggested I call 9-1-1. When I got there the paramedics were working on him. They got his heart started, but I don't know anything more. What can we do now?"

"Just wait. These people know what to do. We have to consider putting Dad into a nursing home soon. I hate the thought, but it is getting to be that time. We could visit him at the place or maybe take him home with us several times a week. It would mean we would both have to clear some time to be more active in his life. One thing for sure, neither you nor I have extra time just now. Whatever we do, we must make it work. Dad won't be with us much longer, and we need to make that time positive for him and us."

"That's a terrible idea. Maybe we could find someone to stay with him at home. Let's wait on those plans until we hear what the doctor has to say."

"Sis, it appears we can't agree on anything these days. If I come up with a plan, you have another idea. It's perfectly clear we must do something to lengthen Dad's life or he won't be with us much longer. Let's not quarrel about what we should do with Dad just now. We're both tired and stressed out. Besides, Dad would have to agree with anything we decide."

6

Cliff left to visit with Brian. He showed his identification to the FBI agent at the door, turned on his wire, and entered Brian's room. When he looked at the bed— it was empty— Brian was not there.

Cliff returned to the door, and the agent said, "That was a short visit."

"He's not here! Where is he?"

"What?" The agent exclaimed.

They returned together to search his room. Cliff looked in the bathroom—he wasn't there. The agent punched a number into his cell. Cliff went to the nurses' station to find out where Brian had been transferred. The nurses checked their charts, and they all rushed back into Brian's room. In about ten minutes Agent Salture came running down the hallway.

"Cliff, what do you know about this?"

"Me? I know nothing. Absolutely nothing! Blame me if it will save your job. He couldn't have disappeared into thin air. I came in, and he was gone. The nurses don't know where he is either. I thought your door guy was supposed to watch over him."

Agent Salture's face reddened. She made no reply. She pulled the agent aside to question him. He had no answers as to where Brian had gone.

Agitated, but unsure about the whole affair, Cliff left to check on his father. Surely they would find where Brian was transferred because he wasn't capable of wandering off by himself. Yet, it was strange the nurses didn't know what happened to him. He made his way to the Emergency room while attempting to put the whole bad episode of his brother out of his mind. Marianne was beside their father's bed when he arrived. His father was now awake and appeared to have recovered from his attack. The doctor approached the three of them.

"You can take him home in a few hours. He'll be just fine now. There's no further damage to his heart, but I suggest you keep someone with him at all times, or put him in a nursing home where they can keep track of him 24/7. He could have passed on if Marianne hadn't found him when she did."

Another cliffhanger, Cliff sighed.

Now was the time for Cliff and Marianne to take control of their father's life. His father had refused help in the past, but the time had come to make some immediate changes regardless of his father's objections.

Cliff reached for his father's hand. His father had always been active in his children's lives until their mother passed. Since then, everything had changed, and their father had changed too. It was like he didn't want his children to be around him any more. He would ask about Brian, then not mention his name again for days.

"Dad, did you hear what the doctor said?"

"I heard him. I'm not going into any nursing home. I'll do just fine at home. You needn't worry about me. I can take care of myself."

"Dad, it's obvious you can't. I know it is hard to accept, but we all have to face adversity some time in our lives."

"Son, I faced adversity before you were born. I don't believe you have the right to tell me what's good for me, and what's not."

Marianne listened. She had nothing to add. She knew Cliff was right in his thinking, but didn't want to enter into the discussion.

Cliff couldn't tell Marianne about Brian being missing. She had enough to worry about with their father's health issues. He needed to get his father's situation settled first—then he could return to Brian's room. Regardless, urgent decisions needed to be made concerning their father's future.

"Dad, I'll move in with you for a while if that is okay with you. Nothing needs to change for the time being. I can be there every morning to fix your breakfast, and see you are up and about. I will be home after work, and we can have dinner together just like when Mom was here. We could have someone come in during the day to sit with you. Are you okay with that arrangement?"

"You mean someone to baby-sit me. No way. I can manage my own life. I like the idea of you moving back home."

"It's set. We'll handle one change at a time. I know you'll be all right by yourself. Keep in mind, Marianne and I have concerns with your wellbeing. This makes the second time in the last month Marianne had to call 9-1-1 for you."

"Enough! Cliff, don't you understand me? I don't give a damn if my heart stops or not."

Cliff, dismayed and frustrated with his father's actions, left to see what was happening with Brian. His family was falling apart, and he didn't have a solution for any of it.

When he arrived at the corridor the FBI had blocked off the hallway where Brian's room was located. He looked for Agent Salture, but couldn't find her. He called her on his cell. It was her responsibility to see that Brian was kept safe. She didn't answer. He angrily punched in her number a second time. She answered.

"Agent Salture."

"Do you know where Brian is at this very moment?"

"No, I don't. I'm too busy to talk just now."

She hung up. Cliff snapped his cell shut in a flurry of outrage. *How dare she treat me like that!* He swore under his breath.

He looked down the hall to see three men in suits, Agent Salture, and Doctor Marsh huddled together. He gazed down at the parking lot below secretly wondering if Brian had left the hospital.

Wishful thinking—he would need outside help to do that, muttered Cliff.

His cell vibrated.

"Cliff, sorry about my hang up. I didn't have any answers for you then, but I do now. The agent at the door told me he had to relieve himself, and he left his position for only a few minutes. When he returned he didn't look inside to make sure Brian was in his bed like he should have done. After an exhaustive search I know your brother has left the hospital. Without any doubt on my part, I believe he needed help to leave. I don't know anything more about this, but in time, I'll have an answer. Two questions: Do you think he had a reason to leave the hospital, and do you have any idea who might help him do so?"

"He was in no condition to be moved. Also, he values his life too much to pull a stunt like this. Someone must have kidnapped him or something. He's still missing a piece of his skull."

"Kidnapped him? That's highly unlikely. I need a list of his closest friends, and the phone numbers of the people with whom he worked. He needed help to get out of the hospital, and help with his transportation too. I would think he would call on his closest friend, and that would be you."

"Hell, I discovered him missing. Is our relationship so fragile you don't trust what I'm telling you? Brian gave me no indication he wanted to leave. This is totally unlike him. He always put his health before everything else. I strongly believe he was kidnapped. I doubt he had the strength to leave the hospital on his own. Look beyond me for your answers. I don't have any for you."

"Don't get your dander up. I am exploring all the possibilities. My badge is on the line. If I can't locate him, and get him back in the hospital, I could be taken off this case."

Cliff and Agent Salture had reached an impasse.

"I'll be available if you need me. I have to see about my father now."

Disturbed with the news about Brian, Cliff left to talk with his father about where he may have gone. He arrived at his parent's home and went upstairs to his father's bedroom. He was resting, but Cliff woke him and explained Brian's departure from the hospital.

"I don't blame him for leaving that damn hospital. I didn't like it there either. As to where he could be hiding, I think he would go up to the mountain cabin to get away from everyone. Brian always liked the forest this time of the year. If he was able, he went to the cabin."

"Good idea, Dad. I hadn't thought of that. I'm going to look for him now. Will you be all right here by yourself for a while?"

"Son, I don't need a babysitter. I'll be all right, now go and find your brother. You better stop and get some food and wood on the way because I left the place without supplies. Besides, it's quite chilly up there during the nights. Oh, one more thing, the shotgun is on the top shelf in the kitchen and the shells for it are in the box on the second shelf."

"Dad, why would you think I would need the shotgun?"

"Just precautionary, Son. I keep it there for a reason. Brian leaving the hospital doesn't make sense either, does it? Get my keys from the kitchen cabinet. You'll need them because only Brian and I have keys for the gate and cabin. You probably don't remember where we hid the keys close to the gate in case we forgot to bring them, do you?"

"I think I do, but it will be dark by the time I reach the gate."

"Bring him here if he is up there, will you?"

"Okay Dad, I checked your refrigerator. There is plenty of food in there for you. I'm off. Call Marianne if you have any problems."

Cliff got his four-wheel drive truck before starting up the mountains. On the way he thought about his father's remarks about the shotgun. It would make him feel safer if he needed to spend the night alone in the cabin. Brian had always scared him with his wild stories, and he hadn't felt safe overnight in the cabin since. Going up to the cabin to find Brian was a shot in the dark, but he had no other ideas. Brian wouldn't come all this way unless something had gone horribly wrong in the hospital, or if he was hiding from the FBI, or from some unknown person. Brian had a brilliant mind, and he must have thought his whole situation through rather thoroughly or perhaps he was a hostage. But if that were so, he wouldn't be at the cabin, or would he? Those fractured thoughts tortured Cliff as he drove faster up the mountain grade.

Nevertheless, Brian left the hospital for a reason. If he was kidnapped he wouldn't be at the cabin, and this trip would be entirely futile.

It was a five-hour drive to reach the driveway to the cabin. Cliff's whole trip was filled with what-ifs. The chain across the road was down, indicating someone was at the cabin, because Dad always put the chain up and padlocked it when he left.

Hope surged within him.

He got out of the truck to check the padlock. It was unlocked and not broken. Hope for finding Brian surged within him. It was still a ten-minute drive to the cabin because the road hadn't been repaired for several years and the undergrowth had encroached on the road.

The darkness slowed his travel on the frontage road. When he arrived at the cabin Cliff sat in his truck for a few moments surveying the cabin and its surroundings. An unrecognizable car was parked near the porch with the front door on the driver's side wide open. Both fear and anxiety gripped him. If Brian were kidnapped he would have to deal with the kidnappers. He looked for lights inside the cabin, but the cabin was completely dark. Surely if someone was inside the fireplace would be aflame, and he would see the light from it where he was sitting. He saw no activity in the cabin or the area surrounding the cabin. The door to the screen porch was wide open. *Most unusual,* mused Cliff. He knew Brian would never leave the screen door open if he were alone inside the cabin because of the pesky critters living close by. Cliff retrieved his flashlight from the glove compartment along with his pistol. He approached the cabin door with caution, and turned the knob. It was unlocked. His father had taught them both to always lock the door. He flashed his light around the inside of the cabin. There was no sign of Brian or anyone else. But if that was so, then why the door was unlocked and a strange car out front? Could it possibly be an intruder? And if so, how did he have the key to the chain lock on the driveway entrance, and a key to the cabin? He aimed his pistol in the direction of the beam of light. A noise in the kitchen caught his attention—the beam from his flashlight caught some movement. His finger nervously gripped the trigger. Some pans from the upper shelf rained down on him as he caught a glimpse of a raccoon fleeing toward the front doorway. In his search he saw nothing else in the cabin. He closed the front door, locked it, and lit a kerosene lamp. He would have to stay alone for the night. He returned to the kitchen to retrieve the shotgun his father had told him about. The shotgun wasn't where his father told him it was kept. *Most unusual,* he mused. He returned to his truck for wood and the food he'd bought on the way. He was fearful of staying in the cabin without his father, because the forest creatures clawed at the screen door and walked on the roof during the night, keeping him awake all night long. His father thought it was funny, but it wasn't to Cliff or Marianne. He recalled the nights when he and Marianne huddled close to Brian when the pesky critters were extra noisy and active.

It took a while to start the fire, because the newly cut wood wasn't dried properly. His father had left everything clean just like he said. It had been over a year since he and his father visited the cabin. With the fire started, he reached for a cushion piled high on the couch. When he picked up a cushion — the pile moved. He gripped his revolver, and removed another cushion—and then, another —Brian was buried under the pillows. Lying next to him was his father's shotgun. He picked it up and checked the safety. It was turned off. He placed the shotgun on the mantle and turned his attention back to Brian. He'd covered himself with cushions to keep warm. Cliff shook his shoulder.

"Brian, wake up. Did you drive up here yourself? Is there anyone else here with you? Tell me, it's important, I need to know, are you okay?"

There was no response. Cliff thought about the bottle of bourbon his father always kept on the shelf in the kitchen. He shook the empty glass to get months of debris from it, poured a small amount of the dark brown substance in it, and rushed back to Brian. He lifted his head and put the glass to his lips. Brian coughed, but swallowed some of it. Brian was not a whiskey drinker, and it didn't go down well. His eyes opened. Cliff could see he was completely exhausted.

Cliff rushed to the kitchen to make coffee and sandwiches. When he returned, Brian was attempting to sit up.

"I hope no one followed you up here. How did you figure I would be here?"

"Dad suggested it. What made you leave the hospital, and who helped you? I know you couldn't leave by yourself."

By now Brian was strong enough to sit up. He looked at Cliff.

"I know you want answers, but I'll tell you later if you promise not to laugh at me. I appreciate you found me, but I don't want to answer any of your questions right now."

"Okay bro, I understand. Thank God I found you. Are you here by yourself? You needed a good reason for leaving the hospital. You can tell me all about it when you are ready, okay Bro?"

"I drove here by myself. Let's have another shot of that bourbon in the coffee, shall we? It helped strengthen me. We had some good times with Dad here, didn't we?"

"Yeah we did. Dad had another heart attack, but he is okay now. He's at home, and as ornery as ever. When I asked him where you could have gone, he said, 'the cabin.' And that's why I'm here."

Brian and Cliff sat in silence while they watched the flames lick the logs Cliff had started with some kerosene.

Brian poured more bourbon in his coffee, and downed another sandwich.

"Thanks Bro, for being here for me in my time of need. You're probably wondering why I pulled a bizarre stunt like I did. Something was going on at the hospital I didn't understand. Hours on end I couldn't remember anything, even you guys' names. Other times I would get terrific headaches and have flashes of unbearable pain that would last for hours. Sometimes when I woke up I didn't know who I was, and if I don't know who I am, how can I function in my work? Sometimes when I woke up Doctor Ulsheeh was giving me a shot and asking me about my work. The Lab is expecting me to return like nothing has happened, but I feel like a different person. That accident did something to my brain, and I can't get a handle on it. I'm a problem solver, and I can't solve a simple little riddle.

Equations flow through my head like a fast moving stream, and they have no meaning to me. In other words, I feel useless for the first time in my life."

"Brian, you need a crystallization moment. You're still recovering. It will take more time. Try not to rush it. Your brain was scrambled from the accident and it needs time to properly heal. It's like those football players who get a concussion. They feel it for a while, and then it all goes away. With your smarts, I'm sure you'll figure it out, and everything will turn out okay, you'll see."

"I need to rest now. Let's talk more in the morning."

Cliff covered his brother with a couple of blankets, and sat in the chair facing the couch. He poured another cup of coffee for himself. The heat from the fireplace felt good as it warmed his backside. He couldn't fall asleep, no matter what. The heat from the fire soothed him. He recalled the evenings filled with hunting stories his dad always told him, Brian, and Marianne. He placed another log on the fire and recited a short prayer he'd learned as a youngster. It would be a long night, but he vowed to stay awake to take care of Brian if he needed it. He didn't understand why Brian was acting like a fugitive. He had always been a rational thinker, but fear of some kind was eating on him. He tried to call Marianne, but his cell didn't work this far up in the mountains. Cliff thought about his practice as he fought dozing off from the warmth of the fire.

He awoke to his brother talking in his sleep. He was quoting formulas. It was just like Doctor Ulsheeh had said. Cliff scrambled to get a pencil and paper to copy them down, but became frustrated with his lack of math understanding. He soon quit.

Morning arrived and Cliff hadn't formulated a plan. One thing he knew—he needed to get his brother down the mountain grade, take him to a hospital, and call the FBI. He needed to get Brian to agree with his decision. He made coffee and breakfast, and told Brian about his plan.

"I need to get the piece of my skull put back, and then we can talk with the FBI. I don't want to get an infection—otherwise everything Doctor Ulsheeh did will be lost."

"Let's go home. I'm sure Dad will be able to help us. Do you feel strong enough to travel?"

"I'm okay. I'm ready whenever you are. You'll need to help me out to the truck."

"Brian, whose car is that?"

"Don't laugh Bro. I stole it. That's right, I stole it. I went down the back stairs and when I got to the parking lot I saw this car with the door open and the keys inside. I got in it and drove away. Right after that I decided to come up to the cabin. I must say it was pretty exciting."

"Bro, I would never take you for a felon. Also, I don't understand where you got the keys for the driveway and the cabin."

"You forgot! I can't believe it. Dad hid a set of keys under that log near the driveway entrance long ago. Remember, we came up to the cabin once and I forgot the keys. Dad called us a couple of loggerheads. He put them there when we left so it wouldn't happen again. I had a hell of a time finding them because when I bent down I got dizzy."

"We need to leave the car you stole here. I'll lock it up, take the registration, and talk with Agent Salture to get you off the hook. Brian, you could be charged with a felony for stealing that car. You were lucky it had enough gas to make it up here."

"Don't remind me. The blackouts, memory loss, my head throbbing most of the time, and now this latest event has put my life in shambles."

Cliff helped Brian out to his truck and went back to lock the cabin and the car. He paused for a moment while he thought of all the good times he, Brian, and their father enjoyed on their trips to the mountains. He drove down the driveway, put the chain back in place and locked the padlock. Once he reached the foot of the mountains his cell worked again.

"Agent Salture, I have Brian with me. We need to find another hospital for him. He says things are not right with Doctor Ulsheeh. I'll explain everything when Brian's injury is repaired to his satisfaction. I'm worried about him getting an infection in his head."

"Thank goodness. I'll find a hospital and get back to you. I want to talk with Brian as soon as he has a mind to talk with me."

His father was pleased to see his two sons. He examined Brian's head and told Cliff he needed attention as soon as possible. Marianne walked into the room.

"What's going on here? Why is Brian here? He should be in the hospital."

"It's quite complicated. I'll explain it to you when I have an hour or so. Just be patient for a while."

Cliff's cell vibrated.

"It's Agent Salture. I need to know where Brian is right this second, and I need to talk with him now! I will send an ambulance for him after we've talked."

"Brian needs care right now! He is in no condition for your questioning. I'll need your word on that."

"Damn it, Cliff. Why can't you do something my way for a change? Okay, we'll play by your rules for the time being. I'll call for an ambulance now. I'll have a couple agents with it to protect Brian from any harm."

The ambulance arrived and the paramedics took Brian with them. Agent Salture had kept her end of the bargain. Brian was on his way to another hospital, and Cliff sat down with Marianne and explained what happened to Brian. She couldn't believe what Cliff was telling her. Cliff returned to his office and found Doctor Ulsheeh waiting in the hallway.

He unlocked the door and said, "Come in. We need to talk."

"Yes we do. Did you help your brother leave the hospital?"

"No, I didn't, but I helped him after he left. Brian said you were constantly seeking information about his work. He is confused about what is happening to him. He has constant memory lapses, and quite often he has flashes through his brain that cause terrible pain. He thinks you are responsible for his confusion. Is there any truth to that?"

"He's not thinking straight. I gave him a shot every day to keep any infections in check and he thought it was to question him. He's delusional. As far as his thinking I was getting information from him, well, that's simply a figment of his imagination. I did copy a few formulas down when he kept repeating them over and over, but I shared them with you, and I intended to share them with Brian at a later date. Believe me, I'm not hiding anything."

"Let's not discuss it any longer, shall we? I'm tired and confused about what's going on with Brian. He tells me he doesn't trust you. Why are you here?"

"I am concerned about Brian. I thought you would be the one he would turn to when he was troubled. His recovery isn't going as well as I expected. He is harboring thoughts that I'm going to cause him harm. I just want him to recover as quickly as possible, and get back to work. If his behavior continues, I will have to go in and reexamine his brain tissue to see if he has developed some internal bleeding in his brain. With his type of condition some very small blood vessels in his brain tissue may have developed microscopic leaks on their own, and in time, a great amount of blood will distort his thinking."

"He is seriously concerned about his memory losses and black outs. Brian has some apprehension about your care. I don't know what happened between you two, but he believes you are inquiring about his work a lot of times when he is sedated."

"That's true. I am doing a study on the rate of recovery of my patients. I ask questions about their fields of endeavor because they are most familiar with that subject. I am not trying to get information about his work. He has memory losses, and when he wakes up he doesn't know who he is. And then, his hallucinations take over. I haven't had a recovery go so astray. When you're through making accusations, I would like to know where Brian is at this very moment."

"You'll have to talk with Agent Salture. He is presently under her supervision."

"Well! I see I'm not making much progress here. He is still supposed to be under my care, and I feel responsible for his recovery. You are my attorney and I expect you to act for my benefit, not against it."

The mild-mannered doctor left Cliff's office in a huff.

Cliff sighed—*another unhappy client.* Each day brought new challenges. He needed to take a walk to clear his thoughts. He locked his office and went to the elevator. When the door opened two men were getting out. It appeared strange because his office was the only one on the floor. He stepped in the elevator and punched the button for the next lowest floor. He got out and walked up the steps to his floor, and cautiously looked into the hallway.

The two men were standing near his outer office door. They were dressed like FBI agents normally dressed, but Cliff had no way of knowing who they were. He watched them for a couple of minutes as they walked down the hall toward his office door.

He waited in suspense.

One of the men pried his office door open. Cliff called Agent Salture. No answer. He left her a message. The two men entered his office. He approached the open outer door and peered in. The two men were searching his inner office.

What shall I do? What could they possibly be looking for? And who were they? And where in the hell is Agent Salture? Cliff considered.

7

Not knowing why these men were searching his office set Cliff's mind on fire. Years of hard work were being destroyed in a matter of minutes. He had no idea why they were going through his files in such a haphazard way. They would look at a file, then toss it up into the air so when it landed the pages would be scattered all over the floor.

What could they be looking for, or were they just wrecking his office? Cliff heaved an expressive sigh.

When he could no longer stand to watch what was happening to his office files he made his way to the stairway to call Agent Salture again. No answer—*damn it!* He grumbled. His patience ran amuck, and he closed his eyes for a moment of peace. That moment didn't arrive.

Agent Salute's voice mailbox remained full, and it wouldn't take another message. Frustration flooded his mind. These strangers were searching his office, appearing to enjoy their work, and he was left without an answer. Agent Salture's phone was constantly busy. Brian was taken to an undetermined hospital, and his mind was like a ship without a rudder.

Cliff searched for his mild-mannered self—and, unable to find it, he sighed heavily. As confident an attorney as he was, he felt he was losing it all. Again he called Agent Salture's cell— no answer—and her voice mailbox remained full.

Cliff waited in the stairway to view his office door, still not understanding why anyone would search his office. In about ten minutes the two men came out. As he watched the men depart he saw one of them had some of his papers under his arm. He wanted to go out and grab him by the throat and get his papers back, but the man was too large to challenge. The two men talked leisurely for a few minutes, pressed the elevator button, and then entered.

When the elevator door closed behind them Cliff rushed inside his office. All of his files were strewn around his office like a cyclone had been through, leaving all of his files covering the floor. It would take a month of Sundays to clean up the mess. The clutter completely covered his floor and he didn't know where or how to begin cleaning it up. He rushed to his window to see if they were still in the parking lot. It was too late. He looked around in dismay. There appeared to be no end to his troubles. He picked up his overturned chair, eased himself into it, and looked around. His office was completely dysfunctional. It would take the better part of a week to get things back to where they were before all this happened. He made a cursory check through his papers, but couldn't determine what was missing. Disgusted, he looked at his broken office door. It would take a carpenter and a locksmith to put it back in order. He made the call to them both. He'd used a security firm in the past and he called for them to send someone over until he could get his door fixed. He waited ten minutes, and no one arrived. He called again, and they assured him their man was on his way. In the past he thought about a security camera, but dismissed the idea when he considered it unnecessary. There was nothing of any value in his office. Disgruntled, he sat on the hallway floor and waited for the security guard. He was in no mood to pick up the strewn papers. Waiting gave him time to decide what to do. The security man arrived, looked inside the office and commented.

"Do you want me to guard this pile of rubbish?"

"Aw, you're funny. Yes, guard my pile of rubbish."

Cliff punched the button for the elevator and waited. Nerves frazzled, mind disturbed, and unsure about his next move, he felt like a wind-blown straw trying to find a place to land. His troubles had mounted to a point where it was getting beyond him to continue his practice. Three years of hard work building up the business were being destroyed.

His mind explored for a starting point—*but where*, he asked himself? Different ideas flashed through his mind like bolts of lightning searching for something to strike. Sorting through his recent failures, he hunted for answers—answers about his next move.

Finally, a plan came to mind—question Doctor Marsh about the two operations on Brian. He had assisted on them both, and he had also assisted on Brian's rehab routine. Perhaps the two doctors were conspiring together. If he found anything suspicious he would dig deeper into the doctors daily schedules. And perhaps he would question Doctor Marsh about Doctor Ulsheeh's outside activities. He needed a break—a break— to rebuild his confidence once again.

He went to the hospital to begin his search for information. The nurses informed him Doctor Marsh would be off duty for a three-day weekend. The loss of two days, possibly three, challenged his plans. The answers he sought were too pressing to be delayed. While driving to Doctor Marsh's residence he rearranged his plans. After knocking a number of times he heard a neighbor yell, "Quit, will you, he's not home."

He asked other neighbors who weren't too disturbed with his knocking about where the doctor could be. Several volunteered he loved skiing, and if he wasn't home, he would be up on the slopes for the weekend.

Cliff's questions couldn't wait to be answered. He needed answers now. A recent snowfall had covered the local mountain area with a good powder. Doctor Marsh could be a long way off, and if so, he would be gone for three days. His decision was almost instantaneous. He gassed the truck, refilled his coffee thermos, and started for the only ski resort within a day of town.

Surely he would find him there. His mind filled with pressing unanswered questions. As he made his way up the mountain slope his mind actively engaged in stringing together the questions he wanted to ask Doctor Marsh. He had driven in heavy snow many times before, and he cursed at the drivers going at a snail's pace, no doubt because of their lack of experience. His cursing didn't take the edge off his frustration, but only added to it.

Without warning, his soft side arrived rather unexpectedly. He turned off the radio and its warning about the weather and his thoughts turned to self-control. He must regain control of his normal self. Repeating it a number of times wasn't enough. He would have to practice it while questioning Doctor Marsh. The recent crisis fed his anxiety. Since Brian's accident he hadn't acted like his normal self. His approach to the Doctor needed to be muted and filled with calmness, understanding, and compassion. He took in moments of silence and vowed to approach Doctor Marsh in a calm and gentle way. As a defense attorney he had developed several sides of his personality. He needed to use the skills he had mastered in his years of law practice.

He arrived at the Lodge only to find Doctor Marsh was snowboarding on the slope. Another delay. He calmly waited outside the lodge, hoping to see Doctor Marsh when he arrived from the slopes. Hours passed and he didn't show up. Cliff swore to himself, but kept his calm. He went inside the lodge, chilled to the bone, and ordered a hot cider, because he hadn't brought the right clothing for the weather. He sat in front of the roaring lounge fire waiting for Doctor Marsh to return from the mountain, and he fell asleep. Exhaustion took over his mind and body.

A heavy hand squeezed his shoulder. He woke with a start.

"Cliff, what the hell are you doing here? It's Doctor Marsh. The receptionist said you were inquiring about me."

"Oh, yes I was. We need to talk. What time is it? I must have fallen asleep."

"The clerk at the desk said you've been creating some disturbances with your snoring. It's rather late, you know. I wasn't aware you were a skier."

"An amateur at most. A lot has happened in the last few days. We need to talk about Brian. Are you aware my brother left the hospital?"

"Surely so. It stood the hospital on its ear for a while, but everything returned to normal when we heard he was found and transferred safely to another hospital. I'm pleased everything turned out well for you both, but I'm not familiar with what happened to him from the time he left our hospital."

"For your information, it hasn't turned out well."

"It hasn't? What do you mean? Agent Salture came by to pick up Brian's medical records, and she told me he was doing just fine. Also, she said Brian would not be returning to our hospital."

"That part is true, but not entirely. I'm here to talk with you about the operations Doctor Ulsheeh performed on my brother. Brian is upset with Doctor Ulsheeh for a variety of reasons. You and I need to talk this thing through. Let's have a cup of coffee, and talk about my brother's operations and his delayed recovery."

"You mean right now? No way. I have a companion waiting for me in my room. I don't get much private time and I need to take advantage of it when it comes along. Your questions will have to wait until morning."

"They can't wait. There is a lot I need to know. I came all this way to ask you about Doctor Ulsheeh and other things."

"Put it on hold. I'll answer all of your questions in the morning. I'm on my time now. My girlfriend is waiting for me. Goodnight!"

Doctor Marsh left, and Cliff sank deeper into the couch, disappointed with the Doctor's remarks. The registration clerk approached him.

"You can't sleep here all night. Either register or leave."

"I'll register. Can you give me Doctor Marsh's room number?"

"You know I can't do that."

"Hey, I found this twenty lying on the floor. I think you dropped it."

"Oh, I guess I must have. Come up and register."

The clerk turned the registration log in Cliff's direction. He quickly scanned the register and found Doctor Marsh's room number.

Cliff was up early to question Doctor Marsh. He sat in the dining room waiting for him to come down for breakfast. He didn't. An hour and a half passed.

He went up to Doctor Marsh's room and saw a tray filled with dirty dishes outside his door. He knocked. No answer. He knocked again. No answer. The cleaning lady came by and Cliff asked about the occupants.

"Oh! They left real early this morning. I am getting ready to clean their room. There is a big storm approaching, didn't you know?

Cliff handed her a ten spot and rushed down the hall to the registration desk.

"Did Doctor Marsh check out early this morning?"

"He received an early morning call, and left a short time afterwards. Also, it's a good thing he did because a heavy storm is about to sock us in."

"You seem familiar with him. Does he come up here often?"

"Oh yes, he does. He is a generous tipper, we don't forget that, and he always brings a beautiful woman with him."

"Interesting, I need to check out too. Here is a twenty for your helpful assistance."

"Any time sir, you're also a generous tipper."

Cliff started his truck engine, turned on the heater, and went back inside the resort for a couple minutes to fill his thermos and to allow the heater to take the chill out of the cab. The weather had turned frigid during the night in the wake of the oncoming storm.

The parking attendant closed his truck door after he got in and commented, "You better get yourself down the mountain because the storm will hit us shortly, and the Highway Patrol will close the road. With the weekend over, a lot of our guests left earlier this morning. Most of our guests don't know how to drive in bad weather."

Cliff's truck was a four-wheel drive, and he had driven off-road and in bad weather before. The attendant's warning didn't faze him in the slightest. The mountain road was narrow with steep cliffs on the driver's side. He eased up on the gas pedal as the thick, fat flakes fell from the sky, creating the most beautiful picturesque scene imaginable. He needed to pay attention to his driving and let his thoughts of the recent events seep from his troubled mind. His windshield wipers were pounding at full blast, but weren't keeping his windshield clean. He slowed again, and cursed the wet snow clogging his windshield that also made the road extra slippery. He cautiously checked his brakes. He passed several cars and swore at them as they slowed to a crawl. He glared at the occupants, but the wet snow blurred his vision. He cursed again. It didn't help. He didn't know what kind of car Doctor Marsh was driving, and he scolded himself for not checking with the attendant before he left.

His dad had taught him to drive in worse storms than this one. He slowed again as he passed more stalled cars. He couldn't stop and be delayed by the storm—there was too much to do, and too many unanswered questions that needed answering. Doctor Marsh's leaving without answering his questions raised his dander and stuck in his craw. Halfway down the mountain the snow let up, allowing him to press harder on the gas pedal. Finally he rounded the last curve before reaching the valley floor. He stopped to gas up, unwind, refill his thermos with coffee, and call Agent Salture. It had taken two torturous hours to get down the mountain.

Agent Salture still didn't answer his call. His trip to the ski resort was a complete waste of time and energy. However, thoughts of why Doctor Marsh left the resort without talking to him fueled his thoughts further about a possible conspiracy between the two doctors.

Cliff went straight to his office. He called the locksmith to find where he had hidden the new keys. When he unlocked the door and entered his office, nothing had changed. It was still in complete disarray. He exhaled heavily to relieve his built-up tension. He looked around to see if he could detect anything missing. He concluded it must have something to do with Doctor Ulsheeh. He searched for his written files on the doctor and they were missing.

Doctor Ulsheeh must be behind this. If so, why would he do this? He must have something to hide. Cliff declared loudly to himself.

His office door swung open and Agent Salture entered. "You need to be a little more tidy. If you're looking for something, I don't see how you would ever find it in this mess. Where in the hell have you been? I have been trying to call you for days."

"Really. You're funny. Guess we've been playing phone tag. I must have called you a dozen times too without an answer from you. Check your cell—your answering log has been full."

"What happened here? It looks like you had some visitors."

"Yeah, two men. What do you make of this?"

"I have no idea."

"No idea huh? I haven't been able to reach you by phone, and thought you may have been taken off the case. Tell me, has anything happened since we were together last time?"

"I don't like to be the bearer of bad news. Brace yourself, will you? Brian has left the hospital again. We're not sure how it happened. I'm here to find out what you know about it."

"This is getting old. Every time something happens you come straight to my door. I've been gone. I haven't seen Brian since you transferred him to the other hospital. After the last time you promised to watch him more carefully. What did you do wrong this time?"

"It all happened in one of those moments— a moment when I let my guard down. A shift change occurred. I expected the regular nurses to come on duty, but was surprised when six new nurses came on duty and I hadn't checked their backgrounds before. It takes about ten minutes each for me to verify their history."

"Yeah, yeah, get on with it. The agent guarding Brian's room didn't have anything to do with helping you, did he?"

"Of course not. I am just telling you what happened during that period of time. If you don't want to hear it, tell me so."

"Are you making this up as you go along?"

"No, I'm not. Quit being so distracting. I'm trying to explain what happened. Here it is; one of the new nurses was immediately assigned to tend to Brian before I had a chance to interview her. Brian was in need of some kind of medical help. Our agent allowed her into his room thinking I had checked her out. After a few minutes she asked our agent to go to the nurses' central station to get another nurse to help her. She told him the call button wasn't working properly. When he returned from the central desk, Brian and the nurse were gone."

"That doesn't make sense to me. I thought the door agent's duty was to watch Brian, no matter what happened."

"Nurses rule the floor in the hospitals, and they need to move around like lighting sometimes. The attending nurse asked for my agent's help, and he responded. This case is enough to test any agent's ability. I am doing the best I can. Please don't be critical of me. It won't help your brother."

Cliff sighed, while Agent Salture walked to the outer office to receive a call. It appeared she was on top of the case once again, and he shouldn't blame her for Brian's absence. Brian had been acting weird ever since the accident. Perhaps it wasn't all the FBI's fault. Agent Salture closed her cell and paused, unsure what to say to Cliff. The screwed look on her face alerted Cliff there could be more bad news coming.

"Spit it out, will you? You look like you just swallowed a hard boiled egg."

"More bad news. Our investigations have uncovered some startling news. The nurse attending Brian recently came from Iran. She was one of the new nurses, and the hospital hadn't informed us she was here on a visa. We have the license number of the car they left in. There are seven agents presently assigned to the case, and we should have some answers soon."

"Do you have any idea about what's going on? This is all getting too weird for words. I don't understand why Brian would leave the hospital again. Do you think he was drugged or forced to go?"

"We have no idea, but we'll know in time. Be patient while we sort through the facts. This has turned into a very complicated case. It would be best if you didn't interfere with our investigation from here on in. In time, I will keep you abreast of any new discoveries we make."

Agent Salture left, but Cliff sat and pondered, more confused than ever. It wasn't Brian's nature to be swayed by another person's thinking unless…

Marianne opened the door and came in.

"Cliff, why haven't you been answering your cell? What's happened here?"

He looked at his sister thinking he couldn't expose her to all of the recent news.

"Quit looking like a scalded turkey and answer my questions."

"I wish I had some answers for you. There are so many unanswered questions I can only speculate about what is going on."

"Get on with it. I have to pick up the kids from school in a few minutes. I hadn't seen you recently and you haven't answered your phone."

"Sorry Sis. All hell is breaking loose. Someone broke into my office causing all of this, Brian is gone again, and no one knows where he is. Sis, I'm worried. Brian has changed in a way that I hardly know him. He is doing the most unpredictable things of late. The FBI has a number of agents searching for him right now. We need to depend on them to do the right thing."

"Ted is very upset with me for being away from the house so much lately. How did you let this happen, and when?"

"Come on, I wasn't here. Brian left the hospital again yesterday, only this time, with some Iranian nurse. He must be afraid for his life or…something else is driving his actions."

"Cliff, we need to have faith in God's doings, and if we have patience enough to see what develops, God will give us a sign. We can't give up hope. Brian loved his work too much to give it up so easily. There must be a good reason why he's doing all of this. Let's have faith in God to do the right thing. It looks like you need some sleep to let your heart slow down."

"Sis, I do. You know all the signs, don't you?"

Marianne left. Cliff had a heavy heart knowing his sister was hurting as much as he. They both loved their elder brother more than they would admit. He called an attorney friend to take over his cases for a while. One of his cases was due to come to court in a couple of days. His mind was so fragmented he couldn't concentrate on anything except Brian and his unusual behavior. He went home, took a sleeping pill and slept for twelve hours. A knock on the door woke him.

"*It might be Brian,* he speculated as he came out of a thought-provoking dream about him. In his dream he was rushing here and there in search of his brother. He opened the door to find a stranger facing him.

"Cliff Mercer?"

"Yeah, I'm Cliff Mercer. What is it you want?"

"I'm Henry Burrell. I was Brian's assistant at the Livermore Lab. I went to the hospital for a visit, and he was gone again. He is acting so weird the Lab has terminated him. He often talked about you, and I thought he might be here."

"He isn't. I don't know where he is at this moment. Firing him was poor thinking by his superiors. How can I help you?"

"He's already been replaced by another administrator, and I have been assigned to him. Through the years Brian helped me with my career. I couldn't have worked with a more knowledgeable boss, and I feel I owe him so much for all he did for me. I need to explain to him what is happening at the Lab."

"It's nice you've stopped by. Brian recently confided his displeasure with me that none of his superiors at the Lab visited him."

"In a way, that's understandable. We're so busy at the Lab we hardly have time to take care of our personal needs. He should be aware of that."

"Give me your cell number, and I will have him call you. I'm sure he will be upset with your news. You know, he prized that position very much."

"I know. Be sure to tell him I came by, will you?"

"Of course. Thanks for your thoughtfulness."

Cliff closed the door. The sleep had cleared his mind. After breakfast he drove to the office. He hadn't cleaned up the mess left by the intruders. He slumped into his chair as he put his papers back in their proper places and he searched for a reason someone would so haphazardly go through his files without a care about how they left them lying on the floor. He looked out of the window and saw a black SUV parked across the street. He decided to walk to see if it followed him. He occasionally turned around. It was following him. He called Agent Salture, and she answered.

"Someone is following me in a black SUV. Is it your crew?"

"No, it isn't. Tell me where you are, and I will have it checked out."

"I'm two blocks south of my office on Manchester. I will be walking back to my office."

Cliff glanced back. The SUV was no longer following him. When he returned to his office Agent Salture was sitting across from his desk.

"It wasn't us, but we know who was following you. It was an SUV from the Iranians Consulate's office. They were driving away when we arrived. I checked out the license plate. We know where Brian is right now."

"Well tell me, where is he now? I'm dying to know."

"He's in the Iranian Consulate's home. We keep a 24/7 camera on the street in front of the Consulate's home, and we have film of a black SUV arriving with Brian inside shortly after the time he and that nurse left the hospital. The car drove into a fenced compound where we couldn't see him getting out of the car, but we viewed the film a number of times and we are sure he was in the back seat. We are now coordinating our efforts with the CIA, because this case has turned international. Tell me, Cliff, has your brother ever indicated any leanings toward the Moslem religion?"

"No, he's a straight-forward apple pie American. I have no idea where you're going with this line of questioning, but I'm getting a dark view of it."

"We know the nurse couldn't have carried him out of the hospital, so we must assume he willingly left with her. There's more—our Government has no diplomatic relations with Iran. However, Iran keeps a consulate office in the city because their country belongs to the United Nations. The Consulate's home is a haven for them to carry on covert activities in our country."

"God, what next? He willingly left two hospitals, and now he is inside an Iranian Consulate's compound. That said, where do we go from here?"

"I don't presently have an answer. We're working on it."

"It sounds like the puddle gets deeper as we go. Brian's gone, my apartment has been searched and my office ransacked—what could happen next? There seems to be no answer to anything. And you say 'We're working on it.' Before Brian's accident life was so simple. Since then, his life is a total wreck, his life is in shambles, and his family is torn apart. I'm so upset I don't know what to do about it."

"Problems like this one can't be resolved overnight. You need to be patient. Everything will work out for the best. Like I said, we have a number of good people working the case now, and we will get a handle on all of the loose ends in time."

"I have no idea what you think about Brian, but I can assure you that he is not an evil man, and he would do nothing to harm his country. After 9/11 I had to discourage him from joining the Armed Services that very day because he was so upset."

"Well, you would know Brian better than anyone. Keep in mind people can change, you know."

"People are my business. There is something very strange happening to my brother. He was level-headed, smart, careful about his health, and he would never act like he is now on his own."

"I believe you. Let's let this case play out, shall we? Sometimes things begin to fall into place and the case gets quickly resolved. Let's hope that is what will happen in this case."

8

Agent Salture got up from her chair, walked to the window, and looked out. Cliff could see she was troubled, but he didn't know how to help her. He blamed her for all Brian's problems, yet he felt silent remorse.

"A dime for your thoughts."

"I was working up the courage to ask you to do something very special for me."

"And what could that be?"

"It could be risky, and it might not accomplish anything positive."

"What the hell, if you have something to say—say it?"

"Time is passing swiftly, and we don't have a clue about what is happening to Brian. My boss just nixed my going in posing as Brian's sister because Brian may not accept that. We have no idea of his state of mind at this time. I was thinking that perhaps you could go into the Consulate's Compound to talk with him, and maybe get a slant on his situation. That's what I have on my mind."

"That doesn't sound too difficult. I'll just walk up to the door, knock, and ask to see him. I can handle that."

"It isn't all that simple. These are difficult people to approach, much less strike up a conversation. Our country's relations with the Iranian Government are close to the breaking point over their nuclear development. The only reason they have a consulate in our country is because the United Nations insisted on his being here."

"I don't know or care about all of that international crap. If my brother is in there, in danger like you suspect him to be, I want to help every way possible. Is there something special I should ask whoever answers the door?"

"There are Iranian soldiers at the door. You'll have to work your way past them to get to someone of authority. Be pleasant, not aggressive, and possibly humble. Don't be like your recent self, but calmly ask to speak with your brother. If they allow you to speak with him, try not to be overly aggressive with your questions. Remember, everyone from Iran has an opinion about Americans."

"I can do that. If I can get in to see him, I can read him like a book. We've thought alike since we were kids. Drive me over there, and you can coach me on the way. Brian isn't the only one with brains in this family. I can memorize anything you want me to ask."

"I have to clear this with my superior. He may want to talk with you before you go in. If that is okay with you, I'll call him for permission. Give me a few minutes."

"Who are you calling? I have never met your superior. Perhaps we should all have a talk. I have a lot of marbles in this game too."

"Hog wash! I am the agent in charge of this case."

"That's funny, if you're the head guy, so to speak, why do you have to check with anyone?"

"The more I'm around you the more I dislike you. I don't have to answer your foolish questions."

"The more you're around me the more riled up you become. That is a sure sign you're falling for me or something like that?"

"That's a laugh. Do you live in fantasyland? Don't venture there. Perhaps I should ask for a transfer. Agents are forbidden from becoming too familiar with their clients. I have no interest in you as a person. You are the brother of my client; and that is it!"

"Wow! Now we have cleared the smoke, who were you calling?"

"I'm not calling anyone. I'm moving ahead on my own."

"I don't want you to get into trouble on my account."

"Personally I don't like you badgering me at every turn. That said, I'm perfectly capable of making major decisions on my own.

If you feel you are able to talk with your brother it might move the case forward."

"The sooner the better. I'm anxious to find out why Brian would willingly go with that Iranian nurse. It is totally unlike him to go with a stranger, especially a young woman."

"It is most important you identify his state of mind. Like, is there any change in his overall demeanor? Is he freely able to share his present condition with you, or does someone else answer for him? Does he use his hands the way he normally did in the past? If he should be under the influence of drugs he will generally fold his hands in front of him and keep them in a rested position throughout the interview, also—his appearance. Is he nervous or calm? Does he appear to be drugged? Find out his future intentions, and don't get overly anxious while talking with him about his plans. Space your questions apart, and talk slowly and deliberately, so he doesn't know you are searching for answers."

"You want me to get into his head to find out what is behind his latest bizarre actions. I get your over-anxious message. You've made your case completely clear to me. I'm an attorney too, remember?"

"Be serious. Your brother has been acting irrationally. He left the first hospital without sharing his thoughts or reasons with anyone. If you hadn't found him he might have died. Somehow we need to identify his state of mind. You say he wouldn't willingly go along with a young woman, but he did. You need to interpret how he has changed and relay that back to me. Your interview with Brian will give us a chance to find out what could possibly have happened to the other scientists. We don't know what came over the other scientists, but they left their families behind, and they disappeared into thin air."

"Sounds like another failure of the FBI to me."

"That doesn't deserve an answer."

Cliff and Agent Salture left his office without another word spoken. They said enough to hurt each other. On the way to the Iranian Consulate's building Agent Salture coached Cliff on being calm and patient no matter what happened. She also assured him if he didn't come out in a couple hours she would make an attempt to come into the building. Cliff felt comfortable with the instructions, but knew well enough she wouldn't be able to help him once he was inside. He would need to put his skills as an attorney to work and conjure up the necessary courage to get the job done.

Cliff approached the door and rang the bell. A large armed soldier answered. He spoke with broken English.

"Do you have an appointment?"

Cliff didn't answer. The height of the soldier bothered him. Cliff felt small standing in front of him.

"Answer—It is a yes or no. What is it?"

"No. I'm here to converse with my brother. He arrived here some time last night."

"What is this word converse? What does it mean?"

Cliff started to speak, but another soldier closed the door in his face. He was left standing outside. He knocked again—no answer. A few moments passed. Cliff glanced back at Agent Salture and shrugged his shoulders.

The door opened and a petite woman stood in the doorway with the soldier standing behind her.

"With whom do you wish to speak, and if you don't have an appointment, I can't help you. Go away."

"My brother was brought here from the hospital last night. I am his brother, and I wish to speak with him."

"I see a black SUV across the street. Did you arrive in a Government car?"

"Yes, I did. May I please see my brother?"

"You are at least truthful. That is something most Americans aren't. Do you have identification on your person?"

Cliff reached for his wallet and conjured up more patience. The large soldier remained in the doorway behind her. This woman was being overly cautious with him. The woman looked at the name and photograph on his driver's license and glanced up at him to see if his face matched the picture on his license.

"It appears you are Brian's brother. Why are you here to see him? I'm quite sure he doesn't want to see you."

"He left the hospital under rather unusual circumstances. I don't know what to make of his decision to be here. I'm here to find out why he left and what he is doing here. Do you have a hospital here?"

"I am not authorized to answer any of your questions. It is my position to identify you, and to seek the purpose of your visit here."

"I wish to speak with the person that can authorize me to speak with my brother."

"I will return in a couple of minutes. Please step inside and stay in front of the guard. If you make any swift movements you will be arrested, and possibly killed. Our soldiers don't have much patience with the likes of you."

Cliff found the expression 'the likes of you' rather amusing. He chuckled inwardly.

Another guard appeared from nowhere to block his path from the hallway. The woman left. He watched her as she walked down the long hallway. Cliff looked around. There were no pictures on the wall. Neither soldier took his eyes off him. Minutes passed slowly, and Cliff stood rigidly erect, trying to look taller. The soldiers were a foot or more taller than he, and they looked down on him. In time, the woman returned.

"Follow me. I'll take you to him."

Twenty minutes had passed and Cliff realized he was on the clock. Agent Salture had said she would intervene, somehow, if he didn't come out in two hours. They walked down the hallway and when they reached a doorway, the woman turned to him and said, "If you do anything irrational or show hostility of any kind you will be immediately evicted. One of our soldiers will be just outside the door. Do you understand? I am warning you for your own good."

"You needn't worry about that. I'm merely here to talk with my brother, and to make sure he isn't held against his will. I am a very patient and calm man."

"Good. Most Americans are very impatient."

She opened the door and Cliff looked around the empty room. Brian was not there.

"Brian's not here. Where is he? I demand to see him."

"You are in the Consulate's house. You demand nothing in here. If you don't shut up and control your tongue, I'll have the guards throw you out of here. Sit down, and I'll bring him to you."

She left the room. The minutes ticked silently by. Cliff realized he was in an uncontrollable situation, and he would have to let patience rule his behavior. He regretted riling the woman that allowed him into the house. He needed to be calm and collected. The room was bare except for four chairs and a table. He looked around for a camera lens and a listening device but couldn't see any, yet he knew they were there. The door opened and Brian entered holding the hand of a young woman.

"I'll be damned, if it isn't my kid brother? What are you doing here?"

"I'm here to take you back to the hospital where you belong."

"I've seen my last hospital. I'm not going back with you. My nurse is taking good care of me. Little brother, I have fallen in love with this lovely nurse. I'm going to say goodbye to the USA forever. I suggest you get your ass out of here. Some of these people aren't too friendly with Americans. I want you and the family to forget I ever existed. You must accept I have died, because I will never return."

"Never return from where? Where are you going?"

"It's not for you to know. I don't know how you got in here."

"Never mind all of that. I need to take you back to the hospital."

"You've always been a little dense. I told you I'm not going back."

"Is this the nurse that helped you leave the hospital? Can't we talk alone?"

"She is, and you can talk in her presence. We will be married as soon as I am well. We intend to have a family together."

"Brian, have you completely lost your senses? You have never made rash decisions like you're doing now. You need to get back to work and be productive again."

"Productive again, you say? That's a laugh. You don't know what you are talking about. I've been working on weapons that destroy people and their cities. I've come to hate what I am doing. I want to become a better person. I have always been different than you, but you could never see it or acknowledge it. You have always wanted to be like me because I was popular in high school and had so many girlfriends. In your mind you've always fantasized you and I are alike, but we've never been alike. It is your illusion. Sorry to burst your bubble, little brother. You've had this desire as long as I can remember. I've let my family guide my life, but from now on I will control the type of life I want to live. I'm leaving for Iran soon, and no one can stop me. I don't imagine I have a job at the Lab any longer, and I've been offered a good job in Iran. I'm going to give up my American Citizenship, and in time become an Iranian citizen."

"Surely you can't mean anything you are saying. I was of the opinion you loved your work at the Lab, and I know you love your country. I don't know what they did to you, but I don't like it one bit. I can't let you do this!"

"You can't stop me. I'm going to a new life—a life not controlled by consumerism and greed. Our country did nothing for me— understand— nothing. You know I'm a man of my own mind. I'm finally letting myself out of the cage I've been molded into since childhood. I went along with Dad's expectations of me, but I can no longer do that. He carved out a life for me because he wasn't strong enough to be as successful in his own life. He is an old man now, has a short time to live, and I no longer care what he does or thinks. I will control my future, and not have him control me any longer. I'll be leaving this compound under political asylum, and I'll never return."

"Brian, this can't be you talking. Can we speak alone without this woman here?"

"No. Emphatically no! Like I said, we will be married. I am in love for the first time in my life. I want you to leave and never look back. Tell the family goodbye for me. You must go now."

Cliff looked at the woman sitting next to Brian. She was a beautiful woman, much younger than Brian. She had been holding Brian's hand ever since they entered the room.

"Brian, I can't leave you like this. Are you under the influence of a drug or something?"

"Love is not a drug. It is a feeling I have never had before. Myia and I are going to build a family together, and I'm going to a place that will appreciate my work. I want to work in an industry that will save mankind, not destroy it. My only purpose at the Lab was to develop deadly weapons to kill people. The United States wants to be the earth's world power, and I hate them for that."

"Hog wash! This is not you talking. I demand that you come with me this very minute. This woman has you under a spell of some kind. Come with me, I can take you out of here."

Cliff jumped up and grabbed Brian's other hand and pulled him out of his chair, and away from the nurse. When he did, he saw an intravenous needle in the palm of his hand with a tube running up the arm of the nurse. Because of the commotion the side door opened and two soldiers entered and restrained him.

"I knew it, I knew it. You are being drugged. Brian, talk with me. Don't let them do this to you. Come with me now!"

The other door opened, and the stern-faced woman came through the door.

"I told you not to get violent—besides, you've been here long enough. It's time for you to leave. You are like most Americans— arrogant and strong-willed, and you won't listen to the truth. Your brother has chosen a new way of life—a life away from all of your consumerism and war mongering ideology."

The soldiers took Cliff by the shoulders and dragged him down the hall to the front door. He shouted back to Brian.

"Brian, I can't leave you like this! I knew it wasn't you spitting out all of those lies. Don't go along with what they want you to do. Fight back. You can't leave Marianne, Dad, and me like this!"

Brian shouted back.

"Go, I have chosen a new life— a life I'll find worthwhile living."

Cliff kept his eyes on Brian until he could no longer see him. All the time he was being dragged backwards by two large soldiers down the long hallway and then through the front door. Outside, the soldiers threw him to the ground.

"Don't come back. If you do, we'll kill you," they commanded.

Cliff scrambled to his feet. One of his shoes was missing. He looked around for it, but couldn't find it. He limped his way to Agent Salture's car parked down the street. With a pained look on her face, she opened the car door for him.

"Cliff, by the looks of you things didn't go well. Did you get angry?"

Cliff didn't answer her question. Instead, he sat dazed, trying to recover his senses. His arms ached. It felt like they had been extracted from his shoulders. He was handled roughly all the way down the hall.

"Cliff, I'm asking what happened in there?"

"I've lost him. Something is terribly wrong, and I can't help him. He was being drugged as we talked."

"Tell me what happened. Did you lose your temper, or what?

"It's too unbelievable to discuss."

"You must tell me while it is still fresh in your mind. Tell me everything that happened inside those doors."

"If you must know, I've lost my brother. I don't understand what's happened to him. He's talking crazy. It's totally unlike him to reject his family, his country. He's talking about love like it was a new discovery. He talked about his job at the Lab as being a curse on society. He was being drugged all during our meeting."

"Were his eyes glazed, and did he keep his hands folded on the table?"

"He acted normal, except the awful stuff he was saying turned my stomach. At first I thought he was pretending to satisfy the nurse holding his hand, but he was so believable. Several times he looked at the door like he wanted me to take him out. I spoke to him in pig Latin, something we used to do to fool our parents, but he wouldn't answer me. After a time I began to suspect he was being drugged." Cliff paused to gather his thoughts.

"He said he wanted to go to Iran to work on inventions that will aid mankind instead of inventing weapons for mass destruction for the United States to use against the world. Also, he wants to marry that nurse. He tells me he's in love with her, and they will be married in Iran. He said he's never been in love before. He says he has been unhappy with the way our father has molded him into a creator of destructive weapons to destroy people. He is going to change his life completely by developing peaceful inventions instead of developing weapons to kill more of the world's population."

"It sounds like he is being controlled. I'm sorry you weren't able to help him. Perhaps I shouldn't have suggested this meeting."

"I'm glad I went in. If I hadn't witnessed it I wouldn't believe it. A month and a half ago he was on top of the world, and now look what has happened to him."

"We did what we could. You have to let go now."

"Unlikely, bull-crap. How can you give up so easily? That wasn't Brian talking all of those lies, but a drug that nurse was administering all the time we talked. When I pulled him up I saw the IV. She was giving him that drug all along."

"Cliff, relax. You're so hyper you'll have a heart attack."

"I need to talk with someone in our State Department that has some real authority. Someone that can help me get him back. I tell you, it wasn't my brother talking, but some evil that has taken over his brain. Everything you have done doesn't mean anything now. Your involvement, or shall I call it your bungling, has cost my family dearly. Brian was an important part of our lives, and now he is lost from our family— lost until I can get him back."

Agent Salture sighed. Cliff's assessment of her role in the case, though totally incorrect and distorted, was meant to hurt her. FBI agents were taught not to get emotionally involved with the people they were assigned to protect, but Agent Salture had done just that. It left her defenseless. Just then a helicopter took off from the Consulate's Compound.

"He's already gone. They're taking him out of the country. I don't have the authority to interfere now."

Agent Salture snapped her cell open and spoke to someone.

Cliff winced. Her words, 'He's already gone,' struck him like a hammer. Because of his disappointment with how everything played out, he chose not to talk with Agent Salture any more. He asked the driver to drop him off at his family home. As he exited the car Agent Salture grabbed his arm.

"I'll do everything possible to get your brother back."

"Sure, like you have handled everything so far. You don't expect me to believe anything you say, do you?"

"Don't be bitter. In our business things don't always go right, but it often does, and that's why we never give up. In Brian's case I had some slipups, I admit, but we had a lot of unexpected things happen too. It was most unusual he got out of our sight two times. I did everything possible to protect your brother. These have been difficult times for me too. I won't give up, I promise."

"Promises, promises. That's all I have ever gotten from you from day one. I'll handle my own affairs in the future. Don't interfere. I'll find a way to bring him back on my own."

The car door closed behind him. Cliff walked slowly up to the front porch of his family home. His inflamed words, barely out of his mouth, coursed through his mind. His disappointment with his visit to see his brother lingered. His body felt drained, and each step seemed a burden.

9

A terrifying thought struck fear in his heart. *How could he explain these bazaar circumstances to his elderly father and sister?* Cliff mulled over the calamity of the last few hours. It would be impossible for Marianne and his Father to believe what happened to Brian. He couldn't believe it himself, so how could he explain it to them? He couldn't even open the front door. His strength abandoned him. His mind fluctuated out of control. He paused, unsure what was happening to him, then turned and sat on the porch swing. His mind jumped from one subject to another like a wild herd in a stampede. An hour passed, possibly two. He'd solved nothing. His talk with Brian left him stripped of self-confidence, and it left him without the brother he dearly loved. He reviewed Brian's unkind words about him and his father that seemed cruel—meant to hurt them both. Brian's words, spoken with such vengeance, impacted Cliff deeply. He placed his head in his hands in an attempt to shut down everything going through his mind.

He heard footsteps, and when he looked up Marianne was approaching the porch. She sat next to him and put her arm around him.

"Cliff, what are you doing outside? It's freezing out here. Didn't Dad call you? He called me, and that's why I'm here. Dad is having a heart problem again, and you didn't answer his call. Come inside with me, and we'll find out what's wrong with Dad."

"Sorry Sis. I'm too troubled to be of much help."

"I've already called 9-1-1. I'm surprised they haven't arrived yet. Come, help me with Dad—Cliff, help me damn it! Don't sit there like a log."

Marianne opened the front door. Ted rushed by her and Cliff. He vaulted up the stairway. Marianne and Cliff followed closely behind. The bedroom door was open, and they entered to see Ted on top of their dad giving him artificial respiration. Ted looked up as they entered the bedroom.

"It looks pretty bad this time. He's having a lot of trouble breathing."

The paramedics arrived and took over for Ted. Critical minutes followed.

"I suggest you three go downstairs until we can get a handle on this. Your father had a massive heart attack," the paramedic instructed.

Cliff sat glumly on the couch and put his head in his hands. He hadn't told his father about Brian. Then he thought, *it might be for the best if I didn't tell him—tell him anything at all.*

Ted sat next to him, but he didn't say anything. The doctor arrived and went upstairs. Marianne, Ted and Cliff didn't talk, but sat silent. No one paid attention to how much time passed. Cliff's mind was blank—free of all the recent turmoil. He stared at his mother's favorite clock on the mantel, but didn't recognize the time. The doctor came into the room.

"He's gone. We did all we could, but I believe he gave up weeks ago. If you want to spend some time with him before we take him, you are welcome to do so now."

Marianne declined, but Cliff slowly made his way up the stairway. His thoughts scattered. He'd lost Brian. Now his father had also left him. The paramedics left the room when he entered. Cliff sat next to his father.

"Dad, on this very day I've lost both you and Brian. Perhaps it's best you didn't hear about his leaving from my lips. I feel so lost not having either of you in my life any longer. How will I go on?"

Cliff threw himself on his father's body, hugged him, and cried loudly.

"Now you can be with Mom. You wanted that, didn't you? Dad, you haven't been happy since she left us, have you? Frankly, I haven't been either. I always wanted to tell you that, but I was afraid you would scold me for saying so. Dad, you've been a great father to me. You did a good job raising the family, and we all loved you for it. Say hello to Mom when you see her. I love you both."

Cliff left the bedroom without looking back through teary eyes. The paramedic patted him on the shoulder as he went downstairs. His thoughts were scattered. He hugged Marianne and Ted hugged them both.

"Ted, thanks for helping Dad in his last moments. I appreciate it."

"I lost both of my parents in a car wreck when I was a senior in high school. I never shared that with either of you. It is painful losing a parent. I know all about it."

"Thanks Ted. I appreciate you being here for us. Perhaps I have misjudged you. Forgive me, if you have a notion to do that."

"Perhaps we can be a family now. It's a time when we need each other. It is a shame Brian can't be here to share this moment. Do you know where he is now?"

Cliff didn't answer his sister, but walked to the front door and sat down in the swing on the porch. He wanted to be alone with his thoughts. His life had completely changed in a single day. His thoughts turned to Brian. Marianne brought a blanket for him, wrapped it around his shoulders, and sat beside him without speaking.

Cliff's thoughts searched for a way to rescue Brian, and bring him back home. There must be a way— a way to rescue Brian. If so, would it be outside of the Government's jurisdiction? It appeared too monumental for his crazed mind to handle now. He put his head in his hands and swung back and forth. Marianne sat silently beside him and didn't interrupt his thoughts. Time elapsed and finally Marianne spoke.

"Tell me about Brian. I know you well enough to know you are holding something back from me."

85

Cliff looked at his sister with surprise. She knew him better than he knew himself, but how could he share the awful truth with her? If he did, perhaps it could relieve his troubled mind from the heavy burden he was carrying by himself. He took her hand.

"Sis, it pains me a lot, but I need to tell you that we've lost Brian too. It's almost too painful to tell you, but I must. I'll explode if I don't."

Cliff explained his visit to the Iranian Consulate's home and why he was taken aback by the way Brian talked about the family and his future life. Marianne sat in silence as Cliff's story unfolded. He tried not to leave anything out. As Marianne listened she sat rigidly by his side, patting his hand as he continued. He exhaled loudly when he was finished.

"Cliff, we must find a way to bring him back home. I haven't given up and I hope you haven't either. I know you will find a way. We both love him a lot, and nothing can take that away from us. Find a way, I know you can."

"Sis, I'm not Superman. It will be far more difficult from here on in. My practice is failing, and I must get back to it. It's now time for the government to do more."

"Have you heard about how those three hikers were detained by the Iranians three years ago, and our Government hasn't been able to get them back? They were arrested and convicted of spying and given five-year sentences. I'm not so sure we can count on the Government to bring Brian home to us. Find a way to bring our brother back to us. I know you can do it. You are smart enough, and you have the sticking power to do it. Promise me, you'll do everything you can to make that possible, will you?"

"Sis, I'll work on it, but I don't want to give up my practice. I'm not sure I can continue to do both. I don't know what I can do just now, but I promise, I will not forget what has happened to him, and I'll search for some way to bring him home. Sis, my mind is so fractured I can't even think about making the arrangements for Dad's funeral. I'm not up to it now. Is there some way you and Ted can do that?"

"Of course. Ted and I will take care of it. He is strong, and I can count on him to help me do the right thing. You take care, and keep in touch. The funeral will probably be in four or five days."

"Okay Sis. Be in touch, will you?"

Ted and Marianne left, and Cliff waited for the coroner to arrive. He went back inside because he was cold. He needed Brian to be at his side during this difficult time, but that was no longer possible. The doorbell rang, and he went to answer it. There stood Agent Salture.

"Cliff, we need to talk."

"My father passed a short while ago. I am waiting for the coroner. We have nothing more to say to each other. I wish you would leave."

"Cliff, I am so sorry for everything that has happened. Sometimes cases like this one don't ever go as expected. I'm sorry for how all of this has turned out. You and your family are hurting badly, and I can feel your pain. What can I do to help take some of the pain away?"

"That is a stupid question. Get my brother back for me. You can't do that, can you?"

"I can't make promises I can't keep. You know I can't. My supervisor wants to talk with you."

"I'm not ready to talk with anyone until my father gets a proper burial. You can tell him that."

"Cliff, I know you are angry with how all of this has played out, but be reasonable. I'm sure you'll want to hear what he has to say about Brian's case. He told me he has some important information that you need to know."

"I hold no ill will toward you or the FBI. I'm upset, and I don't know how to deal with all that's happening in my life right now. You'll have to give me time to work through all of this."

"Of course. I understand. First things first."

The doorbell rang again and Cliff opened the door. The coroner arrived. Cliff invited him inside.

"My father is upstairs in the front bedroom. Please take good care of him."

"We will. I have instructions to take him to Frost's Mortuary. Is that agreeable with you?"

"Yes, my sister Marianne will handle all of the funeral arrangements there are to be made."

While Cliff was talking with the coroner Agent Salture went to the kitchen and poured a glass of water for Cliff.

"Here Cliff, drink a little of this. When was the last time you ate or drank something?"

"I'm not hungry or thirsty. Please go, and we'll talk another day."

Agent Salture closed the door behind her. Cliff sat in his father's recliner. He hadn't done that in the past, because he knew his father would throw a fit. That was coveted territory for his father only, and Cliff knew it. He inhaled, and every smell reminded him of his father. His dad's one and only pipe and pouch of tobacco lay on the table next to the chair. He picked up the pipe and handled it. He recalled the family ceremony when the family gave the pipe to him for Father's Day many years ago.

Cliff closed his eyes to recall more of those happy events. Now, it was all in the past. The coroner and his assistant came down the stairs, interrupted his thoughts, and asked Cliff to sign their release. They closed the door behind them, and Cliff sat alone.

He thought about what Brian said about their father. He knew Brian didn't mean it, and he found it baffling that he blamed their father at all. Brian's education came about because he wanted a career in Engineering. His father wanted him to go to West Point where he could follow his dreams for him, but Brian rebuffed him.

Cliff sat alone and bathed in the quietness of it all. Time passed, the sunlight fled, and darkness came without his being aware of the changes. His family had enjoyed many good times. His mind traversed back through time when his whole family was there. The Christmases, the barbeques, the birthday celebrations, the graduations, and his parent's marital celebrations all came to mind. They were etched into his family history, but could never occur again. His mother's passing had changed all of that. And now, with his father's passing, he knew family functions would be few and far between. He'd never given a thought to starting a family of his own.

The doorbell rang and it startled him. He rose to answer it.

"I'm a messenger from the Iranian Consulate's office. I have been instructed to leave this package with you."

He handed the package to Cliff, turned, and left.

Cliff returned to his father's recliner and turned on the light. It was a small package, wrapped in plain brown paper with a string around it to keep it closed. He carefully opened it. Out slid Brian's college ring, his watch, and a note. Cliff unfolded the note and recognized Brian's handwriting. Almost afraid to read what Brian said in his note, he laid it in his lap for a moment of reflection. His courage returned, and he opened it carefully.

'Cliff, I'm sure you are disappointed with my decision to make a new life for myself, but I do so with my own free will. That intravenous needle in the palm of my hand was not a drug. It was a medication to keep me from getting infected. I will not be allowed to wear my jewelry in Iran. Take care my dear brother, and take care of Marianne too. Explain to her why I needed to leave the family behind. Tell Dad what you want. Please, don't try to bring me back.'

Taken aback by the closing of Brian's message, Cliff sat quietly holding the ring and watch in one hand, and the note in the other. Time passed, and he fell asleep. He woke later and turned on the light. It was a few minutes past midnight. He read the note again, still puzzled by its meaning. Brian sounded more at ease with himself in the note than the person he'd met with many hours earlier.

Brian doesn't want me to bring him back— I don't understand? Cliff loudly exclaimed, as his voice echoed throughout the room.

He got up and paced the living room floor. The thought of never seeing his brother again was too outrageous to accept. He went upstairs, washed his face, changed his clothes, and went into the kitchen while reviewing Brian's final message in his mind. He was hungry for the first time in days. He gathered the makings for a sandwich from the refrigerator, fixed some coffee, poured a cup, and opened his cell. After checking, he found six unanswered messages. Three were from irate clients angered because he had missed their court dates. One was from Doctor Ulsheeh, one from Doctor Marsh, and the last one from Agent Salture.

The missing court dates were inexcusable. It was the first time he had ever let a client down. He thought about how he could rectify their unhappiness. It was the wee hours of the morning, but he couldn't let it go. He called an attorney friend of his and left a message on his cell asking him to take over their cases.

Next he listened to the message from Doctor Ulsheeh. "I need you. I am being arrested by the FBI, help me." Cliff leaned back in his chair. *A new development! I wonder what the FBI has found out about him?* He deliberated over the Doctor's pleading message.

He then listened to the message from Doctor Marsh. "Cliff, did you have something to do with Doctor Ulsheeh's arrest? I need you to call me right away. I don't give a damn what time you call."

Cliff punched in his number. It rang and rang. No answer.

"It's Cliff returning your call. Call me."

Frustrated with how his life had spiraled down in just weeks, Cliff slammed his cell down to vent his anger. Nothing came to mind about how to fix anything. Doctor Ulsheeh's arrest presented a new problem, and he needed to attend to it immediately. He was besieged with thoughts of why he'd taken him on as a client.

The doorbell rang.

As Cliff strode quickly through the living room to open the door he glanced at his Mother's clock on the mantle. It was 2:00 am.

Who could be at the door at this time of the morning? He questioned. He looked through the glass door. A young woman was standing there.

Hesitant, but curious, he opened the door.

The woman held a card in her hand. It was too dark to read it and Cliff's eyes went right back to her face.

"It's 2:00 am in the morning. Do I know you?"

"I have been sitting out in my car for a number of hours working up the courage to ring your doorbell. I saw your lights come on a short while ago. I knew you were up and about."

"Bravo for you. You did it! You caught me in my pajamas. Come in, I'm cold. Want a cup of coffee? I am eating breakfast, or is it lunch, or dinner. I haven't eaten in days."

They made their way into the kitchen. Cliff got a cup from the shelf.

"Do you drink it black? I don't have any milk."

"Black is fine."

He set the cup in front of her. Her cheeks were rosy from the chill in the air. She was young, maybe a couple years younger than him.

"Well, why did you ring my doorbell at this early hour?"

"I will tell you if you promise not to laugh at me."

Her name card lay on the table in front of him. He looked at it and flinched. Her name was Jo Ann Roxley, a reporter for the Inquirer. He looked up at her and smiled.

"A reporter? Well, that's a responsible job. I'm curious. Why did you arrive at my doorstep at this time in the morning? I am far from the most popular person in our town."

"Remember, you promised not to laugh." She took a sip of her coffee. "I saw your light come on a short while ago, and it took me a while to work up the courage to face you. You are my first assignment. I understand you are Doctor Ulsheeh's lawyer. Earlier this evening I waited outside the Federal building for a number of hours to interview you, but you didn't show up. I looked up your address and here I am. My boss wants me to find out why the doctor was arrested, and when he will be released on bail so I can interview him in person."

"I can tell you neither. I was going down there at a decent hour in the morning to find out that very thing."

"You are making fun of me. I better go."

"No, please stay, I could use the company. If you stay I promise to give you my first interview after I talk with Doctor Ulsheeh. Are you hungry? I make a mean sandwich and promise it won't make you sick."

"Well, if you don't mind. My stomach has been growling for a while. I haven't eaten recently either, but please don't make fun of me."

"Good, promise, I won't."

Cliff turned, opened the refrigerator and finished making her a sandwich. He set it in front of her and then looked at her. She had a fresh face and appeared to be right out of college.

"Did you graduate recently from a local college?"

"A month ago I graduated from Duke. I want to be a television commentator. You have to start somewhere, and this was the only job open."

"I'm sure you will succeed wherever you go."

She bit into her sandwich and didn't put it down until she ate the whole thing.

"You either liked my sandwich or you were terribly hungry."

She laughed. Cliff hadn't heard any youthful laughter for a while. Her company lifted his spirits.

"Jo Ann, I am quite busy these days. I haven't been keeping regular hours for a while now, and when I woke up I was terribly hungry. That's why I am up at this hour."

"My boss told me I would have to work for twenty-four hours in a stretch if I wanted to be a good reporter. That's why I am here."

"I will be going down to the Federal Building at nine in the morning. I promise to give you the first interview after I talk with Doctor Ulsheeh. I could call you."

"Promise? That would be great. I better leave now and let you get prepared for your work. One question; is Doctor Ulsheeh in some kind of trouble with the FBI?"

"It's a little too complicated to discuss here and now, but I'll give you more details after I talk with him. If I could get him released maybe I could get you an interview with him. I know you'll do well in the career your have chosen. It seems so many years ago, but it hasn't been that long since I took on my first case. This morning you brought back some of those fond memories— moments with my first client, my first court appearance, my first failures, and on and on. Failures will help build your character."

"I'm out of here. Thanks for the sandwich, coffee and friendly advice. And I thank you for your understanding, you know, my ringing your doorbell at 2:00 in the morning."

Cliff closed the door behind her. He found himself smiling. Unrestrained happiness was foreign and joy had become a rare commodity for him. He picked up his coffee and tasted it— it was cold. He needed to extract himself from the situation he had mired himself in. He reminisced about his recent years as an attorney. He enjoyed the challenges, the successes and failures; however he'd learned a lot from his failures. Now Jo Ann was just beginning her career. She would have her ups and downs too.

Secretly, he wanted to see her again.

10

Cliff was reluctant to return Agent Salture's call. He momentarily thought about it, and decided not to call her back. She couldn't rescue his brother, and the pain of her failure ravaged his thinking. His law practice had suffered woefully because of his lack of attention. Cliff fingered through his briefcase files to focus his mind on work. He'd lost three clients and called the most pressing ones to apologize for his lack of attention to their cases. He used the excuse of his father's death for his negligence. Afterwards, he laid down his cell, feeling badly about his lack of attention to his work, and stared emptily into space.

His mind returned to his work, but he found it always wandered back to Brian, Doctor Ulsheeh, and Doctor Marsh. His cell vibrated.

"Cliff, this is Doctor Marsh. The FBI has arrested Doctor Ulsheeh—you're his lawyer— surely you received his message? Get down there and find out what's going on. He won't take being in jail, charged with a Federal crime, to his liking. I've seen him angry a few times, and it isn't pretty. He is a master surgeon, and he's not a criminal. He believes he is being harassed and arrested by the FBI because he practices the Moslem religion. Get down there and get him released. His family is totally upset with what has happened to him."

"Doctor Marsh, he called me too. I'll find out what's happening. We're dealing with the Feds, which makes my job more difficult, and makes his release more questionable. They don't make an arrest unless they have some solid facts against the suspect. How did you hear he was arrested by the Feds?"

"One of his church members called me when they arrested him on church grounds. I'd like to know what the hell is going on. Doctor Ulsheeh is my mentor. He surely couldn't do anything wrong. You need to protect his civil rights."

"I'll look into it right away, and be back with you in a day or so. My father passed, and I'm dealing with that right now."

"Sorry, I hadn't heard."

Cliff put down his cell and thought about this new development. It appeared he couldn't put Brian and his difficulties behind him. He called the courthouse and pushed back some of his upcoming court dates, grabbed his briefcase, and drove to the Federal building. He scanned the directory and found the jail was located on the fifth floor. When he entered the elevator someone called, hold it! It sounded like a familiar voice— it was Agent Salture.

"Cliff, I'm surprised to see you here?"

"Why so? I'm not looking for you. That's for sure. I understand you've arrested Doctor Ulsheeh. I'm his attorney— I'm sure you're aware of that."

"You needn't remind me. My boss wants to debrief you about your brother's visit. Besides, he has something important to tell you."

"As soon as I review the charges against my client and get his release, I'll make time to talk with him. You people just amaze me. You could have called me before you arrested Doctor Ulsheeh, or didn't you think I would find out? Have you been questioning him all this time?"

"Cliff, I did call you, but you didn't answer my call. Quit being so angry with me all of the time. I did my best to protect your brother. Besides, you can't go through life being angry about something you can't change. Your brother decided to go to Iran on his own. He's chosen a new way of life. Quite a few American citizens have chosen the same path. Either this life is too much for them to handle, or something has changed their basic beliefs about our system. There is nothing you or I could have done about that."

"You don't know my brother very well. My brother would never abandon his country like he's doing now. Something or somebody is controlling his mind and body. He would never make statements about his father like he did unless someone controlled his speech. Show me the way to the person I can talk with to get Doctor Ulsheeh released from his wrongful arrest."

"It's on the fifth floor, second door on the right as you step out of the elevator. Will you call me when you're done, and I'll take you to my boss?"

"I'll see how successful I am in getting Doctor Ulsheeh released—then I'll decide whether to meet with your boss or not. Surely you wouldn't put me under arrest too? You guys are ruining a good man's reputation with your strong-arm actions. Did you know that, or don't you give a damn about law-abiding citizens?"

Agent Salture didn't answer Cliff's challenge. She got off on the fourth floor, and the elevator continued to the fifth floor. Cliff stepped out and found the door Agent Salture described.

"I'm Doctor Ulsheeh's attorney, and I demand to speak with him."

"Cool it, no reason to show me an attitude. It will take a few moments. Please have a seat and fill out this questionnaire while you're waiting. I'll see if he is allowed visitors."

"I'm not a visitor, I'm his attorney. I have a right to visit him. Hey, this is a four-page document. Tell me, where does it ask how many times I went to the bathroom today?"

"You are a wise ass, aren't you? I'm calling my boss. Based on your actions, you will take the long road to seeing him."

The attendant left while Cliff reviewed the questionnaire. He scribbled in the answers quickly, with some scribbled illegibly to make it difficult for anyone to read.

A tall black man approached him.

"Are you finished answering all of the questions? Let me review it, and then I'll allow you to see your client. If you would take the chip off your shoulder all of this wouldn't have been necessary."

He turned the page. His eyes rose from the page, and he looked at Cliff, smiled, and shook his head. "You are a hard case, aren't you? Agent Salture called and asked us to give you a green light to see your client, but you chose to do it the hard way. I'm Special Agent Fowler. I'll take you to your client. He has been quite disagreeable and uncooperative since we arrested him."

"I imagine. You've arrested a man of high standing in the medical community with an impeccable reputation, and for what? Has bail been set for his release?"

"He was arrested under the Terrorist Act # 320144. He's not eligible for bail."

"I won't comment because you will probably give me one of your patented answers. Sometimes I think you Federal people are robots instead of people with feelings."

"Enjoying yourself, or do you run off at the mouth all of the time? You are an angry man, aren't you? Here we are. Go in and sit down, and I'll have him brought in. Put your anger on the shelf for now, because it won't get you anywhere in here."

The room was bare except for a table and three chairs. Cliff looked around for microphones or cameras and didn't detect any, but he knew they were there.

The door opened and in walked Doctor Ulsheeh, with a guard behind him.

"I will leave you two here, and I'll lock the door. You have fifteen minutes."

Doctor Ulsheeh and Cliff shook hands. The doctor looked well spent. Cliff motioned for him to sit down.

"Doctor, they may have microphones and listening devices in here, so I will write my questions and I want you to answer them on my note pad. Am I perfectly clear about that?"

Doctor Ulsheeh nodded, and Cliff wrote the first question. *Have they given you a reason for your arrest? And have they presented you with any charges?"*

He wrote. *I know nothing. They questioned me at great length about my operations on a number of people, but I don't know what*

97

they are looking for. He continued writing. *They broke into my home with guns and scared my family, and when I wasn't there they went to the Mosque parking lot to arrest me. I called you, but, you didn't answer my call.*

Cliff studied Doctor Ulsheeh's face. It was etched with hate mixed with uncertainty. He sat with his hands folded in front of him— the very hands that saved his brother's life. Cliff felt compassion for the very skilled doctor, but was unsure about how to get him released.

Cliff wrote. *I'm sorry for the delay in getting here, but my father passed. I have been informed about your charges, and they are serious. Tell me if anything unusual has occurred in your life since we last met?*

Cliff slid the notepad to the Doctor for his reply.

"The doctor wrote. *During the questioning, they kept referring to my part in a conspiracy to kidnap a number of leading scientists.*

Cliff wrote. *If that is so, is there any truth to their allegations? I can't properly defend you unless you completely level with me.*

The doctor wrote. *I know nothing about what they are accusing me of doing. I'm innocent. I've done nothing. I am not a spy like they are accusing me of being. They are treating me like a criminal.*

Cliff wrote. *Have they been questioning you very long?*

The doctor wrote. *Yes.* They *wouldn't give me a drink of water for the longest time. I made two phone calls— one to you and one to Doctor Marsh. You've got to get me released. My family, my reputation, is all at stake. I don't know what anyone at the hospital must think about my being arrested.*

Cliff wrote. *I'll do what I can to get you released, but it will take a while. We're dealing with two Government Agencies—the FBI and Homeland Security. Ever since 9/11 the rules have changed in regard to espionage. The local newspaper is aware of your being charged with a Federal crime.*

The doctor wrote. *Espionage, they said. Is it all because my nationality is Iranian? In Iran they arrest people and then make up charges against them. I hope that is not what they are doing to me.*

Cliff wrote. *They need to charge you with a crime within a certain time or they must release you. I will do what I can to get you released sooner than later.*

Cliff turned the pad in Doctor Ulsheeh's direction.

Doctor Ulsheeh wrote. *My family and I are all American citizens, and I need you to protect our rights under the law. Remember we discussed that very thing when you first took me on as a client.*

Cliff read what the doctor wrote and sighed, knowing what he wrote was valid. He questioned whether he was up to representing the doctor. If not, he needed to get some help from someone, but who could that be?

Back to basics, Cliff wrote. *Why do you think they arrested you?* He turned his notebook in the direction of the Doctor.

The doctor wrote. *It has to be because I come from an Iranian background. The United States has been badgering Iran for a number of years. They may have arrested me by profiling my background.*

Cliff wrote. *Profiling is hard to prove. You haven't given me very much to work on. I haven't learned a single thing since I came in here. Give me a reason for your arrest, would you?*

Cliff underlined the word 'reason'. He turned the notepad in the doctor's direction.

The doctor wrote. *I am a surgeon. I have a wife and three children. I have no idea why they suspect me of doing anything wrong. During questioning they said I was part of a conspiracy to do something about some scientists. I don't have the slightest idea what they are talking about.*

Cliff wrote. *For now they have the upper hand, and you will need patience. I'll have Doctor Marsh talk with your family and tell them what is happening to you. Also, I will do my best to get you released as soon as possible.*

Doctor Ulsheeh nodded his approval.

The guard entered and led the doctor away in handcuffs. Cliff stuffed his note pad into his briefcase. He sat alone searching for a plan to get the doctor released. He would need help from someone who dealt with Federal charges. He walked back to the entryway and was met by Special Agent Fowler.

"I'm told you agreed to speak with my boss. Agent Salture said you agreed to see him."

"Fine. Let's go."

The elevator took them to the top floor. They walked down a hallway, passing several large open offices where Cliff saw a number of people staring at computers. At the end of the hall, Special Agent Fowler knocked on a door.

"Come."

They entered. It was a large corner office. A huge black man with short graying hair sat behind the desk. Cliff looked around. There was a small conference table with chairs off to the side. The walls were covered with plaques of badges with a black ribbon running through them and a name under each of them. Cliff turned his attention back to the man behind the desk.

"Thank you, Special Agent Fowler. Please leave us alone for now."

The agent left, and Cliff stood facing the man behind the desk. He stood to shake Cliff's hand. His height and stature overshadowed Cliff's small frame. The man before him had a stern face, but kind eyes. His black face, in contrast with his short gray hair, gave him an air of distinction.

"Please sit. Agent Salture told me about your father's passing. You have my condolences as well as those of my whole Department. My name is Special Agent Henry Boller, and I am chief of this area. I have been in charge of Doctor Ulsheeh's case for a number of years. I understand you are representing him. It is most unusual for me to be talking with you about this case, but certain circumstances make it necessary for me to do so. What I have to say may change your mind about representing him."

"We'll see about that." Cliff replied sternly.

Mr. Boller pressed a button on his phone and asked the receptionist to send in Special Agent Salture.

"You've been working with Special Agent Salture for some time now, and I want her to hear what I am about to tell you."

The door opened, and in walked Agent Salture.

"Let's move over to the conference table. There is coffee and water on the side table if you would care for either."

"Before we discuss anything I want to know why my client can't be released on bail?"

"We'll get to that in time. Please be patient with me. I want to bring you up to date with Doctor Ulsheeh's activities and the circumstances involving your brother's departure to Iran. Since I was first assigned to this case four years ago a series of noted scientists, including your brother, have left the United States to work in Iran to further their armament programs. I've concluded it wasn't entirely by their individual choice, but something else made it possible."

Cliff readjusted himself in his chair. At last he was being told the whole truth. Agent Salture had told him bits and pieces as the case progressed, but Henry Boller had led the investigation for four years. Perhaps this case was more complex than Brian's decision to go to Iran.

"This file is getting rather thick, isn't it?" He smiled, paused, and waited for some response from either Cliff or Agent Salture, but neither of them commented.

"Four years ago Donald Sutherland, a noted atomic scientist, was run off the road, suffered a severe brain injury, and was operated on by Doctor Ulsheeh. During his recovery he suffered blackouts and memory spells similar to what Brian recently went through. However, Brian was mentally strong enough to recognize something was terribly wrong during his recovery, and he reacted in a most explosive way and bolted from the hospital on his own."

"Getting back to the Donald Sutherland case. In a matter of weeks after the accident Donald Sutherland mysteriously disappeared, and his family and friends didn't know what happened to him. We started a search for him at that time. Four months later the CIA found he was working within the nuclear program in Iran. How that came about, no one had a clue. This was our first real suspicion a most unusual plot was being carried out. Some people might call it profiling. It wasn't considered profiling by my Department because Doctor Ulsheeh was attending the same Mosque that produced other known terrorists, and he had operated on Donald Sutherland's brain. Doctor Ulsheeh immediately came under our radar. And then, two years ago, Claude Windsor, a noted electronic scientist was run off the road. He suffered multiple injuries, was operated on by Doctor Ulsheeh, and two months later the CIA reported he was living in Iran. A year and a half later another scientist by the name of Jeffery Wilbur was run off the road, and again Doctor Ulsheeh operated on him. He was later found to be in Iran working on their rocket development. And now, we come to your brother's case. I understand he was working on Laser weaponry. As you know he is already in Iran. That makes four of our top scientists who were working on different sensitive projects that are now working in Iran. All of this is intolerable and impossible for the government and me to accept. I regret it has taken this long to apprehend and arrest Doctor Ulsheeh."

"Agent Salture told me about the other scientists, but she didn't tell me they were working in Iran."

"No one knows they are in Iran except the highest level of law enforcement—not even their families. Agent Salture crossed the line and allowed you to visit your brother at the Iranian Consulate's office. We've placed the three earlier scientists on our missing persons list to fool the Iranian Government. I trust you will keep our secret."

"My only mission in life is to get my brother to return home to his family. The rest of your story has no bearing on my resolve. Frankly, I don't want to interfere with your investigation, but I'm going to get my brother back home."

"That's why I'm leveling with you now. Your interference could jeopardize all of their lives, including that of your brother. The question that bugged me on those first three scientists, is why and how could they end up in Iran? They were all brilliant men with exceptional brainpower, and I don't understand how they were persuaded to give up their citizenship to work for our enemy. Something happened to their brains. In the past, we questioned Doctor Ulsheeh on a number of occasions, and didn't get any answers. Recently Special Agent Salture suggested we question Doctor Marsh because he assisted Doctor Ulsheeh on Brian's surgery. We did, and after many hours of grilling he admitted seeing Doctor Ulsheeh put something into Brian's brain during the operation. Later, he reviewed the x-rays and MRIs of Brian's brain but couldn't detect anything. He thought it was a clear, rather thin article. He later asked Doctor Ulsheeh about it. The Doctor denied putting anything in his brain. Later Doctor Ulsheeh told Doctor Marsh it was all his imagination. Days later Doctor Marsh almost had a fatal accident. Whether the two incidents had any correlation or not we haven't been able to determine. I have concluded our renowned brain surgeon is directing this cycle of getting these scientists to his country to develop armaments that will eventually be used against us. I have discussed this with a number of brain surgeons, but I've gotten nowhere because Doctor Ulsheeh is held in high esteem. I've had a number of renown brain surgeons study the MRIs on the four scientists and they haven't been able to detect anything wrong."

"If you knew all of this, I don't understand why and how you let my brother slip through your fingers, or did you allow this to happen just to incriminate Doctor Ulsheeh?"

"We didn't. Believe me, we didn't. In our business unexpected circumstances happen. It all started with Brian leaving the hospital on his own. His actions caught us completely off guard. We considered Doctor Ulsheeh was behind that move. Later you became involved and straightened out that part of the case for us. We then assumed Brian left on his own because he suspected something was wrong with his brain. There is one more thing I understand—you're somewhat of a hothead, and your actions throughout the case have hampered our progress. I want you to control yourself when I tell you the rest of the story. If you're agreeable to my conditions, I'll continue."

"You make it sound rather sinister. I promise not to voice my opinions so forcefully until I've heard the rest of your story."

"When we transferred Brian to the second hospital I visited with him. He agreed to help us rescue the other scientists. He is quite patriotic, and was willing to go along with my plan."

Henry Boller looked at Cliff to view his reaction.

The blood drained from Cliff's face. He picked up his water bottle and took a sip. He couldn't respond to Boller's last statement. His brother had been so convincing. But why would he risk his life for three scientists he didn't know?

"Brian completely fooled me with that spiel about his unhappiness with our country, his family, and his job at the Lab. Inwardly, I couldn't accept the thought he could give up his family to be with that young Jezebel. If everything you're telling me is true, then why did you have to put me through the wringer like you did."

"You've interfered with our investigation from the very beginning. Agent Salture took you to the Iranian Consulate's residence because she became emotionally involved with your brother's case. I'm asking you, plain and simple don't interfere with our operation in the future. There is an ongoing plan already in place. First, you know nothing about foreign diplomacy. Second, any action by you would hinder our plan to get those scientists and your brother returned to the United States. You could jeopardize your brother's life in doing so."

"You're asking a lot from me. I am not pleased with the way my brother's case has progressed. I believe it borders on gross negligence by the FBI."

"I'm sorry you believe that, but your thinking is all misdirected. In our business situations are fluid and can go awry without warning. Sometimes we are able to immediately rectify it, but sometimes we can't. Believe me, we never give up. It appears you have lost confidence in our handling of the case. I certainly hope it isn't so. I could use your help, as well as Brian's, to get this case put to bed. I am presently waiting to hear from Brian. Once he is secure within the community he will get in touch with me. We don't know where the other three scientists are located within Iran or if Brian will be able to contact them, but we're hoping he will find a way. He has a brilliant mind. This is a very delicate operation and a single hitch in our plan could cost all four scientists their lives."

"Brian has put his life in immediate danger so you can solve your case? You want me to butt out and go on with my normal life while Brian is risking his life in Iran to solve your case for you. I'm not able to do what you ask. Your Department has made so many errors along the way I can't butt out."

"You need to give me time to get my plan in action. Brian is in Iran already. That is something you can't do anything about that. I gave you the information on my plan so you wouldn't go half-cocked and mess up our plans. Agent Salture told me you were planning some rescue attempt of your own."

"I did tell her that, but she had no right to share it with anyone. You people are something."

Cliff rose from his chair to leave.

"Don't leave. I need an answer now."

"If I went along with this travesty what promises would you make?"

"I don't understand what you mean?"

"Something like: if you didn't make any progress in a month or two, you will not interfere with my rescuing Brian."

"Law enforcement doesn't work that way. As an attorney, you should recognize that."

"I can't make you any promises, but maybe I could help you in a different way."

"How is that?"

"If you could get Doctor Ulsheeh released to my custody, then perhaps I could gain his confidence."

"That sounds interesting. Sit down, and give me a moment to consider your offer."

Cliff sat again, and took a sip of water.

"It's foolish of me to think I can trust you, but we didn't get anywhere with his questioning. If he should slip from under your radar, you would be held personally responsible. Are you willing to accept that responsibility? The only reason I am considering this is because everything we've tried in the recent past concerning the good doctor has failed. He's slippery as an eel. The longer those scientists are in Iran the more harm could come to our nation."

"I'm cut from the same cloth as Brian. We are both 100% American. You can count on me. If this is a way I can help Brian, then I'll follow your plan."

"Okay, I'll go along. I'll release him to your custody, but I'll keep you on a short leash. I won't have you two followed, but you'll need to keep me informed about what is happening."

Agent Salture sat in silence throughout the whole conversation.

11

Pleased with the outcome of the meeting with Special Agent Henry Boller, Cliff left in haste to spring his client from his unlawful arrest. Special Agent Boller suspected Doctor Ulsheeh of espionage, but he had no solid evidence. The doctor's arrest was based solely on his association with the people of his faith.

Second thoughts invaded his mind, causing him some anguish. Special Agent Bolller shared some high level information with him to win his loyalty, but was it enough? Brian had agreed to work inside Iran to release the other scientists. Cliff felt betrayed by his brother for not leveling with him at their last meeting. He could have signaled him somehow—maybe with a message in Pig Latin. And yet, he didn't. Brian was complicated, and difficult for him to understand at times, but why and how could he jeopardize his future with such a dangerous choice? Since Brian was already in Iran, there was little Cliff could do about getting him back. Cliff threatened interference with Special Agent Boller's plan in an attempt to get more leverage. It worked, and he was pleased with the final outcome of the meeting. He needed to shelf his brother's quandary for now and get on with his own life, but could he find a way?

The doctor would think of him a hero, and it allowed him to feel good about his ability to get his client released so quickly. However, Special Agent Boller made it perfectly clear that Cliff would be responsible for any wayward actions of his client in the future. By the time he reached the jail floor Doctor Ulsheeh was dressed in civilian clothes and sitting in the foyer ready and waiting to accompany him.

"Cliff, you certainly know your business. It didn't take you long to get me released. Thank you. I appreciate what you have done for me. I'd like to know what strings you needed to pull to get me released so soon."

"Sometimes our system makes mistakes while trying to do the right thing. I would suggest you be more selective about your associates. It seems that was the crux of the Federal Government's concerns."

"This is a free country. Those men I worship with are just like me. We have done nothing wrong. Are you telling me I shouldn't practice my religion in the way I choose?"

"I'm merely suggesting that you need to be more discreet about those with whom you associate. Perhaps practice your religion at home with your family."

"I won't. These are my friends and we have done nothing wrong, and I can't do what you ask. Here we are at my home— drop me off here."

Cliff stopped the car, unsure what to do next. His cell rang. Doctor Ulsheeh opened the car door and Cliff snapped open his cell.

"Cliff, it's Marianne. Dad's funeral is tomorrow morning. We need to get together today. I want you here to finalize the funeral plans."

"Just a second," He held his hand over his cell and spoke to Doctor Ulsheeh. "We need to get together to discuss the conditions of your release."

"Conditions, my foot. The Feds have nothing on me. That's what you said."

"You need to be more cautious than before."

Doctor Ulsheeh slammed the car door and walked to his house, ignoring Cliff's last statement and leaving him with a moment of regret.

"Sorry Marianne. Something came up."

She had hung up— obviously upset. Cliff called her back.

"Cliff, are you too busy to talk about your own father's funeral?"

"Sorry. I'm coming your way. Sis, be patient with me right now. I'll be there in a couple minutes."

Those minutes allowed Cliff to settle his thoughts. He must put the Doctor out of his mind and prepare himself to deal with his father's funeral.

Ted was waiting on the front porch to usher him inside. Marianne was sitting at the desk with an array of papers in front of her.

"Cliff, it's about time. Where the hell have you been lately?"

"Sis, it doesn't matter. I'm here now. Let's go over the arrangements."

"Well, it is costing a lot more than I figured. The funeral home wants their money before tomorrow. It is $8500. Ted and I don't have that kind of money. Do you have access to Dad's bank account?"

"Here's my credit card. Just charge on it, and we'll settle his estate later. Charge whatever is necessary on the card, and we'll settle up later. I'm going down to the funeral home to make sure everything is properly arranged. Do you want to go with me?"

"Of course, give me a minute."

"Ted, are all of the funeral arrangements made?" Marianne asked.

"I believe so." Ted answered, and he turned to Cliff. "Marianne has been in a state fretting over the costs. Also, we need to get together to order an arrangement of flowers from the florist. Maybe you and Marianne can do that on the way to the funeral home."

"Good idea. We'll do just that. Marianne, let's go, I haven't got all day."

"I don't see you in days and you're rushing me. What's going on with you, anyway?"

"Sis, you read me like a book, don't you?"

"I always could. It's terrible about Dad dying, isn't it?"

"It happened too fast. Let's stop at Hendley's and get some flowers to put on the casket."

"I'm game. These last few days have been hell for me."

"I'm sorry I wasn't here for you, but Ted was there for you."

"He's good for me. I couldn't have done better."

"When my turn comes to find a mate I want you in on the action."

"I didn't know you were close to being ready."

"I'm not, but when the times comes, you can start looking for me."

"It's good to talk alone. It's going to be tough without Dad to push our buttons."

"Sure is. I'll let you pick out the flowers. Mom said 'Dad always like wildflowers. You know, purple, white, and yellow'."

"I'm picking, let me pick."

"Better yet, I'll wait in the car while you pick it."

"Coward."

"Don't be too long."

Marianne closed the door behind her and went into the flower shop. He and Marianne always had an understanding between them. Cliff's phone rang.

"Yeah."

"Agent Salture here. Do you know where Doctor Ulsheeh is at this very moment?"

"Am I supposed to know?"

"He's at the Mosque with his friends."

"I left him at his home with his family. He was concerned about his family."

"Special Agent Boller won't like him going to the Mosque."

"I asked him to pray at home and he gave me the freedom act. Don't expect miracles from me. I will do my best to keep him in line. My sister is coming, I got to hang up."

"Cliff, who were you talking with?"

"Just a pissed off client. I'm losing a lot of them these days."

"Dad should look good in his blue suit and red tie. I hope you will say something about him being a good father to all of us tomorrow."

"I haven't decided what I'll say yet. Has the VFW contacted you at all?"

"No, they haven't. Maybe you should call them after we see Dad."

Cliff and Marianne went into the mortuary and spent time viewing their father and talking to the Funeral Director, who told them about the upcoming ceremony. Cliff dropped Marianne off at her home, and then went home to look for his Dad's important papers.

He opened the door and Agent Salture was sitting on the couch.

"Christ, can't you leave me alone for the time being? I'm grieving for my father, you know."

"Cliff, you can't put anything ahead of our National Security."

"I can and I will. My family is the most important thing in my life right now. After the funeral I'll work with you. I would appreciate it if you would leave now."

Agent Salture closed the door behind her without replying to his request. He sat alone with his thoughts—his business had hit a new low, his family's structure was in ruins, and the thought of Brian not being able to attend their father's final rites greatly disturbed him. He knew he had to come up with a final message for his father's eulogy. He sat at the desk to write it. It needed to be brief, which required him to choose his words carefully.

The day of the funeral arrived and Cliff entered the church. It was mostly full, and the usher walked by his side. On his way down the aisle he saw Agent Salture and Agent Boller. He sat momentarily, then rose and approached the casket. He looked down at his father, his companion, and his mentor.

"Dad, thanks for being there for me. Now I must carry on for you and Brian both. I will miss seeing you every day just as I have Mom. When you get to Heaven say hello to her for me."

He paused and closed his eyes while saying a short prayer. The prayer came from nowhere. It was a number of years since he even thought of praying. He opened his eyes and felt someone standing next to him. At first he thought it was Marianne, but it wasn't. It was a very petite, frail, elderly woman he hadn't ever seen before. She put her arm around his waist and put something in his side coat pocket. She said, "read the note after the service." She patted him on the shoulder and then left. When he turned around to see her she had seated herself at one of the pews.

The eulogies went well. The pastor and Dad had been friends since World War II, the VFW president said a few short words, and now it was Cliff's turn. He approached the pulpit, climbed the stairs, and looked around. He needed to be strong, and not break down. He looked at his sister Marianne for strength to carry on.

"My father has been my guiding light throughout my life. He supported me when I was down, and cheered me on with my successes. Our hunting trips were unforgettable, and our family at the mountain cabin was a continuous learning experience for me. Dad always had the right answers. His marriage to our Mom was a love affair most of us desire. Love was always present in our home. I will miss him more than I can say today. I thank all of his friends who are here to support our family. I would prefer to have a private graveside service later today. Please respect our family's wishes."

Marianne was standing on the bottom step of the pulpit to hug him when he came down. His eyes were cloudy with tears. He returned to his seat with Marianne by his side.

When the funeral was over Cliff looked for the elderly lady that stood next to him at the casket. People crowded around him to wish him well, but he couldn't locate the elderly lady.

Cliff, Marianne, and Ted went to the gravesite along with the Pastor and the VFW representative. The Pastor said a few chosen words and then turned to Cliff for some comment. Cliff placed his hand on the closed casket and silently said a prayer his mother had taught him when he was very young. After the bugler played taps, the VFW representative removed the flag from the casket and gave it to Marianne. They all left except Cliff. He chose to stay until the cemetery workers covered the casket. Marianne left for her house to oversee the reception.

On his way to the reception Cliff's cell rang. He glanced at the number —it was Agent Salture. He ignored her call. Before he arrived at Marianne's house Agent Salture called repeatedly several more times.

At the reception he looked for the elderly lady, but he didn't see her anywhere. He thought about her message. He chose to leave early because the note in his pocket seemed urgent.

Cliff sat in his car and reached for the note.

Meet me at the empty house on the corner of Juniper and Rose streets at seven this evening.

Seven was four hours from now. His cell rang again. It was Agent Salture. He didn't answer it, but returned home. He needed a stiff drink. He sat in his fathers' recliner thinking about their hunting trips together, and fell asleep. He awoke with a start. It was already dark. He checked his watch and it was 6:45 pm. He went upstairs, splashed water on his face, combed his hair, and put on a jacket. He drove to meet the elderly lady. He parked and surveyed the house. He saw a candle shining through the window. He reached into the glove compartment to retrieve his flashlight. A bright light and a weapon in hand suited him. He put the pistol in his side pocket.

He opened the front door, expecting a greeting of some kind, but none was forthcoming. He stepped inside, turned on his flashlight, and walked toward the shining candle.

"Glad you came." A voice came from the darkness. Cliff shined his flashlight in the direction of the voice.

"Please turn that off. This is an abandoned house, and I don't want law enforcement to know we've broken in."

"There's a candle in the window, what's the difference? Why are we meeting here at all?"

"Frankly, I can't stand a complainer. I'm moving the candle out of the window. It was there to let you know I was here. I'm from out of town, and we need the privacy. The FBI hasn't followed you here, have they? If not, sit down, and let's get on with it, shall we?"

"Okay, I'm sitting. What's next?"

"It's my business to be aware of things before they happen. At times it gives me a great advantage. I am a psychic. Your sister hired and paid my standard $10,000 fee. I visited your brother Brian in the hospital at your sister's request. She felt Brian was acting unusually strange, and she hired me to find out why. From my visit with Brian I found him to be quite smart, and we hit it off rather well. He told me about his offer to go to Iran to rescue the other scientists. I'll answer your questions now."

"If you are as smart as you say you are, I want you to tell me where Brian is right now."

"If this is a quiz, I'll gladly answer. He's in Iran in search of the three scientists. He went voluntarily to find a way to get them back to the United States before they do further damage to our beloved country. Does that sufficiently answer your question?"

"My God. How do you know all this? Special Agent Boller said only top level people knew about his mission."

"It's my business to know a lot of things. I talked with Brian at great length before he left with that Iranian nurse."

"You talked with Brian, and he told you what he was going to do?"

"Yes, he did. I told you we got along well. Marianne hired me to get Brian and the other scientists safely returned to the States. She is afraid Brian might end up in prison in Iran. I'm telling you all this so you won't interfere with my mission. I would like your word on that."

"I don't even know your name and you're asking me to butt out of my family's business. By the size of you, you couldn't do what you promised my sister you'd do. Are you working in conjunction with the FBI on this? You appear to know a lot about what is going on."

"I know something that might shock you. While you were at your father's funeral, Doctor Ulsheeh boarded a plane to Paris."

"No way. He is under my protective care. He wouldn't do such a thing without talking with me first."

"Call Agent Salture. She has been trying to reach you."

"I'll call her later, if you don't mind. I can't believe my sister would pay you $10,000. Frankly, I think you are scamming my family. How much money do you want from me to keep quiet?"

"I'm not asking you for any money. I want you to stay out of my way, help me at times when I need your help, be patient, and not be your usual impatient self. Is that simple enough for a lawyer like you to understand?"

"You are rather bitchy for an old lady, aren't you?"

"I guess I am. Also, I like things my way. Marianne asked me to level with you before I departed for Iran. I won't need much help from you, but if did, I want you to cooperate with me, and not delay any request I might make of you. Do we have an understanding or not?"

"How do I keep in touch with you?"

"You don't. When I need you I'll be in touch. Now, do I have your word to stay out of my way for the time being?"

"I will, but Special Agent Boller has a plan in action. Your interference might jeopardize Brian's life."

"Let me worry about that. I operate in the dark. I won't work in a way that would harm Brian's life. He and I have an understanding. I would jeopardize my own life before I would put his life in danger."

Cliff sighed. "You have a free rein, and I won't interfere with you for the time being. You have my word on that."

"I'll be in touch from time to time. Be patient. That's all I can promise for the time being. Molly is my name. Is that enough for you?"

"You've got our $10,000 dollars and all you can give me is your first name. I need more. You could leave here and we might not ever hear from you again."

"I'm a principled person. I will give you your money's worth. That's all you need to know for the time being. You'll need to leave now. I will make sure you are not followed. Take good care of your sister for the time being. She is pretty disturbed over this whole thing. She gave me your cell number, and you don't need mine."

"Frankly, I don't fully understand all of what's happening. I would like to stay and talk further about your plans."

"Just leave now. I have nothing more to say. You will hear from me when I have something to offer. Now go."

12

When Cliff returned to his car he called Marianne.

"Marianne, tell me what secret are you keeping from me?"

"Secret? Oh, you found out. You mean Molly. She's a story in herself, isn't she? Ted and Molly went to high school together. They ran into each other at the grocery store several days ago and he brought her home with him. We got talking about Brian and the trouble he is having. She was so confident about her ability to bring Brian safely back home we hired her on the spot. I know you're having a hard time balancing your business and spending time coming up with a way to rescue Brian. She is very talented, and has experience beyond belief. I'm sure you'll like her once you two have talked, or maybe she has been in touch with you already."

"We've talked. Frankly, I don't know how she will be of any help. She is elderly, and not very strong, but I have to admit she has a way about her. It was a bold move on your part to pay her that much money up front. She bowled me over with her knowing Brian volunteered to go to Iran to rescue those scientists?"

"Ted talked with her and made all of the arrangements. I saw her walk up to you when you were at Dad's casket. She talked with Brian in the hospital, and she found out all of that on her own. She is a remarkable, talented woman, and I believe Brian likes her too. Lighten up will you? She can't do any harm, and she certainly could help bring Brian back safely."

"She said she charges $10,000 for her services. Where did you and Ted get that kind of money?"

"I borrowed it from Dad. Earlier, before Dad passed I told him Brian was in trouble, and without question he gave me his credit card. Don't be mad, I am just trying to help Brian, and I know you're having a tough time right now with Dad's passing and all. I love Brian as much as you do."

"You do the praying, and leave the rest up to me. I hope this slip of a woman don't muddy up the waters for me."

He closed his cell and sat in his car for a quiet moment. His cell rang.

"Hello."

"It's Agent Salture. Why in the hell don't you answer your phone? I've been trying to let you know Doctor Ulsheeh has left the country. Did he contact you before he left, or were you in on his escape?"

"Come on now. Your opinion of me is quite jaded. I'm only interested in getting Brian back. The last time I was with the doctor, he was angry with me for telling him where to worship. Anyway, I thought he was wearing one of those ankle bracelets you people put on criminals."

"Smart-ass! He's your responsibility, not mine. I'm just trying to protect you. You vouched for him, and it is up to you to keep track of him every minute of the day or night. By allowing him to leave the country you have committed a felony offense. I hope Special Agent Boller doesn't ask me to arrest you and bring you in to headquarters."

"As of this moment I don't care what you're told to do. The promises I made were only to get Doctor Ulsheeh released from jail. You people had no reason to arrest him. If you need to arrest someone, then come and arrest me."

"You are being difficult with me. I'm trying to work with you. Doctor Ulsheeh leaving the country and leaving his family behind is a bold move on his part. If he visits Iran and returns to the States, he will be immediately arrested, and you won't be able to get him released."

"Goodbye." Cliff snapped his cell closed in a moment of anger.

Days passed with Cliff hearing any thing about the case. He tended to his clients, and it felt good to get back to his normal routine. Even Marianne hadn't been in touch. The end of the day arrived, and Cliff sat alone nursing a beer. He went to bed thinking about his appearance in court the next day.

At 2:00 am his cell rang. He rolled over in bed to answer it.

"Yeah, what is it? It's the middle of the night, you know."

"It's Molly. I have some new developments for you."

"It's 2:00 in the morning. Are you out of your mind?"

"I've located your brother. He and I had a short chat. Everything is fine with him. He is already working on the Iranian laser program. He is getting settled in, but hasn't started looking for the other scientists yet. Also, I saw Doctor Ulsheeh."

"You saw Doctor Ulsheeh? Where are you right now?"

"I'm in Iran. I did a double take when I saw Doctor Ulsheeh talking to one of the atomic officials. Did you know he was here?"

"I knew he flew to Paris. His family is here, so I know he will return to the States."

"I need some money. Please wire it to the Olivine Hotel in Istanbul. I will be there tomorrow, and don't be skimpy. I've had to pay some handsome bribes to locate Brian. The normal population here in Iran is hurting badly because of the sanctions the world has put on them. A number of important people will do anything for money. It is time to strike while they are in the mood. I will be at the hotel early tomorrow, so wire it first thing in the morning, and don't be skimpy. I am making good progress."

"You tease me with a tiny bit of information, and you're asking for more money. I am not a money tree."

"Grow up, Sonny. Join the real world. This is no longer a two-bit world we live in. It costs money, and my exceptional efforts for you won't be cheap. I can't operate in my usual way unless I have your full support. I work 24 hours a day, so quit whining about the time I called. Send the money!"

"Okay, I'll send it first thing in the morning. Oh! I don't know your last name."

"Promise not to laugh—it's Moonshine. Molly Moonshine."

"Molly Moonshine—doesn't that beat all. I don't know how Marianne found you, but you've won me over with your straight-forward talk and actions. Be careful, it could be dangerous over there."

"I can take care of myself. Don't worry about me. Send the money."

Cliff closed his cell and lay in bed thinking about his conversation with Molly. She was a fireball, and she could bring Brian back if anyone could. He thought about Doctor Ulsheeh and why he'd gone to Iran. What could he be up to? And would he return to the States? And why did he flee like he did? Perhaps he went to Iran to make way for his family to return there. If he left the States completely no one would find out what he did to those scientists to make them go to Iran. Before going to sleep Cliff decided to visit Doctor Ulsheeh's family first thing in the morning. Perhaps they had some answers for him. And maybe he could find out why he'd left in such a hurry. Sleep didn't come easily, and Cliff woke up tired and grumpy.

As he sipped his morning coffee he put his day's activity together. He needed to wire the money to Molly. He decided to send her another $10,000 dollars. He needed to talk with Marianne about his father's estate. He wanted to visit with Doctor Ulsheeh's family, and he had a court appearance late in the afternoon. The day wouldn't be too rushed. His toast popped up and he went to fetch the jelly. His cell vibrated.

"Cliff, where is Doctor Ulsheeh at this very moment?"

"Who is this, and how did you get this number?"

"This is Special Agent Boller. Where is Doctor Ulsheeh right now?"

"I don't know. I'm not his baby sitter."

"Don't get smart with me. I'm sending a couple agents over to his home right now. If he's not there I'm coming to arrest you."

With his problems multiplying by leaps and bounds Cliff decided to put off his visit to Doctor Ulsheeh's family and call Marianne.

"Marianne, have you heard from Molly?"

"No, I haven't. I gave her your cell number, and she said she would work with you."

"Guess what. She wants more money. What do you think about that?"

"It is what it is, don't fret about it. Brian can pay us back when he gets settled and he's back to work."

"Nothing, and I mean nothing fazes you does it, Sis? We need to get together to discuss Dad's estate. I will pick up his will and papers from his safety deposit box and be at your house by eleven. Is that okay with you?"

"I'll make it okay. I would like to get Dad's estate settled as soon as we can."

Cliff finished his second cup of coffee and was cleaning the sink when the doorbell rang. He walked to the front door. The bell rang nonstop. He looked through the door window and two men dressed in dark suits were standing there.

Cliff opened the door.

"Cliff Mercer, you are to come with us. Is there anyone else in the house?"

"What? Who are you?"

The lead man reached into his pocket and brought out a badge. He quickly flashed it, and returned it to his pocket.

"I didn't see it. I still don't know who you are. Let me see that badge again."

"We're with the FBI, and we don't need any of your smart talk. Special Agent Boller sent us to bring you to his office."

The other man grabbed Cliff's arms, turned him around, and put handcuffs on him.

"This is totally unnecessary. I asked a simple question, and I expected a simple answer."

"You'll stay in the cuffs until we deliver you."

Cliff was loaded into the car and he didn't dare say anything on the way. They arrived at the San Francisco FBI Headquarters.

"Take the cuffs off this man. I told you to ask him to come in to see me."

"He gave us some resistance."

"I apologize for their behavior. Please sit. Would you like something, water, coffee?"

"I'm fine. It was a little misunderstanding."

"I'm just curious. Something has come up in your brother's case. Have you been interfering with the CIA and the FBI's efforts to bring back your brother and the other scientists?"

"Me, no. I thought you had everything under control."

"There is a Molly somebody in Iran who is paying some high officials for information about Brian and the other scientists. Is she working for you?"

"My sister hired her. I had nothing to do with it."

"I'll ask again. Is she working for you?"

"Well, technically I guess she is."

"I know she is, because she called you at two this morning for additional money. I would like you to tell me what she is up to in Iran. She hadn't checked in with our Embassy in Iran."

"I haven't the slightest. She is like a loose cannon. I believe she will get all of them back safely."

"That's a laugh. How could an elderly woman accomplish more than our CIA and FBI? Was she standing next to you at your father's casket?"

"Yes, she was."

"I called you here to talk about Doctor Ulsheeh. Do you know where he is right now?"

"According to Molly he is in Iran discussing nuclear power."

"Impossible. We are following him in Paris at this very minute."

"Molly told me he was in Iran."

"I'm getting irritated with your smug answers. It was your responsibility to make sure he stayed within the city limits. You failed to do that, and you could be charged with a felony."

"I was as shocked as you when I heard the Doctor left the country."

"His actions prove he is definitely involved with the conspiracy to abduct those scientists. We're unsure how he did it, but in time we will find out. Furthermore, your associate Molly whoever is muddying-up our search for the scientists. I understand she has bribed a number of Iranian citizens seeking information about Brian and the other scientists. It is against the law for a United States citizen to bribe a foreign elected official. If and when you're in touch with her, I want you to advise her of that."

"Some of those scientists have been in Iran for four years. You haven't got them back, and you're relying on Brian to bring them back on his own. And now, you're complaining about my representative breaking a few rules. Personally, I'll get my brother back by any means. It has been four years and you haven't figured how Doctor Ulsheeh enticed those four scientists to work for their government. Get real, will you?"

"I don't need a lecture from you on how to do my job. I work within the law and sometimes it moves slower than other methods.

We're getting nowhere here. We need to work together. Molly is interfering with Brian's ability to locate and get those scientists back and she is putting Brian's life in danger. If the Iranian Secret Service should find out he is working for me, then he will be executed. Now, do you understand my concern?"

"I hadn't thought of that."

"Get her back here and keep her out of Iran. Let me properly do my job. I have two CIA operatives working with Brian at this very moment. Your brother is quite smart, and he will get the job done better than anyone I know. He is a true patriot for taking on this assignment."

"I'll have to wait until Molly contacts me again because I have no way of getting in touch with her. I wouldn't want to jeopardize Brian's life."

"I trust you. For now I'll let you go. Please keep me informed about what progress you make on the case. Get that Molly out of Iran, and keep her off my case."

Cliff left. A smile erupted from within. Molly was making significant progress, and he decided not to interfere with her at this time. He didn't understand how she had done it, but she had busied herself with the case. He went to the bank, wired the money to Molly, picked up his father's documents and headed for Marianne's home.

Cliff sat at the desk and opened up all of the papers he took from the security box. His father had several insurance policies, a deed to the house, and a number of investments. By the looks of it, it would take a while to get his estate settled. Their father's will stated his estate be divided equally between the three of them. Without Brian present Cliff was reluctant to divide up their father's estate. Before Cliff left, Marianne and he decided to cash in the insurance and investments and for Cliff to stay in his father's house for the time being. Cliff left and sat in his car while he thought about what a great man his father had been. It would be hard for him to work on the estate, but he was trained to do just that. He decided to go to the cemetery to visit his father and mother's gravesites. Since Brian was gone his family life hadn't been the same. He loved his sister, but Brian was his closest sibling, was in danger, and might not be able to make it back.

Cliff went to court with his client and won the case, which made him feel good. He went home and waited for a call from Molly. *What would he tell her when she called?* The question weighed heavily on his mind. Should he follow Special Agent Boller's orders, or let her proceed on her own? It would be bold to let her continue on the path she had chosen, but would it actually put Brian's life in danger?

The house was quiet and Cliff listened for every noise, even the slightest. He heard someone on the porch. He grabbed the gun from his father's side cabinet and approached the door. Just as he reached the door, the doorbell rang. He looked through the glass and saw a stranger outside.

"Who is it?" Cliff asked through the closed door.

"I work with Molly. I need to talk with you."

Cliff opened the door and allowed the stranger to enter.

"My name is Teddy Marshall, and I work with Molly. I talked with her a short while ago, and she asked me to meet with you."

Cliff showed his guest to the living room and offered him a beer.

"Molly wouldn't like me to drink on the job. I will take a glass of water."

Cliff returned with the glass of water and asked, "What is this all about?"

"Molly thought I should meet with you immediately to tell you her latest information."

"Well, get on with it. Give me her message."

"Molly met with Brian in Iran, and he told her someone here in the Livermore Lab is a spy, and he's feeding all of the latest information about the laser project Brian was working on to an Iranian scientist."

Cliff sat back in his fathers' recliner to absorb what Molly's agent just told him. The news was shocking.

"Did Molly tell you what she expected me to do with this news?"

"She said Brian wanted this information passed on to your FBI contact."

Cliff took a sip of his beer while his mind grappled with this latest news.

13

After getting Teddy Marshall's phone number, Cliff showed him to the door and returned to his father's recliner. Thoughts of what he could do with this latest news coursed through his mind. Brian's decision to go to Iran to rescue the other scientists was getting more complicated as time went on, and Cliff was thrust into the middle of it all. He decided to sleep on it and make a decision in the morning about what to do. His thoughts were always clearer and crisper in the morning.

Cliff tossed and turned throughout the night as the news Teddy delivered the evening before replayed over and over in his mind. A spy at Livermore Labs was beyond his ability to deal with it, but the news Brian risked his life securing just couldn't die without his following up on it.

He didn't have access to the Lab, much less have a source to interview anyone working there.

He finished his second cup of coffee and decided to call Special Agent Boller for an appointment. He wasn't sure how he would accept Molly's discovery, but Boller was fair with him in the past. He arrived at the Federal building and was ushered into Special Agent Boller's office.

Questions about how to present the news about a spy working within the confines of Livermore flashed through his mind. He sat before the distinguished-looking Agent Boller, but wasn't sure how to begin. Agent Boller sat quietly and waited patiently for Cliff to explain the reason for his urgent visit.

Finally he asked, "Cliff, why did you come to see me?"

"Molly, my contact in Iran, has come across some very disturbing news. In a conversation with Brian he disclosed to her that a spy in the Livermore Labs has been passing secret information to the Iranian government."

Cliff sat back and waited for a response from Agent Boller.

He observed the look on Agent Boller's face—a mixture of surprise and doubt.

"There seems to be some misunderstanding here. To date I have no news from our CIA operatives in Iran about this situation at all. If Brian was aware of this why didn't he tell our CIA operative instead of going through your contact?"

"That is something you need to find out for yourself. There must be some distrust existing between Brian and your operatives. I can't think of any other reason."

"Regardless of how you came across this information, it greatly disturbs me. It's not that I don't believe you, but to have a spy working inside Livermore is an intolerable situation. All projects within their confines are listed as secret and our Department screens each person working there very thoroughly. Also, the news that Brian does not trust our CIA implanted agents in Iran is disturbing. I find both quite bothersome. Our two agents there are Iranian born citizens who volunteered for our service a number of years ago, and I have no reason to doubt their loyalty to our cause. I don't understand Brian's distrust of them."

"If that's so, my news is of little or no value to you. If not, I suggest you start working on the news I brought you."

"I intend to, believe me. Do you have a name we can work with, or do we have to begin work in the dark?"

"My source didn't disclose a name. This news is all I have. I believed it to be so critical that I wanted to tell you right away."

"We have a number of security agents assigned to Livermore, and I'll be in touch with their supervisor within the hour. I thank you for bringing it to my attention. We've been on opposite sides of the table for a while, and it is refreshing to have you on my side for a change. Keep a rein on your contact in Iran because terrible things could happen to him if he is discovered. A number of their leaders are quick to administer justice to anyone spying in their country. I know all about this because we have lost several capable agents in the last few years."

"It isn't a him, it's a her. In fact, she's an elderly woman. A woman you would help across the street. I had my doubts about her ability when I first met her, but I've changed my mind since. She has been able to discover this news when your trusted operatives couldn't. I believe that's why my brother trusts her so."

"Unbelievable! It would be doubly difficult for our State Department to get her released if she was caught."

"I'll let her worry about that. She is quite capable of taking care of herself."

Cliff returned to the house to work on his Father's estate. He needed to close it and get it behind him. However, his mind kept returning to Brian in Iran. His brother's life was in constant danger. Molly could create a situation where Brian could get killed. She was constantly active and at odds with the CIA operatives in Iran. His cell vibrated.

"Cliff, it's Teddy. I have a first name of that spy at Livermore. His name is Roger. That's all Molly has at this time. Molly wants to know what you've done with her information."

"Tell her the FBI at Livermore working on her news. I will pass on this latest information to my FBI contact. Tell her to keep safe. If she should get caught she might tell them about Brian's mission."

"She's been doing this kind of undercover work for a number of years. I'm sure she is careful about her activities. I wouldn't worry about her."

"Good. I'll pass on this information to my source. Thanks."

Cliff called Special Agent Boller.

"This is Cliff Mercer. I have a name of that spy at Livermore. His name is Roger."

"Impossible. Off hand, there is only one Roger I know of at the Lab, and he is the Chief scientist at Livermore. You've presented me with an impossible situation. There is no way I could question his integrity. I will immediately look into his recent activities."

"I don't want you to do me any favors. I hand you this startling bit of news and you appear fearful to act on it. I would suggest you check to see if there is more than one Roger at the Lab. That would be a hell of a starting point."

"Cliff, you're a wise ass, you know. Leave the detective work to me. I appreciate your information, and I'll check into it." He signed off.

Days passed without a word from Molly, Teddy, or Special Agent Boller. Cliff's cell vibrated.

"Cliff, it's Marianne. Have you heard anything about Brian lately?"

"No news. I have been thinking about going over there myself. Time goes by, and I feel we are losing him more as each day passes."

"I wouldn't do that, Cliff. Surely Molly will be able to help bring him back. I couldn't stand to lose you too."

"Aw Sis, I can take care of myself. I feel lost without Brian and Dad around. How are all of the kids?"

"They're all fine. Cliff, I don't want you to go over there. Do you hear me?"

"I hear you. I have Dad's estate almost finished. Maybe we can get together by the weekend and discuss it. I gotta go."

Cliff worked on the estate till late in the night, and went to bed.

He got up to go to the bathroom and heard a noise from downstairs. He grabbed his baseball bat from the closet and quietly made his way down the creaky stairs. Someone was in the kitchen. He slowly approached the kitchen doorway where he could see a light coming from under the door. He smelled coffee, and heard the rustle of a skillet. He opened the door, ready to slug the person in the kitchen, but no one was there. Suddenly someone from behind grabbed the bat from his hand. He turned to face Molly.

"You should be more careful with that bat—someone could get hurt."

"Molly, what are you doing here? I could have knocked your head off."

"That would be difficult because I heard you and took the bat out of your hands."

"Molly, you scared the hell out of me."

"Really, you scare easily, Sonny Boy. I went up to your bedroom and you were sleeping so soundly I didn't want to wake you."

"You were in my bedroom, and you didn't wake me? I thought you were still in Iran with Brian."

"You snore when you sleep on your back. I would suggest you sleep on your side. I'm starving right now. Let me finish my cooking, and I will explain it all to you. The coffee is done, help yourself."

"Why not? It's my coffee."

"Are you grouchy all of the time? Don't be like that. We're both on the same team, aren't we?"

Cliff grumbled something and finished pouring himself a cup of coffee. He knew his embarrassment was showing as he sat at the table to view this remarkable woman. Most women her age had trouble going to the store, driving a car, or crossing the street, but this woman had just returned from halfway around the world, and was cooking breakfast in his kitchen at three in the morning. He remembered locking the front door before going upstairs.

"Molly, how did you get into my house?"

"Get yourself a good lock, Sonny Boy. That piece of junk you call a lock could be picked by my granddaughter. I've uncovered some disturbing news. News I needed to deliver in person."

"I'm not used to being awakened in the middle of the night by a strange person cooking in my kitchen."

"Sonny Boy, I'm not a strange person, I'm on your payroll, remember? I move around at will to get things done, and I never look at the clock."

"My name is Cliff. I don't like you calling me Sonny Boy."

"Boo Hoo, you have mighty thin skin."

Molly finished her cooking and sat directly across the table from him.

"The real truth is —I ran out of money. It's something you don't want to hear, I know. I tried to get some from Brian, but they don't pay him over there. They provide him and that girl a place to live, and the Government buys their food. Besides, I have something real important to tell you."

The toast popped up and Molly went to fetch it.

"Do you want some toast?"

"I want to know about Brian, quit stalling, will you?"

"This is the first meal I've had in a day and a half. Pass the jelly, will you?"

"Is there anything else you need?" For God's sake tell me about Brian. That's what I'm paying you for." Cliff said with a touch of anger in his voice.

"I told you, I ran out of money. I divorced my second husband because he was always grouchy. Maybe you are not paying me enough. Besides, I'm not accustomed to being talked to like you're doing. You don't seem to like me the way I am—you should see me when I get mad! Give me a moment. I've been on a plane for twenty some hours without anything to eat. You are supposed to be a lawyer, and I always thought lawyers were supposed to have unquestionable patience."

"Okay, I don't need a lecture about my character traits. I'll wait until you are finished. Do you want another cup of coffee?"

The doorbell rang.

"It's three in the morning. Who could be at the door?"

"It's Teddy. I called him to come over. Let him in while I finish up here, will you?"

Cliff grumbled as he made his way to the front door. *"It's three in the morning, and you would think this is Grand Central Station."*

He peered through the glass and saw Teddy at the door.

"Don't you have a key to my door too?" Cliff asked sarcastically.

"Molly called me. Are you out of sorts?"

"That sounds like something they would say in the United Kingdom."

"I was a spy for the Majesty for over twenty years. That is how I first met Molly."

"Come in, Teddy. Molly is making herself something to eat in my kitchen. I hope you're not hungry too."

"I could use some hot coffee, otherwise, I'm fine. It's cold out this time of morning. Molly wanted to brief me at the same time she briefed you."

"We don't want to spoil any of her plans, do we?"

Molly was just finishing. "Hello Teddy, glad you could make it. Help yourself to the coffee, and we'll get started."

Cliff and Teddy sat down while Molly pulled a folder from her purse. She appeared older than he remembered. He recalled her being thin, but the wrinkles in her face were deeper than he recalled. Cliff had only seen her once before and it was by candlelight. She fingered through a number of 8 X 10 photographs, set some aside, and pushed a couple of them across the table in Cliff's direction.

Cliff picked them up, unsure what he was about to see, and looked at the first one. It was a picture of Brian. He appeared to be in good health. His clothes were wrinkled, and he had grown a beard, but he looked healthy and fit.

"I hired you to bring Brian back, not bring me photographs of him."

Cliff glared at Molly, and Teddy squeezed Cliff's forearm.

"Let her finish!" Teddy warned.

"Sonny Boy, it is like a rattlesnake nest over there. Every direction you go there are Government people checking. Brian is under constant watch day and night by his wife and three other operatives. He would leave me a signal when we could meet by leaving the postal box door open. Most of the time we met in the middle of the night. On this one night we were able to meet because his wife was out late. He believes she works for their intelligence group. They are watching him so closely he hasn't been able to look for the other scientists. After a few moments with him he asked me to leave because he was expecting the two CIA operatives. Just as I was leaving Brian saw them coming up to the front door. He asked me to hide in the closet. Within minutes Doctor Ulsheeh opened the door and came in while Brian was talking with the two CIA operatives."

Molly leaned back, took a sip of coffee, and took a deep breath. She shuffled through the pictures and picked out two more photographs and slid them toward Cliff. He picked them up. One was a picture of Doctor Ulsheeh, and the other was a picture of Brian holding a gun with two dead men lying on the floor.

"I don't understand."

"Brian killed them both. Doctor Ulsheeh handed Brian the gun, told him they were spies and he should kill them both. Without hesitation, Brian shot both men in cold blood."

Cliff sighed heavily. He dropped the picture on the table, and put his face in his hands.

"Brian would never hurt anyone. You have this all wrong."

"I witnessed it. Doctor Ulsheeh told him to shoot the CIA agents, and Brian did just what the Doctor told him to do."

Teddy picked up the photographs to look at them.

"You've talked with Brian, does he appear normal to you, or do you think he is under some kind of spell?"

"Teddy, you've been through some bizarre days in your hitch with international operatives. I imagine you've seen all kinds of weird things happen like this, haven't you?"

"Yes, but this is different. It appears Doctor Ulsheeh had some control over Brian. I can't see his eyes in this photograph. It generally shows in the eyes. If someone is under a narcotic or a spell of some kind it will show in the eyes."

"This is my brother you are both talking about! He is no weirdo. He is an intelligent scientist. Years ago, he couldn't shoot a deer when he had it in his sights. He would go hunting with Dad and me, and he could never shoot a living creature. He couldn't have possibly shot those men."

"It pains me to tell you this truth, but I am just doing the job you and Marianne pay me to do. If you want me to discontinue my services I will do so."

"Give me time to digest all of this. I can't understand why Doctor Ulsheeh didn't have him shoot you too."

"I'm sure he would have if he knew I was present. I shot this picture from the closet I was hiding. Doctor Ulsheeh went to get the authorities, and I came out of the closet and shot the picture of the two men on the floor. Brian agreed to meet me the next morning. I left right after that."

"Tell me you didn't witness Brian shooting the two men. You were in the closet, and couldn't see any of what was going on. The Doctor probably shot them. My brother could never kill another person. You don't know my brother. I can't accept what you are telling me."

"I saw it all. There was a half-inch space in the closet doors. I didn't see Brian's eyes like Teddy suggested, but I witnessed the Doctor giving Brian the gun, and Brian shot both of them. Without hesitation, he did just that. I don't blame your brother for any of this happening. I'm sure Doctor Ulsheeh has complete control over his brain."

"Does Brian know why the Doctor is in Iran?"

"I'm of the opinion he was called over there to control Brian's state of mind. Brian might not be agreeing with everything they want him to do. All of this is only speculation on my part, but it appears to make sense, doesn't it? His girlfriend is with him all of the time except when he can slip away from her to meet with me."

"I don't understand how he would accept you if all this is true."

"When Marianne and Ted first hired me I asked them for a personal item Brian would recognize. She gave me your mother's cameo pin. When we first met I showed it to him and he immediately accepted me."

"My God, you have all the answers, don't you? So, you say you actually saw Brian shoot those two operatives?" I'm asking because the news could get back to Special Agent Boller."

"Yes, frightfully so, I did."

"Would you be willing to meet with Special Agent Boller when I tell him about losing his two operatives?"

"The pictures speak for themselves. He might not take kindly to my being on the case. I'm sure he has told you so."

"Tell me, do you think Brian could be in trouble for shooting the CIA operatives?"

"He might be given a medal for his contribution to the Iranian cause. I'm sure Doctor Ulsheeh will stand up for him. They will watch him much closer for a short while, and it will make my job harder, but I'll find a way to be in touch with him. I'm sure Brian gave the supreme effort to stay the course, or Doctor Ulsheeh had full control over his brain. It will be your job to convince Special Agent Boller of that."

"I hope I'm up to the task. What are you going to do now?"

14

"I'm a hot commodity in Iran right now. I need to regroup, come up with a new plan to re-engage in Brian's and my hunt for the other scientists. The longer this thing goes on the more likely they'll discover Brian's mission."

"Brian covered my back for all the years we grew up together. No matter what, he was there for me. Sometimes he took the blame when I caused the problem. Now, it's my turn to cover his back. I don't understand why he shot those operatives, but whatever the reason, I'm sure Brian was right to do what he did. It is hard for me to wrap my head around it, and it will be even harder to tell Special Agent Boller what actually happened."

"Teddy, get him a glass of water, and we'll come up with a plan to tell this Agent Boller what happened."

Silence overcame the kitchen. The problem hung in the air like a thick charcoal cloud bringing rain.

Cliff broke the silence. "Brian couldn't have changed in such a short time. Frankly, it is impossible for me to believe Brian is capable of doing such a thing. Tell me again, did you see Doctor Ulsheeh tell him to shoot them, or what? If you say you saw him shoot them without any word from the doctor I'll have to take your word for it."

"I witnessed it all. Doctor Ulsheeh handed him the gun, and Brian shot them both. I am not totally sure Doctor Ulsheeh said anything to Brian. He may have been acting as a puppet of Doctor Ulsheeh's bidding. It all took place in seconds. There's no way for me to determine what caused him to do such a thing. I do know Brian shot them both, just like I told you. There wouldn't be a reason for me to lie. The picture speaks for itself. Brian is holding the gun and the two operatives are lying on the floor. The question we have before us is; what are you going to do about it?"

"I don't know. I can't tell Agent Boller my brother shot his operatives. Who knows what goes on over there? I'm beginning to question my own sanity. Unless… I put the picture in an envelope and mail it to Agent Boller. I know it would be a cowardly way of doing it, but what the hell. That's what I will do."

"I'm beginning to believe you are getting your head into the game."

Teddy laughed. Cliff had a screwed look on his face. Molly took another sip of her coffee.

"We need to come up with an overall plan. I don't believe in reacting to a situation, but to always control it. In time, I will return to Iran to protect Brian from those overbearing intelligence officers the Iranian Government has assigned to his case. He is intelligent, but he has no experience with the people surrounding him. I believe his girlfriend is his most immediate threat. I consider her the most dangerous of them all. A word of advice—mail the photograph in the next county, and don't leave any fingerprints or DNA on the envelope."

"Thanks a lot, you have a lot of confidence in my ability to play your game. Do you think I fell off the turnip truck when I was a teenager?"

"My God, you're sensitive, aren't you? You're paying me for what I know, and what I can do for you. Don't find fault with my every sentence. I know you're upset about what has happened, but accept the facts and move on, will you? Lighten up—it will pay off, or you'll go crazy thinking of what you could have done. Teddy and I have been in this business for well over thirty years. We've made our share of mistakes, that's for sure, but we've learned from each mistake. Now, we're passing our knowledge on to you."

"Now that I have lesson 101 on espionage, I need to know how much money you are asking for this time."

"You're funny. Money is only currency. It is meant to flow from one person to another. That's why they call it currency. I'm not in this caper for money. I love the company I rub elbows with, and I enjoy the sweet taste of victory when I came out ahead of the bad guys. Now that you've asked, a round figure of $10,000 for the time being will do just fine."

"Does that include Teddy's services too, or do I pay him separately?"

"He works for free. He enjoys the game too. I do all of the traveling, and I incur the expenses along the way. Believe me, I work cheap, anything to do with international costs lots of greenbacks. The American dollar is sought after by a lot of influential people."

Teddy wiped the photograph free of prints and DNA with a special cloth he removed from his pocket, and placed the photograph into the envelope.

"I will address the envelope, so they can't trace the handwriting back to you."

"I hadn't thought of that. I'm sure Agent Boller investigates all angles, don't you imagine?"

"I'm sure he does, and he has an army at his disposal to help him. You'll get a call in a few days asking about the photograph. You're to act dumb, and pretend you know nothing about what happened in Iran. Tell him your operative returned to the United States weeks ago, after his lecture about her meddling, and she doesn't intend to return to Iran."

"According to you guys I won't have any trouble acting dumb."

A smile erupted from Molly's face.

"My God, she's human, after all. In all my time with you Molly, that is the first smile I've ever seen." Teddy laughed, and asked if Molly had anything else to show him and Cliff.

"Have your fun. Let's get back to work. This is a jaw dropper. From the information I've gathered Brian has turned over a number of accurate formulas to the Iranian officials. I don't know whether he considered them unimportant, or he did it to whet their appetites for the possibilities yet to come, but I've run them through my educated sources, and they have found his formulas to be authentic. It means at this stage of the game, Brian is cooperating with them to the fullest extent possible. He may be doing it to avoid suspicion, or maybe he is under the doctor's influence, or it may be what Agent Boller has instructed him to do. There is no way for me to determine which one is correct."

"The waters keep getting muddier and muddier, don't they? How did you find out all of this information?"

"Never mind about that. I have proof right here. Unless you are a scientist it won't do you much good to look at them." Molly slid a packet of papers toward them. Cliff flipped through the pages and looked up.

"I don't even know the formula for table salt let alone all of this stuff."

"The formula for table salt is NaCI. Didn't they teach you anything in law school?"

"I know the law and I don't need to know all of this other stuff. Molly, I need you to stay on the case. I want you to concentrate on getting Brian back to the United States. I'm willing to pay you for whatever it costs to bring him back. That has to be your singular mission once you return to Iran. As each day passes his chances of being found out multiply ten-fold. I'll give you the money provided you work toward getting him back to my family. I don't give a damn what he has done or what formulas he has turned over to them, I just want my brother brought back home in one piece."

"I had him on the crust of coming home when Doctor Ulsheeh arrived. I suspect the Iranian Intelligence Services were suspicious of Brian when he first arrived, and they called on Doctor Ulsheeh to take control of his brain. I witnessed that control when he shot the two CIA operatives. You know, Doctor Ulsheeh risked his entire career by coming to Iran at this time. He must have been ordered by some very influential Government people to go to Iran to take control of Brian's brain. His shooting the two CIA operatives gives the Iranian

Intelligence force reason to control Brian's future actions. Also the good doctor has jeopardized his future career in the United States."

"I don't know if you realize it or not, but I put my reputation on the line for him. I had no idea the good doctor would leave for Iran like he did. My future could be in jeopardy too. Agent Boller made it clear to me when he agreed to let him out on bail. The last time we talked I don't think he knew Doctor Ulsheeh went to Iran—he thought he stayed in Paris for a doctor's conference."

Cliff left to inform his sister what happened to Brian. He wasn't sure if he would tell her about Brian shooting the CIA operatives or not. On his way to her house his mind reviewed everything Molly had told him. He knew Marianne couldn't accept the fact that Brian was now a killer, so what could he tell her about his horrendous actions? His mind, searching for a way to tell Marianne, had no solution as he approached her front door.

"Hi Sis, we need to talk without the kids and Ted present?"

"At least say hello to them, then we can go into the study."

"Hi kids. Hello Ted, how's it going? I came over to brief Marianne about Brian, and I don't think the kids should hear what I have to say."

"I understand. Go on into the study. Marianne has been calling you for a day and a half."

Cliff sat directly across from Marianne. "Sis, I have been avoiding your calls for a reason, and I'm sorry. This whole thing about Brian has got my mind doing flip-flops. Molly is back in town and has spent several hours telling me about Brian. She has been in Iran for a couple weeks, and has been in contact with Brian a number of times. Molly is of the belief Brian's girlfriend works for the Intelligence group and reports on his daily activities. That's why Molly hasn't been able to spend much time with him. Frankly, it seems to me that he may not be coming home for some time. We have to prepare ourselves for that outcome."

"Well, I guess all we can do is to pray for his safe return. I need to smile again, feel good again, and laugh again. All three would be pleasant surprises for me. I question when all three will become a reality again. Ted has taken over the kids for me, thank goodness;

otherwise I wouldn't know what to do. My mind is constantly occupied with thoughts of Brian. I guess we must let Molly do what she can for the time being and get on with our lives."

"Right now I don't believe prayer will help him much. As for when you will get back to your normal routine, I can't predict that either. I know my life hasn't been the same since Brian's accident."

"You shouldn't say that prayer wouldn't help Brian. Remember Mom used to say 'God will get you for saying that.' Is Molly doing the job we expected her to do?"

"Yes. If anyone can get Brian home, Molly will do it. According to her the possibilities of that happening are getting slimmer by the day. You and Ted did a good job finding her. Be sure to tell Ted that. She has been expensive, and at times I doubted her abilities, but I believe she will get him back. At first I was reluctant to give her more money, but she convinced me what we are doing is the only way we'll ever get him back."

"I'll keep praying for him. I know we'll get him back, but I don't know if he will be the same brother we had before the accident."

"You could be right Sis. You do the praying and I will do all I can to get him home. Give me a hug. I need some of your strength to get through all this. My practice has gone into the toilet, my nerves are constantly on edge about what might happen next, and I haven't called Annie lately. Will you call her for me and try to explain the reason for my neglect?"

"Of course. Come here, little brother. I'll call Annie. She believes everything I tell her. Maybe you two could get together soon."

"I hope so. I need something to take my mind off Brian and his troubles."

"I could invite both of you for dinner some evening soon."

"Forget it for now. I wouldn't be very good company these days. We'll get past this, and someday we'll look back on this time and laugh. Let's hope everything turns out the way we want it to."

Marianne walked Cliff to the door. They hugged once again and Marianne warned Cliff to eat his vegetables. He laughed and closed the door behind him. Vegetables were the furthest thought from his mind. Entering his car, he sat quietly, letting his mind settle. He hadn't told Marianne the whole truth, but he excused himself from that burden. Marianne said she hadn't laughed for a long time and he hadn't either. She had shouldered Brian's and her problems, but Cliff couldn't. His thoughts remained with Brian. His mind wandered into the past. If he learned anything about life since he graduated from college it was that life was filled with painful lessons, and the future wouldn't come with a printed guarantee. He started the car and drove home.

A couple days passed without any earth-shaking events, and Cliff became engaged in his practice once again. The day was winding down and Cliff put the last document in his briefcase when the door to his outer office swung open with a bang.

"We need to talk." Special Agent Boller emerged from the darkened outer office. His hand held the envelope Teddy had mailed to him.

Cliff looked at his huge frame. His eyes wandered up to his face. Agent Boller's eyes appeared lit up and were not the kind eyes he remembered from his previous meetings.

"What's up?" Cliff causally replied.

"Don't play dumb with me. You know damn well what's up!"

He slammed the envelope down on Cliff's desktop.

"You sent this to me, didn't you?"

"Never saw it before. Do you want me to look at what is inside the envelope?"

"Damn right. Take a look, and maybe you can tell me who is behind all of this."

Cliff pushed his brief case aside to open the envelope.

His mind flashed back to his high school days when he wanted to become an actor. He needed to call on that ability once again to convince Agent Boller he'd never seen that envelope before.

"I don't understand." Cliff removed the picture from the envelope. He stared at it with a raised eyebrow.

"Are they dead? Have they been shot?"

Cliff looked up at the tall agent with the question painted on his face.

"Damn right. Brian has a gun in his hand and my two CIA agents are lying on the floor. What do you know about it?"

"Nothing. I know nothing. I've never seen these men before. When and how were they shot?"

"Don't play coy with me. You know when and how, so just tell me. I know you sent that envelope to me. I'm asking what you know about this?"

"This is unbelievable. You can check my handwriting if you wish. Was Brian hurt in all of this fracas?"

"I'm asking if your agent in Iran witnessed this killing, and if she took this picture. I want to talk with her."

"I brought her home weeks ago when you told me to butt out. You said your agents would take care of Brian. I did what you asked. I discharged her over a week ago."

"I want to talk with her. I need her name and address."

"I haven't the faintest idea where she is living. Her name is Molly Moonshine."

"You gotta be putting me on. Molly Moonshine. No one has a name like that."

"My sister hired her, and I only met her one time. She is an elderly woman, weighs about 100 pounds soaking wet, and she wears thick glasses. I doubt if she would be involved with this violence."

"I'm tiring of your charade. First you vouched for the doctor to stay in town, and he went off to Paris. Now you're telling me you or your agent had nothing to do with my agents getting killed. Everything that's happened will not bring your brother back, but will put his life in further danger. Tell me, where can I locate Molly Moonshine?"

15

Agent Boller turned and walked toward the outer office. Cliff exhaled a silent sigh of relief. He'd pulled off answering any more of his questions. Inwardly Cliff felt good. He'd succeeded with the best acting of his life. The outer door closed behind Agent Boller. Cliff picked up his phone to tell Teddy about his successful acting.

The door burst open. Agent Boller entered before Cliff was able to speak with Teddy.

"I don't want to burst your bubble, but you are a lousy liar. Who are you calling? Give me your phone."

"Identify yourself." Agent Boller said into the phone. Click. The person at the other end hung up. He laid Cliff's cell down and stared at him.

"I don't get riled easily, but your nonsensical answers are grating on my nerves. I can read you like a book. You know how my agents got killed, and you won't tell me how it happened. Now, your brother is in Iran without protection, and if he gets killed or sentenced to a long prison term you can blame yourself, or you can level with me now to avoid the consequences of the truth when it comes out sometime in the future. Do you have anything further to tell me?"

"I've told you what I know. I don't understand why you keep insisting I know more. I don't."

"I've been in law enforcement long enough to know when someone is lying to me, and you are lying to me now. Tell me the truth, and I'll overlook your belligerent attitude."

"Your crystal ball, or whatever you're reading, is all wrong. I've told you what I know. Let's leave it at that, shall we?"

"I've talked with Agent Salture and she tells me you have been full of half-truths from day one."

"Believe what you wish. I have nothing more to say."

"I need to have Molly Moonshine's cell or address right now!"

"I don't know it! It was your idea to pull her out of Iran and for me to discharge her. You made that crystal clear to me. If I knew where she was, or if I had her cell number, I'd give it to you, but I don't."

"I know you have her cell number."

"She trashed the cell she had in Iran so it couldn't be traced. Isn't that something you guys do all of the time?"

"You think you have all of the answers, but you don't. Perhaps I need to talk with your sister. Earlier you said she hired this Molly. She must have the information I need. Give me your sister's address and cell number."

"W-e-l-l, I don't know about that." Cliff dragged out his answer. "She's not involved with any of Molly's activities in Iran. Besides, she's very sensitive, and she has no answers for you."

"If you won't cooperate, maybe I should arrest you, and she will come down to bail you out. I believe I'll do just that. Turn around so I can put the cuffs on you."

"Slow down. I will try to find the information you want. Give me a day or so, okay?"

"You claim you and your brother are so much alike. I don't agree. He is a patriot and you impede my every move to find a workable solution for your brother's safety. Your brother volunteered to help me bring the other three scientists home. My two agents were killed, and now I don't have any resource to protect him. And I believe you know exactly what happened to my agents."

"Please leave. I will try to get the information you are seeking."

Agent Boller closed the door behind him, and Cliff put his head in his hands. He hadn't fooled him in the slightest. He called Teddy.

"Teddy, the FBI just left. I didn't fool him at all. I'm glad you didn't answer him. He wants to talk with Molly. What do you think I should do?"

"She's already in the Middle East. I'll tell you what. I'll pretend to be her brother, and I'll tell him she is South America right now. I'm the best fibber on the planet. Just give him my phone number, and I'll deal with it."

"I hate to put all of my troubles on you, but if you don't mind, I'll take you up on that."

Cliff called Agent Boller and gave him Teddy's cell number.

He leaned back in his chair. His troubles mounting, his head full of what if's, he closed his eyes for a silent moment of peace. In a month his life had changed so much…so much.

"*What next.*" He murmured to himself. His cell vibrated and he answered it.

"Cliff, it's Molly. What's wrong? I can tell by your voice."

"My visit with Agent Boller didn't go well. He didn't believe a word I said. Teddy is going to call him. He desperately wants to talk with you."

"I can't be bothered right now. I have some disturbing news. Are you sitting down? I arrived in Iran and I haven't been able to locate Brian. I've had my people looking for him for two days now, and no one knows where he has gone. I can't approach his wife, and I have no sources at the penitentiary. This all happened while I was home. Wait… Someone is in my hallway. I'll call you back."

Cliff's mind churned, coming up with all kinds of scenarios. Maybe Molly wouldn't be able to take care of herself. After all she was old, fragile, and a wisp of a woman, but she was extraordinarily smart. Should he call her back, or just wait as she asked him to? The minutes ticked by. The silence was deafening. Cliff rose and paced the floor. This was not his world, but a world filled with foreign intrigue. He called Teddy to describe what happened on the phone. His cell was busy. An anguished moment ensued, with his nerves still running asunder. Cliff's hand remained on his cell, waiting for an answer—an answer of some kind from Molly to relieve the tensions he'd developed.

Cliff's cell vibrated. He turned it on, and waited for someone to say something.

"Cliff, it's Agent Salture. Special Agent Boller called me and wanted me to talk with you. Is it okay if I come over to your office?"

He was receiving another call. "Yeah." He closed his phone, and opened it for the incoming call. It was Teddy.

"Cliff, I just got off the phone with Molly. She is in trouble of some kind. It sounds like she has been injured. I am leaving for Iran within the hour. I will need a credit card or money in a hurry. Can you meet me at the International desk at the airport? There is something terribly wrong with Molly."

"Sure, I'll meet you there. Cliff closed his cell and stared into space for a five-second count. Should he call Agent Salture back, or what? His thoughts were short-lived as he rushed out to his car and on to the airport. On the way his cell vibrated. Cliff answered and it was Agent Salture.

"I'm at your office and it's locked. Are you in there?"

"Hell no! I'm picking up a friend at the airport. I thought I would be back before you came over. Sorry about that..." his voice faded away. "I'll call you when I get back. Okay?"

There was no return answer. He knew Agent Salture was pissed. They had been around each other long enough to know each other's shortfalls. He arrived at the airport and met Teddy.

"Teddy, do you know what's going on over there?"

"I know Molly is in trouble, and I'm going over to help her. She doesn't know I'm coming, but it is something I must do."

"I understand. Here is my credit card, and I have only a thousand dollars in cash. Be in touch with me, will you?"

"I'll call you in a day or so. Control your feelings. Don't get too anxious. Oh! By the way, I wasn't able to talk with Agent Boller. You'll have to deal with him for the present. I'll find Molly, and get back to you as soon as I can."

Cliff felt abandoned. Molly and Teddy would be in Iran and he'd have to face the full force of the FBI alone. He left the airport behind and drove to his office. He met Agent Salture in the hallway.

Without saying a word Cliff unlocked the door and held it open for Agent Salture to enter. He plumped down in his chair and began.

"What is it now? I have to get back to my law business. It is going down the drain with all of the pressure you people are putting on me."

"Just cool it, will you. I'm on your side. You should know that by now, however, I have certain obligations I need to fill. Special Agent Boller called me and told me about your non-cooperation with revealing all you knew about this person by the name of Molly. He is of the opinion she had something to do with the slaying of his two CIA agents in Iran. Will you be open with me, and tell me the truth?"

Cliff responded with a clipped reply. "There is nothing more to say. I don't know where the photograph he received came from. He acts like I mailed it. If I did, my fingerprints and DNA should be all over it."

"He checked all of that immediately upon arrival. It was not your handwriting either. Level with me, will you? If you don't give me the right answers you'll have to deal directly with Special Agent Boller. You'll find him more difficult than me. Just tell me where I can contact this Molly character, and we'll forget all of those other lies you have been telling Agent Boller."

"My operative Molly was not in Iran at the time his CIA agents were shot. I explained that clearly to Agent Boller. It appears he doesn't believe me. Instead he's accused me of lying. Agent Boller demanded that I return her from Iran and discharge her. He said Brian could get killed if she interfered with his investigation. Molly returned and destroyed her cell so nothing could be traced from her cell. She told me she was going to South America for a vacation. That's the truth. She is somewhere in South America, and cannot be reached for about a month. I swear that is the truth."

Throughout his statement Agent Salture made futile attempts to interrupt him, but Cliff kept talking.

"Many times, especially recently, you've lied to me, and ever since Brian went overseas, I've felt you have blamed me for his leaving. He volunteered to go there—so quit blaming me. I had nothing to do with his leaving. And yet, you continue to blame me."

"My life is in shambles. My mother and father have passed, and Brian, Marianne's and my elder brother, is overseas where he could be killed at any moment. You continue to pretend you have made no mistakes that allowed this situation to develop, and your only excuse is Brian volunteered to go to Iran. That's what galls me."

Agent Salture looked contrite. It was obvious Cliff's remarks hurt her deeply. Agent Salture's cell chirped loudly. She gave Cliff an oh-well look, and reached into her purse to answer it.

Cliff rose from his chair and went to his outer office so she could speak freely. He looked at her and saw a frown develop on her forehead. His cell vibrated.

"Cliff, it's Marianne. Get over here right now. The FBI is here and they're arresting me. What is this all about? Ted is at work and I need someone to watch the kids. They're talking about putting them in child protective custody. Tell me...tell me, what's happening?"

"Call Anne to watch the kids. I'll meet you down at the Federal Building. I don't know what's up."

Cliff looked up and caught Agent Salture's eye.

"I'm here to arrest you too. You know the routine so I won't repeat it."

Another agent stepped in from the hallway and placed handcuffs on Cliff. He conjured a rebuttal to the agent's swift actions, but it fell on deaf ears. Agent Salture walked behind them to the car. She buckled his seat belt and sat next to him.

"I gave you a chance to clear the deck with me, but you didn't."

"You had your orders the minute you walked into my office, didn't you?"

"Stop right there. You're crossing the line. You can be prickly at times, you know. I've tried to give you every consideration, and throughout the whole time you've made everything most difficult for me."

Cliff's irritation vanished as quickly as it arrived. Perhaps Agent Salture was right. The rest of the trip was made in silence. Cliff sought an answer to cajole Agent Salture's hurt feelings before they reached the Federal Building but none was forthcoming. Cliff was rushed up to Special Agent's Boller's office. The door opened and he saw Marianne sitting at the conference table looking distressed.

"Cliff, what's happening?"

"Nothing serious. Let me handle this." Cliff looked at Special Agent Boller with a pained look on his face.

Agent Salture stood close to the door. Agent Boller looked in her direction.

"Go. I'll handle it from here."

Cliff rose and poured a cup of coffee for himself, and took a bottle of water for his sister. He sat next to her, and held out his hand. "Nothing to worry about Sis, okay?"

"Comfortable? I didn't bring you down here to make yourself comfortable. You've made it necessary for me to play hardball. I will order an investigation of your friends, your clients, your family, and whatever comes to mind. I've ordered an investigation of both of you from the first days you wore a diaper. We'll see what comes up. I'm having you both arrested for obstruction of justice. You can spend the next 120 days in a Federal lockup until that investigation is complete. I have been overly patient, but you have resisted me from the very beginning. For your information Doctor Ulsheeh is back in custody, and you won't be able to get him released so quickly this time. I will ask you a simple question. What was Doctor Ulsheeh doing in Paris?"

"I simply don't know, probably some doctors conference. That is what brain surgeons do for recreation, isn't it?"

"You're rather glib, aren't you? A few hours behind bars for you and your sister will change your attitude."

"I don't know what you want from us."

"I told you in your office. I need Molly Moonshine's cell number and where she is at this time. I want to talk with her about my agents being killed in Iran. I believe she is involved somehow. Is that simple enough for you to understand?"

"We're entitled to legal counsel, aren't we?

Agent Boller didn't answer Cliff, but turned away and sat at his desk to look at the papers on top of it. The silence was deafening. Cliff glanced at Marianne. He could see she was on the verge of panicking. There was a knock on the door. Agent Boller went to open it. He talked in whispers to the person outside the door, and he faced Marianne.

"Marianne you can leave now. I have made arrangements for you to be taken home."

Tight-lipped, she hugged her brother and went to the door. She hesitated momentarily, looked at Cliff, and left. There was a knock on the door. It opened, and Teddy was pushed into the room ahead of an agent. The agent left.

Cliff looked at him, defeated.

"Cliff, you see, we have our ways. You've been unreasonable up to this point, and now you know we are aware of all your recent activities."

Teddy had been roughed up. His clothing was torn. However, he didn't appear to be rattled or unglued.

"It's time to level with me, and quit acting so obtuse."

Cliff looked at Teddy. "Tell him what he wants to know. There is no other way," Teddy said.

Surprise was written on Cliff's face. He considered what Teddy said, but it caught him by surprise. Unsure about what to say, he hung his head.

"Damn it Cliff, tell him. If you can't tell him, I will. Brian shot your two CIA agents." Teddy blurted out.

Shocked, Agent Boller looked at Teddy, and then at Cliff. "You say Brian shot my agents? That is unbelievable! He and I had an understanding. He was to work with my agents to get the scientists back alive."

Teddy continued. "This is how it all came down. Brian told Molly to hide in a closet when your two agents knocked on the door. Brian and your two agents talked for a very short time, and then Doctor Ulsheeh opened the door and came in. It was almost like he and the doctor had planned all of this ahead of time. The doctor whispered something into Brian's ear, and slipped him a gun. He shot them both, and Brian handed the gun back to the doctor. The doctor left without another word. Molly took the picture from the closet you received from me. You now know all we know."

"I need to talk with Molly. I don't understand why Brian would do such a thing." Agent Boller replied.

"You should know. The good doctor went over there to control Brian's thinking. Brian would have no reason to kill your agents, unless the Iranian Intelligence Service is behind all of this. Because of the shooting they got rid of your agents, and took stronger control of Brian," Teddy retorted.

A hard knot formed in Cliff's throat. The secret was out, and he couldn't do anything about it. Brian could now be charged with murder. His brother, the brilliant scientist, could be tried and convicted for murder should he ever make it back home, and if tried and convicted in a foreign country he could serve a lifetime in prison or be executed. At the moment he could think of no way to defend his actions.

"I was afraid something like this might happen. I still don't understand why you would defend the good doctor like you have done. A few minutes ago you told me he was in Paris at a doctors' conference."

"It was foolish of me, I know. I was protecting my brother. The truth? What is the truth? We have no way of understanding the real truth by what we have seen or heard."

"I'm aware your brother was under the influence of the doctor, so for the moment I'm not putting the blame on your brother. However, it has created a dilemma for me and for Brian too. We have to work together to put the doctor behind bars for good. He has disrupted the lives of four brilliant scientists and their families."

Skeptically, Cliff looked at Teddy, and then at Agent Boller.

"He's my client, and I must defend him. You need to release him."

"Cliff, I've been doing this work for a couple of decades. I believe you about what happened to my agents, and the first words out of your mouth are, 'release my client'. You're unbelievable!"

His words were unyielding, as if written in stone. He'd spat out a reply like he was expecting loyalty from Cliff for releasing his brother from blame.

Cliff remained mum. There wasn't anything more to say. Everything was out in the open—there was nothing more to be said. He felt a hand on his shoulder as he was pushed toward the door. It was Teddy.

"Enough, said and done. It's time to leave."

Cliff gazed at Special Agent Boller as the door closed behind them.

Teddy was suspiciously quiet. Words failed Cliff too.

Both were uncomfortable with the situation, the time, and the place. Teddy was an action type of guy, and Cliff felt his intolerance for dealing with authority. Cliff's mind was ablaze with questions for Teddy. And Teddy, he was a man within himself, complex and difficult to understand. Cliff knew little about him. It was the same with Molly. They were all about the business at hand, and wouldn't reveal anything about their feelings, their past, their present, or their future. They lived for the minute, hour, or day. Cliff felt uncomfortable being around either of them. Teddy was his only lifeline to Brian now, but could Teddy find him and bring him home like Molly tried to do? He was fearful something happened to Molly, and if so, would Teddy be the one to bring Brian and Molly back home?

"Agent Boller doesn't know Molly is in Iran, does he?" Teddy inquired with a sense of urgency in his voice. The wrinkles in his forehead indicated his concern for Molly's welfare.

"Not to my knowledge, he doesn't."

16

"I don't understand how the FBI found you at the airport."

"Simple enough. They have a tap on your phone. They overheard us talking, and when we met at the airport they waited until I boarded the plane then they arrested me. I resisted, but as you can see, they roughed me up some. We need to find a way for me to get to Iran. I've called Molly a number of times, but she doesn't answer her cell. It is totally unlike her to be out of commission this long. I don't like what's happened."

"What would you suggest? This cloak and dagger life is all new to me."

"I need to get over there to find out for myself. Perhaps I could go to another large city to take a flight to Iran. I need to shake the FBI's tail on me, but I'm not familiar enough with the city streets to lose them. Do you have any suggestions for me?"

"Let me think. There must be a way to get you to another airport."

"I'm looking for fresh ideas. Pique my interest about how I could avoid the FBI and get to Iran to help Molly. I'm sure most of my moves are well known by the Feds by now. They had plenty of time to delve into my past."

"Don't know why you would count on me? I don't have a fresh idea anywhere to be found. I would make a terrible covert spy if I were pressed into service."

The minute the words were off Cliff's lips he wanted to snatch them back. The look on Teddy's face screamed for some kind of help. Teddy looked at Cliff with an anguished, pained look on his face.

"Well, are you going to help me or not? Let's get this settled right now. If you're not, I'll get there some way on my own. I'm positive Molly needs help, and I'm the only one who can help her. It would make things easier if you would help get me get to Iran. One way or the other, I'm going over there. I've got to find out what's happened to Molly. She's in trouble. Every minute I delay could be critical."

"I also fear for Molly's safety, but I don't know how to help her or you. I'm still worried about Brian. There's no one looking out for him if Molly is out of the picture. You said earlier she could take care of herself."

"True. She can take care of herself. In this business unexpected things happen, and we're not always equipped to deal with them at the time. If Molly was injured, she'll deal with it. If she's dead, I'll deal with it. Regardless of the present situation I'm going to Iran to work with Molly, that is, if she's alive. Molly shouldn't mean anything to you except that she is an employee doing your bidding."

"Not true." Cliff could feel the blood filling his face, reddening his cheeks. Not knowing how to respond to Teddy's accusation, he sighed. There was no way he'd win this argument.

"Let's leave it there, shall we? You tend to your business, get the doctor released, and I will find a way on my own to go to Iran to help Molly. The plan is simple enough, let's make it happen."

"Wait! I have an idea. Ted, my brother-in-law, knows the back streets really well. He grew up here. He could get you out of town without the Feds following you. Let me call him."

"I'm all for it. Sounds simple enough. I'll go home, put on a disguise, and we'll meet on this corner in two hours. Be sure not to make any calls about this, or the Feds will be all over us."

Cliff left to find Ted. He had to talk Ted into helping Teddy get out of town. He kept asking if he could be arrested for helping. They drove around to make sure the FBI was not following them, and they went to the corner to meet Teddy.

An hour passed. The door to the car opened and a stranger said, "Good, let's get out of here." It was Teddy.

"I've checked the airport and it is swarming with law enforcement people. We need to drive 250 miles south so I can get a flight out to Iran."

They didn't talk much on the way because tensions ran high. They reached the airport, and Teddy got out, thanked Ted for helping, and handed Cliff a cell phone.

"I'll be in touch as soon as I find out something. I appreciate your help. I'll find Molly, and I'll do what I can for Brian."

Ted drove away from the airport. Cliff felt good about what had happened. He knew Teddy could take care of himself and he'd wait for his call. He thanked Ted for his help when he got out at his office.

"Cliff, that was exciting. Thanks for inviting me into your new life."

Cliff chuckled. It had been exciting for him too. He unlocked his office door and entered. Agent Salture was sitting across the desk.

"What have you been up to, your face is flushed?"

"I've been walking."

"Not true. I saw you getting out of a car. Can you tell me where Teddy has gone? We've lost him."

"I don't know. Please leave my office. I need to draft a letter of withdrawal of services to Doctor Ulsheeh. Before I visit him I need to find another attorney to represent him. Would you have any suggestions?"

His cell vibrated.

"Cliff, it's Doctor Marsh. The FBI has arrested Doctor Ulsheeh again. He called me to contact you because he wasn't able to reach you. Do what you can for him, will you?"

"I can't discuss his case with you, but the charges keep piling up. I will leave right away for the Federal Building."... Pause... "Has the FBI been questioning you about Doctor Ulsheeh's activities?"

"Yes, they have. I have been cooperating with them. I don't know what's going on, but I have to assume it is getting pretty serious."

"Thanks for being forthright with me. I'll leave for the Federal Building now."

Cliff laid down his cell and looked at Agent Salture while thinking what he should do next. He felt uneasy about writing the letter with Agent Salture sitting across from him.

"Please leave, you're making me nervous. I need to write this letter to unload some of the baggage I've been carrying around."

"It's about time you saw the light of day. I'll leave for now, but I need to warn you we'll be watching your every move." She rose and closed the door behind her.

His letter was barely started. Pondering whether he should complete it before he met with Doctor Ulsheeh or not crowded his thoughts. *Make it short and to the point, enough is enough*, he concluded.

The words didn't come easily. He'd never written a letter like this before. His practice had always been straightforward, and not filled with so many twists and turns. The case had taken a wrong turn lately, and it was no longer about protecting the doctor's civil rights, but defending him for espionage. He reached for Volume 12 of his law books. It was on page 952 where he found the proper wording. It was short and concise. His fingers flew over the keys of his computer. After finishing, he leaned back in his chair for a final read. It was ready to be printed—one for his file, and one for the doctor.

He folded it confidently, and while putting it in the envelope he thought about how he would present it to the doctor. He made his way to the door with the envelope in hand. The singular thought of not having the doctor as a client lifted his spirits. The thought of being sued for misrepresenting him continued to press on his mind. Traffic was heavy, giving Cliff time to solidify a plan on his way. He would suggest several other attorneys to represent him. He arrived at the Federal Building and just as he was entering the front door, a well-known defense attorney was leaving.

"Maurice, it's been a while. Do you handle a number of Federal cases?"

"Yes, it's my specialty. These days the Feds are into every activity known to man. They are wrong a great deal of the time, which gives me an opportunity to get my client off. Also, many times they overstep the law, and that's where I get them. It's a well-paying occupation these days. What the hell are you doing here? Surely you're not giving me some competition, are you?"

"Heavens no. One of my clients is in the jail here. I'm glad I ran into you. My client has been charged with espionage, and it's completely out of my league. I would like to turn his case over to you."

"You're not known to give away a good client. What's the matter, doesn't he pay well?"

"He's well heeled. This Federal stuff is out of my league. Do you want the case or not?"

"I'll come along and listen. I'll let you know after I hear a little more about the charges. This could be an expensive defense case. You're not expecting a commission from me, are you?"

"No. I'm emotionally involved with the case, and I want out. Isn't that enough of a reason? Charge him your upper fee. He can afford it."

The elevator door opened, and Maurice and Cliff entered the cell holding area.

"We want to visit Doctor Ulsheeh. We are his attorneys."

I know who you are. You made enough of a ruckus the last time you were here. I'll check with my boss first. Be seated and fill out the questionnaire."

"Cliff, you already have a reputation with these jar-heads. You won't win any points that way. They want you to follow their way of doing things, and if you do, they will treat you decently. Patience is my key word. They work at a snail's pace. A visit down here takes four hours of my day. It's an easy way to charge my client while I'm working on other cases."

"Maurice, how long have you been handling Federal cases?"

"It's been almost eight years now. I started by myself, and since then I've hired two other associates. We have an office a block away."

"I need to search your briefcases, or you can leave them here."

"We'll leave them." Maurice crisply replied. "Cliff, it's okay. Put your brief in a locker and take the key. You won't need it. They have a secure interview room."

Cliff removed his letter and put his brief in a locker. Maurice and Cliff entered the room, and waited for Doctor Ulsheeh to enter.

"You mean it is okay to talk in here without it being recorded."

"They wouldn't dare. We have client privilege here. I told you these people don't think for themselves, they go strictly by the book."

Doctor Ulsheeh entered. He looked fatigued, unshaven, and lost, his eyes dulled, and his hair uncombed. Jail time had taken a toll on him. His eyes wandered from Cliff to Maurice, then back to Cliff.

"Cliff, where have you been? I was arrested the minute I stepped off the plane. I've been expecting you for some time."

"Doctor Ulsheeh, I want you to meet Maurice. This case is getting to be too much for me. I am resigning from representing you, and Maurice will be taking over for me. This is his arena of expertise, and it isn't mine. He has been representing clients from unfair Federal charges for eight years, and he knows the ropes, where I don't. You have been charged with espionage, and I don't feel capable to represent you any more. Here is my letter of resignation."

The doctor looked at Cliff, and then at Maurice. "If you believe it is in my best interest, and this change won't hurt my chances to get out of here, I'll accept it. I need to get out of here to tend to my family. The FBI arrested me the minute I got off the plane. Just before I was arrested I called my family and told them I would be home in an hour. It's been a day and a half. I finally got a chance to call Doctor Marsh, and he said he would call my family."

"Doctor Ulsheeh, when you left to go overseas you broke the trust I had placed in you. For starters, I don't know why you would do such a thing, but I can no longer put my reputation on the line for you."

"It was something I had to do. I'm under a great deal of pressure too. I knew you would be upset with me if I told you of my plans."

"Maurice, take over. Doctor Ulsheeh will fill you in on the details. I'll be in touch." Cliff got up and left the room.

When Cliff reached the lobby Special Agent Boller was waiting for him.

"I see you have been visiting with Doctor Ulsheeh."

"I needed to resign. That's what you wanted, isn't it? Maurice Stockton is taking over the case."

"Good, he's tough, but fair. I've dealt with him before. You've made a good choice. One question; where is Teddy? My agents have lost track of him."

"Beats me. I have been busy shedding this case. Cut me some slack. I've done everything you've asked me to do. I need some quiet time, and I need you out of my life."

"You're not completely rid of me yet. I'm working hard to help Brian complete his mission without him getting hurt or imprisoned. I will need your help from time to time to achieve that. Give me your good ear, and listen well. I can't save Brian without some outside help. It is difficult for any known American to work within Iran. That is why my two agents worked out so well—they were citizens of Iran. I don't have any reliable conduits presently in Iran to protect Brian from harm. It is my belief the Iranians suspect Brian is up to something—otherwise they wouldn't have brought the doctor in to help them. Brian is smart, but smart doesn't always get the job done. They are ruthless with foreigners, especially ones that spy on their country. Tell me the truth, did Teddy go to Iran?"

"He's going there. I don't know where he is right now. Can I go now?"

"I need to be in touch with Teddy. Work with me, will you? Don't change cells on me. I'll be in touch. If you hear from him I want to know it."

Cliff exited the building without replying to Agent Boller's last request, or could it be considered an assignment or a threat? He couldn't look back— it was past history now. A huge load was lifted from his shoulders. It seemed centuries ago when Doctor Ulsheeh first walked into his office to pressure him into taking him on as a client. His life had been nothing but trouble since that very day. He was finally done representing him, and the baggage he'd acquired since they first met went with it. The thought that Doctor Ulsheeh controlled Brian's mind continued to disturb him as he visualized the two CIA agents lying on the floor. The FBI knew the whole story about Brian's part in their killing for which he could be prosecuted if and when he returned to the United States. All that in mind, the thought of how Brian could overcome this terrible tragedy was getting more impossible to answer. It would now be up to Molly and Teddy to bring Brian safely home, and if they did, would he be the same person as he was before he left for Iran?

He arrived at his office door, unlocked it, and walked through the darkened outer office. He looked toward his desk, and Agent Salture was sitting in his chair.

"You have the gall! What are you doing here, and how did you get into my office?" Cliff demanded as harshly as he could make his voice sound.

A deep frown curved across Agent Salture's forehead. Cliff's cell vibrated, He looked at it. It was Ted calling him.

"Excuse me. I need to take this call." He walked toward the outer office.

"Cliff, it's Ted. I arrived home and Marianne is gone. Our neighbor was watching the kids. She said a large black SUV picked her up and left. Do you know anything about this? It's not like Marianne to leave without a note of some kind."

"I'll look into it. I'll be back to you shortly. Don't draw any conclusions. There must be a simple explanation for her leaving. Has she been involved with the FBI other than her trip down to the Federal Building?"

"Not that I know of. Do you know why they want to talk with her?"

"I told Agent Boller Marianne originally hired Molly. Perhaps they are still looking for Molly. Ted, don't worry. Marianne can take care of herself."

"I know she can. Brian's disappearance has broken my family apart. You've involved Marianne in all of your doings. It's you who has pissed me off. You and your determination to bring Brian back started this whole melee. Cliff, you're to blame for all that's happening right now. My family is the most precious thing I have in life, and your blundering has got Marianne upset, and now she's involved in your missteps."

Cliff angrily snapped his cell closed. Ted's accusations hurt him deeply. True, he and Marianne desperately wanted to get their brother back. The family had been completely torn apart since the accident and their father's death. Disturbed by Ted's remarks, Cliff's fiery eyes stared at Agent Salture.

"What? You want me to leave? What did I do so wrong for you to be so angry with me?"

"It's not you. It's everything. Things are not going especially well for me. My life is like riding a bucking horse. One day I'm up and the next day I'm down."

"Cliff, that glib tongue of yours could do so much for your own future. Instead you have ventured into territory you know nothing about. Why not put your brother's troubles on the back burner for a while, and get on with your own life."

"I've thought about that so often, but it has become impossible for me to do. The thought of never seeing Brian again would ruin my life. Did you ever have a close brother or sister?"

"Yes, I did. She died eight years ago and it took a while, but I'm over it. I go out to the cemetery once a year and talk with her, but that's the extent of it. I'm not saying Brian is lost, but I'm saying his future is in doubt."

"I need closure. I'm waiting for my contact to call and tell me Brian is okay. He and I had a sense about each other. It's hard to explain. It has been that way since we were youngsters. I feel he is hiding out just like we did when we were kids, and he will come out when he feels it is safe to do so."

"I'm pleased you feel that way. I'm here to deliver a message from Special Agent Boller. Brian's case has been turned over to the CIA in D.C. Doctor Ulsheeh is being formally charged with espionage as we talk, and Agent Boller's office is assisting the Federal prosecutor to build a case against Doctor Ulsheeh for treason. They have arrested three other persons at the Mosque, and they are being charged as part of a conspiracy to abduct those four scientists. And the latest news is the FBI is no longer handling Brian's case in Iran, and I will be removed from the case in a day or so."

"Just like that! The FBI has cast Brian adrift in a foreign country. Where's your sense of honor, duty, and all of that good stuff you people spout all of the time? His life doesn't mean a thing to you people. He was a conduit to get what you think is enough to charge Doctor Ulsheeh and his bunch. I always believed you sent Brian over there to get needed evidence, but it appears you changed your plans. Now that you think you have enough evidence against the doctor, my brother is of no value to you any more. His life doesn't amount to a hill of beans to any of you."

"Sounds like you have unloaded all your troubles on me. I don't know if I have broad enough shoulders to accept it all. Enough said, it is true Brian has been cast adrift along with the other scientists. It was not Special Agent Boller's call. The orders came direct from Washington. When the two implanted CIA agents got killed, the higher-ups took the reins out of Special Agent Boller's jurisdiction."

"Did all of this just happen or has it been in the works for some time?"

"I wasn't informed till this morning. I came directly over here to tell you."

"I appreciate that. Who is making these decisions in the White House? I need to talk with them."

"They're unreachable for someone like you or me. The CIA reports to the Director of National Intelligence. The orders came directly from them. It is the National Security Office that approves or disapproves all of the CIA's decisions."

"I guess Molly and Teddy are my only hope to get Brian back home."

"What did you say?"

"Oh nothing, just day dreaming to myself."

"If I heard you correctly, I suggest you get in touch with them and tell them to back off. They would be fighting an uphill battle with the Iranian Intelligence on one side and our CIA on the other."

"Sounds like you are casting me adrift too."

"I'll be taken off the case today or tomorrow. I hope you'll be able to get Brian back, and it's not in a casket. We've lost some really good guys over there. They were all patriots like Brian."

Agent Salture closed the door behind her.

Another chapter of the case went with her. Cliff relaxed in his chair with thoughts about Teddy front and center. Now he needed to depend on these people he hardly knew to get his brother back safely.

17

Cliff's cell vibrated.

"Hello, it's Marianne. I'm home. Federal agents came to our house and arrested me. They took me down to the Federal Building and kept asking if I knew how to get in touch with Molly. I kept telling them you were the one she was working through. They said I hired her, so I should know her home base. They finally brought me back home. Ted is mad as hell about all of it, but I told him to cool it, because I wasn't harmed or anything. In fact, it was exciting."

"I'm glad you're home safely. Tell me, was it the FBI again or the CIA that picked you up?"

"I don't know. It was a different man that questioned me this time. I was scared to death, but I kept repeating I haven't been in touch with her. Do you know how it is going over there?"

"It's very complicated. I suggest you pray harder for Brian. I have the feeling he will need a lot of prayers in the coming days."

Cliff's voice dripped heavy with concern. "Somewhere along the line I told the Feds that you and Ted originally hired her. I guess they were following up on the information I gave them. Sorry about that. For your information Molly is back in Iran, and I believe she has been hurt, but I can't be sure. Her partner left to find her and Brian, and thanks to Ted for helping get him to the airport. I should hear back from him in a day or so."

"I'll be glad when Brian is home safe, and we can consider all of this a bad dream. How is Dad's estate coming along?"

"I'll be back on it today. I'm getting back to my work this morning too. It has been a while. Take care."

Cliff closed his cell. His life had been hell for the past several weeks. Suddenly his body became restless. He got up and paced the floor for a few minutes before sitting down again. He must get back to his routine, but if so, where would he start? The door to his outer office swung open, and two well-dressed men entered.

"Cliff Mercer. Are you the brother of Brian Mercer?"

"I am. Who's asking?"

The large man in a dark blue suit reached in his pocket and showed Cliff a badge.

"My name is Jerry Ellen. I am with the CIA. This is Hank Dobbins, and he is with the FBI. We'd like to ask you a few questions."

"I'm questioned out. Why don't you talk with Special Agent Boller? He knows everything about the case. His office is on the top floor in the Federal Building. He has all the answers you'll ever want."

"We've talked with him. We understand you want your brother brought back from Iran. I can help you achieve that. If so, would you be willing to work with us to get it done as expediently as possible?"

"I need to know more about what you want from me before I can commit to anything. You see, things have not gone well lately. Are you the two agents that arrested my sister? If so, I don't think I can work with you."

"We treated her well. We brought her to the Federal Building for questioning about the International Agent she hired by the name of Molly Moonshine. That was the starting point of our investigation. There is no need for us to defend ourselves about that simple inquiry."

"You scare the hell out of ordinary people when you emerge out of the blue and arrest someone like my sister. Her husband came home and couldn't understand where she was and why she had been arrested."

"We tried to interview her at home, but she kept complaining that the children shouldn't hear about their Uncle Brian being in trouble."

"Okay, that's settled. What do you want with me? How can I help you get my brother home safely?"

"From what you told Special Agent Boller, your contact in Iran has befriended Brian, and she has been in touch with him on a number of occasions. We want to talk with her. We've completely lost contact with Brian since he killed our CIA agents. To solidify our plans we need to be in touch with him, and it is most important we speak directly with him."

Cliff's body hardened. The thought of working with another Federal Agency disturbed him. He'd just shed himself from the tentacles of the FBI, and now these men wanted his help. Brian's face came to mind. This might be his only hope, but it could put Molly and Teddy in danger. Cliff's new cell vibrated.

"Excuse me. I need to take this call." Cliff walked to his outer office.

"Cliff, it's Teddy. I'm settled in Iran. I am with Molly now. She has a broken arm and shoulder, but I can use her brainpower. As you know, she's street smart and can turn a situation on a dime. Brian is gone, and Molly doesn't know where. She's not sure if the reality of what he did has come back to haunt him, or someone has abducted him. We will start looking for him in another day or so. Anything new there?"

"The CIA has taken over Brian's case. Ask Molly if she wants to work with them?"

"Cliff, it's Molly. I'd considered it. Find out what they want from me, and then I'll make up my mind. Don't worry about me. The guy that did this to me suffered more damage than I did. Call me back on the cell Teddy gave you. We will be here for a couple more hours."

Cliff closed the cell and walked back into his office. The two men were talking in whispered tones. He couldn't hear what was being said, but when he approached his desk they stopped talking.

"Tell me about your plans. You need to be forthright with me—otherwise, I won't cooperate with you. Why do you want to talk with Molly?"

The CIA man spoke. "Since we lost our two agents we have no reliable connections inside Iran, and it takes time and is most difficult to establish new agents that can be trusted. It is hard to hire and train good Iranian people who will not cross you for a higher price. The country is in a constant state of flux, and the punishment for spying is severe and dealt with quickly and severely. Your contact is already in Iran and your brother appears to trust her. That overcomes two major stumbling blocks for us."

"I can see how that would help you, but how would it help me get my brother back? Tell me what you want to accomplish by working with my operative?"

"It is our understanding Brian is alone in Iran, and he couldn't possibly know how dangerous it is to be an American on Iranian soil. Does your operative know where he is?"

"She doesn't. When she returned to Iran he'd disappeared. She will start searching for him shortly. I still haven't heard your overall plan."

"You've cornered me. I don't have an overall plan. We are working on thin ice, and the plan gets built by the day."

"Be frank with me. Would you be satisfied just to bring Brian back home, and if so, would he be tried in an American court for killing your agents?"

Jerry Ellen paused. It appeared he didn't have an answer for Cliff's questions.

"That's what I thought. You have no plan at all. I can't work with you. First off, I don't trust you. And secondly, I have no faith in the system you guys represent. Please leave, I have a lot of work to do."

"We can play hardball if that is what you are looking for. I've soft-pedaled you this morning hoping we could work together. We could arrest you and wring the information from you. I was aware you wanted to get your brother back home safely."

"My brother is a patriot and he volunteered to risk his life to rescue the other scientists, and our government workers have done nothing to help him. I don't know what your motives are about him, but you're going to have to earn your trust with me."

"We'll leave it there. You've had your say, and I've had mine. You haven't seen or heard the last of us." The two men got up and left.

Cliff called Teddy, but received no answer. The decision had been made, and he'd have to live with it. He shuffled through his briefcase trying to find a new beginning for his work. His practice had gone down the drain, and his only choice was to start all over again. His cell vibrated.

"Cliff Mercer, I can get your brother back, but it will cost you a great amount of money. Are you interested?"

"Who is this, and how did you get my cell number?"

"Never mind all of that. For $500,000 I can deliver Brian Mercer to you in two days. I would need $250,000 now, and the balance when I bring him home. Are you ready to deal?"

"I can't deal with someone I don't know. You could be a scam artist who has heard about my desire to bring Brian home. Come to my office where we can meet and discuss my brother."

The phone went dead. Cliff leaned back in his chair. His cell vibrated.

"Cliff, it's Marianne. I had a call from some unknown who offered to bring Brian home for a huge sum of money. I told him to call you."

"I just finished talking with him. I think it is a scam of some kind. He hung up on me. Don't let someone like that fool you or Ted into giving him money."

"I thought only a few of us knew about Brian being in Iran. I hope it doesn't become general news. I wouldn't know how to handle the press and all that."

"Sis, I'm getting tired of all of this ongoing mystery too. It has become a nightmare for me. I've practically lost my practice, and I'm no closer to getting Brian back home. I'm about to wash my hands of it all. It's good we have each other— otherwise, we'd both fall apart. I suggest you work on your home life right now because Ted is upset with all that has happened. It would be a blessing to have Brian home again, but I'm beginning to believe it is impossible." Cliff sighed deeply.

"I'm still praying. Let's trust in God for now. Don't let this get you down. Do you want to come over for dinner tonight?"

"Thanks Sis. I'll be working late tonight. Oh, forget what I said. I'll keep trying to bring him home."

Cliff turned off his desk lamp and sat in the darkness. He dozed for a while, and when he woke he heard someone in the hallway. *Did he lock his door?* He questioned himself. His office was the only occupied office on that floor.

Cliff reached into his top desk drawer. That was where he kept the loaded gun his father gave him after he'd returned from World War II. It was dark, but he saw the outer door open. He slid down in his chair. Someone turned on a flashlight and came in from his outer office. He slid further down in his chair. The person stopped at his desk, and didn't see him. He was almost crunched below the desk by now. Hr gripped the gun tighter. He'd never used the gun before and didn't know how to take it off safety. The person picked up his briefcase and walked out of his office. He attempted to see who it was, but it was too dark. The door closed behind him, and he heard the elevator going down.

There was a streetlight in front of his building. Not pulling the curtains back, he looked out the window. He saw Anne, his girlfriend, cross the street carrying his briefcase. She got in her car and left. Infuriated, he ran out of the office to his car in an attempt to follow her. She was out of sight, so he decided to go to her apartment and wait for her. She lived a dozen blocks away. His foot was heavy on the gas pedal. He arrived on her street, and saw her car parked in front of her apartment building. He got out and felt the hood of her car. It was still warm. He knocked on her door.

"Cliff, what a surprise to see you. It's been a while. Marianne said you were so busy I shouldn't call you. Would you like something to drink?"

"I'd like my briefcase back, if you don't mind. Also, tell me why you took it from my office?"

Anne's face reddened. She looked uncomfortable. She didn't reply.

"I know you have it. Go get it, and give it to me." She started to speak, but Cliff clipped her off.

"My briefcase, I want it now! No talk, no nothing. I want the briefcase now!"

Anne didn't move. Her whole body was shaking. Cliff pushed her aside and went to the bedroom. It wasn't there. He went to the kitchen. It was sitting next to the dishwasher. He picked it up and opened it. Nothing appeared to be missing.

He approached Anne again. She was shaking violently. Her lips moved, but words didn't come out. Cliff slapped her. She stopped shaking and spoke.

"Cliff, how did you know?"

"I saw you. Tell me who put you up to this?"

"I was leaving work yesterday, and as I was getting into my car a policeman and a well dressed man stopped me. The policeman said I had fourteen parking tickets, and he was going to impound my car and throw me in jail. The other man said he could help if I did something for him. He showed me a badge. He said if I brought your briefcase to him he would get the tickets fixed, and I wouldn't be arrested. He gave me the key to your outer office door, so I thought he knew you."

"Anne, we're through over a few lousy parking tickets. I can never forgive you."

Cliff was still fuming as he closed her front door behind him. He stood in the darkened shadows for a few minutes while he scanned the area for activity. He saw nothing. He sat in his car and fumed for a while. Someone tapped on the window. It was Anne.

"Cliff, I'm sorry. Can we still go together? Your brother has caused you to change. I still love you. I know I did wrong, but I was scared to get arrested."

Cliff didn't roll the window down, but started his engine without replying to Anne.

"Step away from the car, I'm leaving." Anne held onto the car handle. Cliff started slowly. She let go of the handle. He looked into the rear view mirror and he saw her standing in the middle of the street when he drove away.

What next? He mused. He and Anne had an ongoing relationship for over five years. She was after him to get married, but Cliff wanted to get his business on sure footing before he thought of marriage and a family.

He drove to his father's house. He hadn't used his apartment since his father passed. The house was dark when he arrived. He generally left a light on in the kitchen because it was central in the house. He was at odds with himself as he unlocked the door. His thoughts were mixed with caution. He strode quickly into the kitchen. He turned on the light, but it didn't come on.

Ah, the bulb has burned out, he mumbled. His mind settled. It seemed like everything was a puzzle for him these last weeks. *Where was the confident attorney that controlled his way of life?* His mind summoned an answer. He opened the refrigerator and took out a beer. It would do for his supper. He walked into the living room and sat in his father's recliner. The day had been stressful. He sipped his beer and thought about his father, then fell asleep and didn't wake up until his cell roused him.

"Cliff, it's Teddy. We started looking for Brian today. We haven't had much luck. Molly hired a trusted Iranian to help us sort through this tangled mess. Everyone we ask for help has a hand out for money. I consider the odds of finding him rather long. I know this isn't the best of news, but I want to level with you. Molly is more confident than I am. How are things in the States?"

"Nothing new here. The CIA is still after me to get Molly to work with them. I don't trust them. Keep on your toes over there. I wouldn't want to lose you guys too."

"Hey, I'm enjoying this action. It's good to get back into the game. I'll be in touch regularly."

Cliff was fully awake now. He showered, made coffee, and planned his day. He needed to be in touch with his clients. He had badly neglected them, and it was time to make amends. Just as he was getting ready to leave, the doorbell rang. He went to the door and looked through the glass. It was Jerry Ellen, the CIA agent. Cliff opened the door with the chain in place.

"What the hell do you want from me now? That sorry stunt you pulled with Anne doesn't sit well with me."

"I'm here to apologize for FBI Agent Dobbins' dumb actions. Involving Anne was a dumb-ass move on his part, I admit. You are withholding information and I need to move my case forward. I came up with another solution to our problem. I spoke with my boss and he agreed to meet with you to find a solution. My boss wants to talk—that is, if you would be willing to discuss meeting with him. Could I come in to explain?"

Cliff opened the door and invited him in. He walked to the living room, and Jerry followed close behind.

"Want a cup of coffee? I'm on my second one, and there is still some left in the pot."

"Yes. That would be nice. Black, please."

Cliff returned with the coffee and sat down. Jerry picked up the cup and took a sip.

"It's good. Thank you. The coffee pot was empty in the office this morning. Cliff, you and I are getting nowhere. You and I got off to a bad start, and Dobbins and I made it worse involving Anne. I talked with Anne this morning, and I told her I would try to patch things up between you two. She really cares for you. I'll admit, we overstepped our authority by approaching Anne the way we did. It was a sorry attempt to get Molly's cell number from your briefcase. We have no way to get in touch with Brian except through her. It's imperative that I speak with her. Brian could get slain, put in prison, or lost within their system. There are a lot of radical people living in Iran. My boss is second in charge of the CIA at Langley, and he wants to meet with you to explain the volatile position Brian is in. Also your contact may be in great danger, and unable to help Brian."

"You mean just him and me? You mean me meet with the man second-in-charge of the CIA?"

"He's a good listener, and you could tell him what you've been withholding from me. You'll find him to be extremely fair. I could set up a meeting today if you're agreeable."

"Okay, I'm on board with it. Let's get on with it. Set it up."

"Here's his restricted number. You'll have to put up with a number of delays before you're able to speak with him because that's how our government works. His name is Larry Ross. Each time someone asks for your identification, just reply code 1717. Display patience with the system, because it will take several minutes before he will answer your call."

18

After Agent Ellen closed the door behind him, Cliff considered whether he should make the call or not. To involve the CIA in Brian's unraveled tattered life could create a major problem for him, and could create a problem for Molly and Teddy too. Unsure what to do— perhaps think it over for a day or two—Cliff pulled back the curtains to see the charcoal colored skies. As he continued to search through his options, he recalled being scolded by his father for not aggressively solving a problem when it arose. It had been his way since boyhood—to put off making decisions for a day or two in the hope an unseen answer would magically appear. Generally it never did. He smiled just thinking about his inborn habit. His dad and Brian could make snap decisions on the spot, but Cliff never mastered the technique.

His thoughts drifted deeper, to high school when he and his brother, on a backpacking trip to the mountains, swore a secret alliance to always look out for each other. He must not procrastinate now. He shouldn't put off this opportunity to rescue his brother from the tangled mess he'd involved himself in. He knew Brian could not commit murder on his own, but like it or not, his brother had actually killed the two CIA operatives. If Molly hadn't shown him the pictures of his brother in the act of shooting them, he wouldn't believe it to be possible. It's true, Doctor Ulsheeh controlled his mind at the time, but who would believe such a bizarre story? He loved his brother, but also knew he could be crafty and smart when he wanted to be.

Their childhood adventures seemed to be surfacing a lot these days. He needed to reconstruct the life he and Brian enjoyed before all of this happened.

Reality struck him. He couldn't think about returning to his previous life until Brian was safely back home. Marianne counted on him to find a way, some way, to make it happen. The FBI made mistakes along the way that allowed Brian to be driven to this sad, sad life. He put his life on the line for the other scientists. The case drifted along for years without a solution, and now, Brian was paying the price for their failures. At the moment, the CIA wanted to take control of his future life. Could he take this next big step, and let that happen?

The progress Cliff made summed up to little or nothing. Brian was roaming alone, unchecked, in a dangerous country. He murdered two men, and based on the pictures, he hadn't flinched a muscle. Cliff had no idea about Brian's state of mind when he committed that awful act. Could he be running from the murders he committed, or was he running away from Doctor Ulsheeh and his unwavering control of his mind? And could Brian be changed in a way Cliff wouldn't know him when, and if, he ever returned home? The answers hung unsolved in the air. And if Brian could emerge from this awful life, would he be the same brother Cliff loved so much before the accident?

He picked up his cell, knowing he couldn't stop now. Both he and his sister needed to have Brian back home. Since his father passed, he missed Brian more than ever. He punched in the number, waited… and waited. Finally a machine answered. He spoke his code number when he heard a click, nothing else— deadly silence. Nothing—Cliff assumed the call was disconnected, and then came an automated voice.

"Is this your National or International code number?"

Cliff was puzzled, but repeated. "National code 1717."

The line went dead again. His impatience rose from his toes to his chest, and he drummed his fingers on the desktop to relieve his tension.

"State your name and code number. Who do you wish to call?"

"Cliff Mercer— code 1717— Larry Ross."

Another wait. His hands impatiently gripped the cell tighter. The line went dead.

"You've reached the office of Larry Ross. Please hold."

Another minute passed, and as impatience raged in him, Cliff sighed heavily to relieve his built up tension. It had taken over five minutes to reach Larry Ross's office, and now he was waiting again. Finally—a live person answered.

"Cliff Mercer, I'm pleased you called. I would like to personally meet with you. Do you have a preference as to where and when we could meet?

"My office would be fine with me. As soon as possible."

"I would prefer to meet at a less populated place. I would suggest The National Cemetery of San Francisco. It is located at 1 Lincoln Boulevard at the Presidio. Would you be agreeable to meeting me there tomorrow morning at 7:00am? It doesn't open until 9:00am, but I'll have the gate open for our meeting. Come alone— I repeat, come alone— otherwise I will not meet with you."

"I'll be there."

Cliff closed his cell. *A cemetery— strange place to meet,* he muttered. Cliff's heart skipped a beat. His mind searched for a reason to meet with this unknown person that took forever to reach by phone and at the last place on earth he would ever think of going. Another dead-end—*perhaps—perhaps not?* Cliff reflected. He was desperate for help. Worth while? Maybe? He needed to give it a shot.

Cliff rose early the next morning. He would have to travel across the Bay Bridge. He shouldn't have a problem with traffic this early. The fog hung just above his car as he crossed the Bay Bridge. He drove to the cemetery gate, put his car in park, and leaned back to listen to the local news on his car radio. The fog clung overhead, refusing to give up its territory. He looked out and the chill in the air caused him to reach for his thermos. He knew he was early, and the wait didn't upset him. Fifteen minutes passed and the cemetery gate remained locked. A few minutes before 7:00 a man came from nowhere and unlocked the gate. Cliff slid through the gate opening without opening it any further, and looked around for the man he was supposed to meet. The fog hung low, and the chill of the damp morning air made him aware of where he was. Silence was all around him as he looked at the gravesites. At this location the sun couldn't chase the fog and chill away until noon on a summer day. Not seeing anyone around, he walked further into the cemetery. The starkness of the place left him feeling dispirited. He was alone, except for the dead. And then, a voice greeted him from behind.

"Cliff Mercer, I'm Larry Ross. I'm pleased you are punctual. It's a lonely place this time of morning, isn't it? There is a purpose for my asking to meet you here. Perhaps we can have our talk now. I have been aware of your case for a very short time, and only since the FBI recently turned this case over to my care. Perhaps you'll be able to fill in the intricate details of Brian's plight in Iran. I'm of the understanding Brian took on a most improbable task —bringing back our notable scientists from a very dangerous country. I gather Special Agent Boller of the FBI was responsible for making the grievous error —of sending an unskilled person to Iran to accomplish a task his more experienced operatives weren't able to achieve. As you know, Americans are not welcome in Iran except in very special cases. Brian's knowledge of some of our Government's most secretive military projects could possibly protect him from danger; however, it might magnify his notoriety in that country. In other words, the politicians could use his capture for their propaganda purposes. All in all, it is a dangerous and inhumane country for foreigners. I pulled our remaining CIA operatives out of there after we recently lost the two by your brother's very hand."

Cliff flinched. True, Brian shot the CIA operatives, but he couldn't be held responsible. It was Doctor Ulsheeh. But how could he explain something so outlandish to this high-ranking CIA official?

"Let's walk, shall we?"

Cliff's mind returned to the present. "Everything you've said is true, but you don't know my brother. He's a patriot beyond belief, and his resolve to finish what he starts is completely off the chart. If anything is possible, Brian will make it happen."

"You make him sound like he's a super-man, but it takes more than smarts to complete a mission like he has undertaken. It takes experience of my kind to survive in a country like Iran. The International community is unpredictable, and they don't think like what we Americans expect of them. We put our life's survival above everything. Furthermore, they play dirty, and we try not to engage in those practices."

"I know little about what you are telling me. The more you say, the more I doubt Brian will make it back home."

Larry didn't respond to Cliff's remarks.

"Let's stop here. This grave is one of my dearest friends. He and I were agents together for over ten years. He was killed in Iran five years ago. We were both sent there to bring back four Americans held in their prison system. On paper it appeared to be a routine operation. We were both skilled in this type of warfare, we had a bundle of money to bribe whomever we chose, and we went in thinking we were too smart to fail. But fail we did. We went in thinking we could easily achieve our goal and return home safely, but it didn't happen. Iran is a crosscurrent of deception. There is no one you can trust. We faced danger at every turn, and before it was done, I returned home without my partner, and without our mission being complete. Every time I come out here I review those mistakes. Mistakes your brother will surely make, and it may cost him his life. That's if you don't allow me to help you."

Larry laid his hands on the cold concrete marker, bowed his head and recited a short prayer. Cliff realized Larry needed a private moment. He walked away and sat on a nearby bench. The bench was cold, and he felt it migrating into his body. He looked around at the rows of silent gravesites. The morbid scene lay before him. The cool morning, the low hanging fog, and the silent gravestones dotted the landscape, and the sight of the Pacific waters lay beyond. The loneliness, silence, and cold invaded his thinking. He needed to visit his father's grave, but only during the day when the sun was shining brightly. It began to dawn on Cliff why Larry brought him to the cemetery. Larry sat down on the bench next to him.

"I can't imagine what possessed Special Agent Boller to send Brian to Iran with only two Iranian backups. He had no business doing that without my permission. Iran is my territory. I have been aware of those scientists being there for some time now, but we didn't have the ability to rescue them without endangering their lives, along with those of a number of our own fighting men."

"It surprised me when I learned Brian volunteered to go there. I was aware he was upset with something that happened at the hospital, but he never got around to sharing his secret with me. I believe Doctor Ulsheeh has controlled his mind—otherwise he could never kill another person."

"Controlled his mind? I can't imagine that happening, but at this time I have to go along with your thinking."

"Reliable sources indicate Doctor Ulsheeh put something in Brian's brain to control his actions. Brian couldn't kill any living thing."

"That's why we're talking. You know him better than anyone—his habits, what he is likely to do, and how he thinks. When I got shoved upstairs I was ordered to send additional agents to Iran. Each time the mission failed to complete the assigned task. On each occasion I took it personally. I'm sorry to tell you this, but Brian has about a five percent chance of ever returning alive. Let's walk."

Larry's last remark drew Cliff's attention. He and Larry walked through the mist. Larry stopped and put his hand on another headstone. Cliff read the engraved writing on the headstone. It read, Edward Ross.

"My brother. I lost my brother in Iran. He and I were the only children of CIA Director Melvin Ross. We grew up in this dark community. It's part of our fabric—you know, like father like sons. We lived with danger our whole life just like our father did. But after my brother was killed I drew back, and they assigned me inside the walls of Langley, and then I was promoted to this position. I guess they award failure with a promotion. Perhaps I've lost my resolve. I can't say, but I am considerably more cautious about sending agents into harm's way than ever before. A number of these new agents are married with families, and it makes it doubly tough to send any of them into areas where they might not come back. Iran, Syria, Pakistan, and Libya are the potentially dangerous countries in which our agents operate, and only our most experienced agents are sent to operate within those countries."

"I'm sorry for your loss. I appreciate all of the knowledge you have given me about the region, but I came here because I thought you had a plan, an answer to rescue my brother, but that mustn't be the case. Your negative comments have not given me reason to believe my brother could actually succeed."

"Believe me, that wasn't my intention. I wanted you to know what obstacles Brian is facing. If he gets arrested it will take years to get him back, if at all. Their prisons are a living hell. A couple of our operatives were held in solitary confinement for months on end and ended up as zombies. His only chance of survival is to give them something—something so valuable they couldn't consider killing him. And that is the knowledge he has in his head. For the time being we'll have to count on that to believe he will remain alive.

A tear appeared on Larry's cheek. He quickly brushed it away with his forearm in an attempt to hide it. Compassion gripped Cliff. He immediately realized he was witnessing a genuine moment. This high-ranking CIA agent was displaying his soft side. Larry knelt down, turned his face away from Cliff, and whispered something to his brother.

"I loved my brother, probably as much as you love yours. Ed volunteered to go into Iran just like Brian did. Two other agents were in trouble, and he volunteered to go in to rescue them. He went against my wishes and advice. Looking back, it was a foolish attempt, but a choice he made alone. He and the other two agents lost their lives. I realize none of this has anything to do with your brother's case, but I wanted you to know first hand what Brian is facing. I don't want to lose another American in Iran. I don't want you to lose your brother like I did. Your contact in Iran is already implanted in Iran and that could be a good starter. I have the know-how, the means, and the desire to bring your brother back safely. Work with me."

His sincerity captured Cliff. They continued to walk through the cemetery. The chill invaded Cliff's body. He shivered to shake off the damp chill of the air and the sad stories Larry portrayed along the way. He was not prepared for sad stories of failure, but was looking and hoping for a plan to rescue his brother.

Larry stopped and put his hand on another gravestone.

"When you're in this business as long as I have been, you ask God why? You question, 'why didn't I get the bullet instead of my partner?' This agent, Tom Shelley, took a bullet meant for me. He did it without a second thought, and I have continued living my life regretting his action. I've thought about getting out of this business, but having a partner like Tom has kept me here. I can't guarantee I'll get your brother back, but I'm willing to make the supreme effort if you'll work with me."

Cliff shook off the chill. Larry appeared to mean everything he said. His sincerity and integrity surfaced and he appeared above reproach.

"Okay, I'm with you. How do we go about getting started?"

"It's cold out here. I'll keep it short. I need you to bring your operative back from Iran for a face-to-face meeting with me. I believe in organization. It is always best achieved face-to-face so we can evaluate each other and learn what each of us is all about. When you put all of your marbles into the game you can't afford to lose. I don't know about your operative in Iran, but I need to meet her. Do you think you could accomplish that for me?"

"My operative is rather independent, but I'll give it my best shot."

"Good. Give me a call when you have her here to meet with me, and I'll take it from there. If she doesn't have the tools to get the job done, I'll let both of you know."

They had circled the cemetery, and arrived back at the gate. Cliff left without another word. He turned his car heater on high and waited to get warm before starting the car. The meeting with Larry Ross had drained him. Sitting and looking out at the cold Pacific with his car heater running full blast, he considered all Larry had said. It wasn't just the chill in the air that made him shiver, but the stories

Larry had shared with him. He stated his case well, and his remarks left Cliff with the impression he was a man of his word. He needed to make a decision about how he would approach Molly with his request. If she wasn't agreeable to meeting with him, what would he do? Perhaps talk Teddy into working with Larry. He decided to call her right away. He called, but received no answer. Disappointed, he drove back across the bridge and returned to his office. He stepped out of the elevator as his cell vibrated.

"Cliff, it's Teddy. Brian has been arrested. We've located him in prison. Over here they keep foreigners in prison for up to six months before they're up for trial for whatever crime they're charged with. We don't have the ability or the funds to get him released. The prison officials won't disclose their charges against him."

Cliff couldn't answer—his hopes dashed. Larry's views about the Iranian prison system vibrated through him. He opened his office door and collapsed into his chair. His morning was draining, and this latest news about Brian hit him right between the eyes.

"Hello, are you there?" Teddy spoke out. Cliff couldn't answer— he was breathless. His mind recalled Larry speaking of the Iranian prison system, and how once inside, it would take years to get released. Brian being locked up in an Iranian prison was too much to accept. The line went dead. Teddy had disconnected. Cliff sunk lower in his chair. All appeared lost. Once Brian was in their prison system his return home could stretch into years. His cell vibrated... he answered it. It was Molly.

"Cliff, are you all right? Teddy said he got disconnected."

"I'm okay. The news about Brian got me for a moment. I talked with Larry Ross, second in command of the CIA, and he wants to have a face-to-face meeting with you. Are you willing?"

"I know that name. If I remember correctly, he's an upright guy. How did you meet him?"

"I met him, that's enough. Can you come back to meet with him?"

"That's why I am calling. Teddy and I are preparing to come home. Meet us at the San Francisco airport tomorrow at 11:00am in the International lounge. We'll be there resting. Arrange that meeting, and I'll fill you in on the rest of my discoveries when we see you. Cliff, all is not lost. It's not all bad—I have some good news to tell you."

Cliff called Marianne to tell her about Brian being in prison. She dropped her cell, and Ted pickup it up.

"Who the hell is this?"

"Ted, it's me. Is Marianne all right?"

"I don't know. Whatever you told her, she is praying and crying at the same time. Has something happened to Brian?"

"He's in an Iranian prison. I'm coming over there." Cliff snapped his cell closed, raced to his car and jumped in.

Ted opened the door. "Cliff, I'm getting tired of all of this baloney. Marianne can't continue to go through all of this bullshit."

"I know. It's pure hell for me too. I don't know what to say. Brian's being in Iran has taken complete control over my life too. I can't think of anything else besides Brian's safety these days. Can I see her now?"

"She's up in her bedroom. Take it easy on her, will you? She's on the verge of a complete breakdown. I find her praying for him while cooking dinner, and I woke up last night and she was in the bathroom praying for his return."

Cliff entered the bedroom and found Marianne on the bed lying face down, crying and reciting a prayer.

"Marianne, we need to talk."

She turned over. "Cliff, I'm done. I can't take any more of these up's and down's with Brian. We've lost him, but what can we do? I can't accept that! We've lost Mom, then Dad, and now it's Brian."

While hugging her he recalled when she fell in a mud puddle on her way to the grade school graduation day. He rushed home on his bicycle, found another dress for her to wear, and rushed back to the auditorium before the ceremonies began. He recanted the story to her. She stopped crying, and began smiling.

"We took care of each other in those days, didn't we? I remember that day. We were always a happy family. I mean we looked after one another. I'm feeling lost now because those times can never happen again. Cliff, what are we going to do?"

"Sis, you have your own family now. You have Ted and the kids. That should be enough for you. We both miss Brian because he used to make all of the decisions for us when we couldn't make up our own minds. Time moves on, and you have to learn to move on with it."

They hugged one another. Cliff realized he needed this special moment as much as his sister did. They sat side by side on the bed without saying anything for a while.

Marianne gathered herself. "Cliff, I appreciate everything you have done to bring Brian home. I haven't told you that before, but I wanted you to know. We both love Brian, but since he went off to college he has changed a lot, don't you agree? I thought it was because he considered himself smarter than us, but that may not be the reason. We need to accept what the Lord will do for him from now on. I think you should go back to your practice, and I will get on with my life too. I would like you to spend more time with my children. You have been an absentee uncle ever since Brian's accident happened. Come over for dinner once a week, and get to know your nephews and nieces."

"Sis, I promise to do just that. I'm leaving now. I'll be in touch. For the time being don't worry about Brian—leave his return to me."

Cliff hugged his sister again, and went downstairs. Ted stood in his way.

"Your family is a mess. Cliff, I blame you for all the misery you have caused Marianne. Stay away from her for a while, otherwise..."

"Otherwise what? We're family, and marriage can't change that. I know you feel left out, but it's our family business—deal with it."

The children came running in when they heard the yelling.

"Uncle Cliff, are you angry with our dad?"

"No, I'm not. Grown men get in disagreements once in a while. It doesn't mean a thing. I'll see you guys later."

Cliff rushed for the door, a bit embarrassed by the scene he caused. He hadn't been himself for quite some time, and this latest outburst had drained him. He sat in his car trying to compose himself. He and

Ted hadn't got along in the past, but during his father's funeral, he and Ted had solved their differences. His cell vibrated.

"Cliff, it's Doctor Marsh. We need to talk."

"I'm drained. I don't have anything to say to you."

"You'll want to hear what I have to say. It's about Brian. How about meeting me at the Golden Triangle on Weber Street in an hour?"

"What's the Golden Triangle? It sounds sinister."

"You've never ceased to have a sense of humor. It's a bar, and you can grab something to eat. They make great sandwiches. Well, are you going to meet me or not?"

"You better make it worthwhile. My favorite is pastrami. You better be right about the food. Yeah, I'll meet you there."

"The sandwich is on me. You'll have to buy the drinks. See you at seven."

19

As Cliff rushed out the door he ran into Anne standing in the doorway.

"How long have you been standing there?"

"Long enough to see your bare bottom. You should close the door when you change clothes."

"You caught me, quit snickering, will you? I have a meeting tonight. I always change clothes when I do that."

"You haven't grown up since you were in high school, have you? I haven't seen your bare bottom for some time. Do you still remember the first time we did it?"

"All I remember was, it was a total failure. Come to think of it, we did have some good times together," Cliff chuckled.

"Cliff, how did we lose those times?"

"We were kids then, now we're grown up. There are too many things influencing our lives now. This thing with Brian has got me tied up in knots. Once I get past trying to bring my brother back home maybe we can start a new beginning."

"Oh Cliff, I hope so."

"I'm on my way out. If you have something more to say, say it—I'm running late."

"I know you, I can tell. You're still angry with me, aren't you? I'm here to apologize. I want things back to where they used to be. Forgive me, if you can. I didn't mean to do what I did. It was plain foolishness, but that FBI man scared the holy hell out of me, and I didn't want to go to jail."

"Anne, I wish I could understand, but I can't for the life of me. You chose the easy way out, didn't you?"

"Come on Cliff, forgive me. Say it, please. You got your briefcase back, no harm done. I told you why I did it—please don't make this more difficult than it has to be for me."

"How long have we known each other, maybe fifteen years? I never thought you'd consider doing something so painful to me, no matter what. If you can't trust someone what's left? We can talk about our history together, but it doesn't mean a thing to me now."

"What do I have to do to get your forgiveness?"

"Tell you what—meet me for lunch tomorrow, and I'll put all of this behind us."

"Cliff, you know I'm working, and I can't do that, and you know it."

"Can we put it behind us, maybe, yeah maybe, and get back to our old routine, you mean? I'll do my best to forget what you did, but there will always be doubt in the back of my mind about when you'll cross me again."

"Cliff, please don't toy with me. I apologized. Isn't that enough? I don't understand, what is our old routine?"

"My spending the night at your place on Thursdays, and you spending the night at my place on Saturdays."

"Cliff, stop teasing me. Will you? We never did that, and you know it."

"My fantasies are working overtime. I'm having a little fun with you. Lighten up, will you? By the way, we haven't been seeing much of each other lately, have we?"

"It's all your fault, not mine. That one time you called I needed to work, and you knew it. Ever since Brian's accident you have been avoiding me like the plague."

"It hasn't been on purpose. Are we here to talk about our high school days? You're still feeling guilty about crossing me, aren't you?

"You haven't forgiven me yet, have you?"

"You're forgiven. Understand, forgiven, or do I have to post it on the front of the building?"

"Cliff, don't be mean with me. I know what I did was wrong. Don't make me beg for forgiveness. I'm still in the dark about that old routine remark."

"Our old routine—well, you were there for me when I broke my leg playing football, and I was there for you when your dress slipped down at our graduation party. I was there to pull it up for you, or, have you forgotten all of those many, many times we did good things for each other?"

"You remember all of our youthful mistakes. We did have fun growing up, didn't we? Somehow we've lost the spark."

"I got to go, I'm late. We'll have to talk, maybe tomorrow."

"I made a bad mistake, and I'll never do it again. Is that enough of an apology?"

Cliff laughed. "Enough! You're forgiven for the fifth time. Give me a hug, and we'll both forget it. You should know I couldn't stay angry with you. We need to talk about our problem another time. I'm running late."

"Give me another hug. I need it."

"Yeah, me too."

Cliff hugged her. Nothing of any value was in the briefcase. It hadn't mattered, but the idea Anne had stolen it continued to bother Cliff. He was pleased they made up. Anne's hug felt good. He and Anne had been close since high school.

Traffic was heavy, and a frustrated Cliff swore at the slow drivers, cursing at times as he made his way through the wet streets to an unfamiliar sector of town, knowing he was late. *"Ah, there it is,"* he muttered to himself. He parked his car on the street because the parking lot was full, locked it and looked around the seedy neighborhood, questioning why Doctor Marsh would choose to meet at this shady location. He opened the well-worn door of the Golden Triangle, looked at his watch and realized he was fifteen minutes late, and shrugged his shoulders to relieve his ongoing frustrations.

The darkened interior, the smell of stagnant air, and the stale odor of tobacco and beer greeted him. It reminded him of some of the seedy bars he'd visited in high school and college. At the time he had little or no money, drinks were cheap, and his friends hung out there. He spotted Doctor Marsh sitting at a corner table. Cliff pushed a chair aside and sat directly across from him.

"How did you find this hell hole to meet at?"

"You don't remember, do you?"

"Remember what?"

"When we were in high school we came down here to drink beer. We were all under age, but this place didn't care. Don't you remember now?"

"You know what? I don't remember much about those days. Is this why you brought me down to this smelly bar—to recall our youthful days? You said you have something important to tell me— surely it isn't about something we did in high school."

"You like everything out front, right away, don't you? Okay, first things first, we'll split the bill. My first name is Reggie, and I'll get around to answering your question in a moment. Surely you remember how you used to tease me about my being named after some Prince or someone of nobility."

"Is this a quiz or something? No, I don't recall teasing you about your name."

"I never liked that teasing, and to be truthful I hated it, but you wouldn't let up. I dropped off the football team because of your constant teasing. In practice you used to say, 'Don't hit Reggie, he's too fragile, he's royalty you know.' Do you remember now?"

"No, if I did that, I'm sorry, I don't recall any of what you are telling me. I don't remember much about those times except playing football and chasing girls. It's a little late, but I apologize if that means anything to you now. Are we here to talk about our youthful faults or what? Tell me it isn't so. I thought you had something of importance concerning my brother to tell me. That's all we have in common now, isn't it?"

"Cliff, you're angry at the world tonight, aren't you? I thought you changed your mind about coming. I've already ordered both sandwiches. Do you still drink beer or have you moved on to something heavier?"

"Jack Daniels on ice. My dad drank it, my brother drank it, and I drink it. I guess you could call it a family thing. With Brian gone I think about those family traditions more often. Our family was always close, but when Mother passed, things changed a lot. Enough of that! I'm here to find out what you have to tell me."

The sandwiches arrived, and the waiter took the drink order. Cliff grabbed his sandwich and started eating it like he hadn't eaten in a while. Reggie glared at him.

In between bites Cliff said, "What do you have to tell me?"

"I'll get around to it. Don't be so damn pushy. Enjoy your pastrami sandwich. You look like hell. Haven't you been eating and sleeping properly lately?"

"Reggie, don't play doctor with me. I don't have to answer your silly questions. Truthfully, I haven't been well. My practice is on the rocks, everyone and his brother is angry with me, my sister is cracking up, and my brother is in an Iranian prison. I haven't been sleeping more than two hours a night, and my girlfriend took my briefcase. Other than that, I'm still the same Cliff Mercer you knew in high school."

"That's a heavy load you're carrying. Sorry, I didn't mean to pry."

The waiter arrived with Cliff's drink. He took the glass and gulped down the drink.

"Waiter, hit me again."

Cliff's manner surprised Reggie, and the waiter too. Trying to mask his surprise, Reggie asked how he liked his sandwich.

"I did eat it all, didn't I?"

"The way you devoured it I thought you hadn't eaten in days. Didn't you stop to taste it?"

"Damn, you're full of questions, aren't you? You're right. I am uptight tonight. I guess the sandwich was good. I haven't been myself lately. That was the first drink I've had in months."

The waiter brought Cliff a second drink. He looked at Reggie expecting him to order another beer, but he didn't.

"That's it. Two drinks is my limit," Cliff voiced. The waiter left, and Cliff asked Reggie again for the reason he'd called him here.

"Cliff, I'm sorry all of this had to come down on your shoulders. As you know Doctor Ulsheeh was my mentor. I found it extremely difficult to accept the truth about what he had done to Brian and a number of scientists before him. It was only this morning that he shared his secret with me. He has extended family in Iran, and if he doesn't follow their orders to the letter, his family in Iran will be killed. In a way I understand his plight, but as a doctor, I can't accept how he has ruined a number of people's lives to satisfy his own personal motives. It is a doctor's lifetime purpose to save lives, not bring misery and destruction to patients and their families."

Frustrated with Reggie and his theorizing, Cliff exploded. "I didn't come here to listen to your stories and ethics tales. It's all bullshit!"

"As an attorney, I'd think you would choose your words more carefully."

Cliff downed his drink, rattled the ice cubes around in the glass, and shouted to the waiter for a refill. The waiter rushed to his table with another Jack Daniels in hand. They exchanged glasses without saying a word. Reggie stared at Cliff with dismay on his face.

"Get on with it. I thought you had something to tell me. I don't want to hear your story about how Doctor Ulsheeh shattered your image of him. I don't care about your disappointments with your mentor, and all of that doctor goodie stuff. I thought you had something important to tell me. Your disappointments are of no concern to me. Either you have something to tell me, or I'll leave right now!" Cliff looked at his watch.

Cliff's outburst caught Reggie off guard.

"I'm sorry. Are you going to meet someone? You keep looking at your watch."

"My impatience is showing, right? It's been showing up a lot lately. Get on with what you have to tell me, will you?"

"I thought you wanted the whole story from the very beginning. I haven't been above-board with you right from the very start. I avoided you in the mountains, because I didn't have any answers for you then."

"You pissed me off when you left the hotel and drove down the mountains without talking with me. It made me suspicious of you then, and you have avoided me since. I'm not here to hear about your high school regrets, or my over zealous behavior. Get on with what you have to tell me."

Cliff called the waiter for another Jack Daniels. Reggie waited until it was delivered.

"Here is what I called you for—I assisted Doctor Ulsheeh the two times he operated on Brian. The first operation was to remove part of his skull so Brian's brain would have room to expand, and not crowd his swelling brain. After that Doctor Ulsheeh assessed his brain for leakage because his brain was full of blood. There were two major ruptures. He repaired the ones he could locate, stabilized his brain trauma, and prepared him for the next operation. Doctor Ulsheeh skillfully repaired both ruptures. I watched in amazement as he examined all of Brian's brain tissues without harming them. There was a considerable amount of blood throughout the brain. He worked tirelessly for almost two hours, getting the brain as clean as possible. He allowed me to clean up after he finished. I assisted and observed throughout the whole procedure. Brian was young and in good health, which helped him through the surgery. Otherwise he wouldn't have made it."

"Did you see anything unusual during the operation?" I mean, were you suspicious of Doctor Ulsheeh at that time?"

"I had no reason to be. I was sent here by Professor Ludwig to observe Doctor Ulsheeh's skilled methods of operating. He's a fine surgeon. I consider him to be one of the ten best brain surgeons in the United States, if not the whole world."

Cliff yelled at the waiter for another Jack Daniels.

"It's good to unwind. My life hasn't been going well recently. The Jack Daniels tastes good. All bad news, if you know what I mean. The drinks help settle my nerves. Do you want another beer?" Cliff's speech slurred at times.

"I'm good. As you said before, you and Brian were close. I'm the only child in my family, and I often wished I had a brother to fight my battles for me."

"Brian was a good brother, but there were drawbacks. He was so damn smart, and at times he would make me feel dumb. School was always so easy for him, but me, I had to struggle for every grade."

The drink arrived, and Cliff downed it in a hurry and told the waiter to bring him another.

"You better take it easy with those drinks if you expect to drive home. Maybe we better stop here, and talk about it another time."

Cliff replied. "I'm fine, get on with it."

"Sure, you're fine." Reggie replied. Cliff laid his head down on the table and passed out.

Reggie called the waiter to help get Cliff to his car. He located Cliff's keys, and drove him to his house. He couldn't lift Cliff out of the back seat, so he lowered the windows about an inch and went into the house for a blanket to cover him. He locked the car and went inside Cliff's apartment to sleep.

Early the next morning Reggie went out to the car. Cliff and his car were gone. He called his cell. No answer. He waited an hour and called again. No answer. The day continued. He called again late that afternoon. No answer. Reggie decided to go to Cliff's office. He opened the unlocked outer door, found Cliff asleep in his chair, and said loudly. "I'm looking for an attorney, do you happen to know one?"

Cliff woke up, and rubbed his eyes. "Oh, it's you. I'm an attorney, but you'd never know it after how I acted last night. I don't remember driving home last night. Did you do that for me?"

"Yeah, it was me, and I slept on your couch last night. I couldn't carry you inside."

"I keep an extra set of keys in the glove compartment. I woke up and drove to the office. What's the matter, you look as bad as I feel?"

"Someone tried to run me off the road on my way over here. It reminded me of Brian's accident. Do you think it's possible Doctor Ulsheeh ordered a hit on me?"

"Well, I don't know. Tell me about what happened."

"I was on the freeway, and I was just about to turn off to your street when an SUV came from nowhere and hit me hard on the side. The whole side of my car is a total wreck. Luckily, I was still able to drive it, and by some miracle I was able to keep from being run into that deep ravine just before the turnoff."

"Scary stuff, huh? Welcome to my world. It's stuff like you just experienced that I've been living with ever since Brian was first operated on. I don't think you ever got around to telling me what you wanted to tell me last night, or did you? Perhaps I was too far gone."

"Not really. It is hard to believe Doctor Ulsheeh could do something so deadly to me. I'm his understudy, and someone who could possibly replace him some time in the future. Or maybe Doctor Ulsheeh's life is tumbling down all around him. What do you think I ought to do about it?"

"Did you report it to the Highway Patrol?"

"No, I came straight here."

"Best to forget it then, and move on with your life. You need to be more careful in the future. After last night I'm a fine guy to give you advice. Hey, I appreciate what you did for me last night."

"You were completely spent. I'm sure you would do the same for me. You're right. I should have reported it right away, but I was so shook up, I didn't think straight."

"I made an ass out of myself last night, didn't I? Was all of that stuff you were telling me about how I used to tease you on the level?"

"It's all true. Truthfully, you ruined my senior year. When we were in that play I think you weren't aware it was me because you didn't mention it after I left the football team."

"Jocks can be jerks sometimes. I guess it is called adolescent thinking."

"Forget it. It's past history. I shouldn't have brought it up, but it has bugged me for a long time. I guess I needed to get it off my chest."

"I understand. Want some coffee? I'm going to make a fresh pot. I have a splitting headache. Let me get my head on straight, and then you can finish telling me what you wanted to tell me last night."

Cliff went into the bathroom, washed his face and took an aspirin. When he came back into the office he poured a cup of coffee.

"How often do you sleep here?"

"Too often. Let's get on with what you have to tell me."

"How much do you remember me telling you about the first operation?"

"I remember enough. Get on with it, will you?"

"The swelling in Brian's brain wasn't receding. Doctor Ulsheeh decided to go in again for second look. We consulted. I was eager for the second operation because I needed the experience. Anyway, he thought Brian had a leak that needed to be fixed. That's what happens when the swelling refuses to go down."

"Yeah, yeah. I know all that. Get on with it!"

"It was during the second operation when I saw Doctor Ulsheeh take something off the tray, unwrap it from a plastic covering, and put it into Brian's brain. It was something most unusual for a surgeon to do because his operating nurse would normally do it for him. He had me busy doing something else at the time and he thought I didn't see him. As a learning assistant I've been taught to observe his every move. After the operation I asked Doctor Ulsheeh about what I saw, but he dismissed it as a foolish question. He asked me whether I was assisting to learn or to question him. Because of my respect for his skills as a surgeon I relented, but my curiosity continued to bug me. The next morning I examined the x-rays in an attempt to satisfy my inquisitive mind about what I thought I saw, but I couldn't detect anything. Later, when I saw him multiple times asking Brian questions while he was still in a coma, it raised my curiosity again. I asked Doctor Ulsheeh about the extra attention he was giving the patient, and he told me to mind my own business. That's when I went back for a second time to review the x-rays. When I couldn't see anything I took the x-rays to Professor Ludwig to see if he could detect anything. At the time I wasn't completely convinced I saw Doctor Ulsheeh put something into Brian's brain. Professor Ludwig couldn't detect anything either, and he reprimanded me for questioning the famous doctor, and warned me if I did it again he would remove me from the assignment. Later I approached Doctor Ulsheeh about my suspicions, and he rebuffed me again. He told me if I wanted to work with him I must believe in what he was doing, and quit being a critic."

"Tell me, did Doctor Ulsheeh find a leakage in Brian's brain?"

"Yes, he did. That's what Professor Ludwig asked me. He said Doctor Ulsheeh had reason enough to go back for a second look. It was bad enough to get on Doctor Ulsheeh's bad side, but to have my Professor get after me because I had no right to question Doctor Ulsheeh's actions. After that, I put my suspicions on the shelf."

"Have you had any second thoughts about forgetting about what you saw?"

"Plenty, and looking back, I think that's why I avoided you like I did. I couldn't share my suspicions with anyone including you. After all, I was the student. Doctors are like police, they don't rat on each other—besides Brian got better. He was out of the hospital and went somewhere, so I got on with my life. Case closed, at least I thought it was closed."

"That's when my life got extremely complicated. You probably didn't know Brian volunteered to go to Iran to bring back the other scientists."

"You mean Brian and the other scientists are in Iran? I didn't know that. I thought everything was done when Brian left for the second time. Then Doctor Ulsheeh came to my apartment the other day and said he needed to talk with me about Brian. He looked like hell, and I asked what was wrong. At first I thought he'd lost a patient. That's how we doctor's feel when we are not successful. It hurts us almost as much as the patient's family."

Cliff got up and poured himself another cup of coffee. Hesitantly, he sat again and looked at Reggie. Pain was written on his face. It appeared he had something important to tell him, but he didn't know how to start.

"I'm a good listener. Tell me what you have to say. I'm numb, beyond hurt, if you know what I mean."

"Thanks Cliff. What I'm about to tell you will ease some of your pain, and I will feel better about it too. Doctor Ulsheeh came to see me because he thought I needed an explanation for what I had been asking him about for quite some time. This is what he told me—'I've just been released for the third time from the FBI lockup in the Federal Building. I want you to take over my surgeries for a while until I'm cleared of all the accusations by the Federal Law enforcements units. The freedom from government interference is what I liked the most about this country, but since the arrests I have begun to doubt the government. Six years ago an Iranian spy came to my house. He told me that my grandparents, my uncles, my aunts, and my wife's immediate family still living in Iran would be killed unless I cooperated with them. I went home and talked it over with my wife, and we decided I should do as they say. They would single out a noted scientist, find a way for them to have an accident, and then I was to operate on their brain to insert a chip, which he called Artificial Intelligence. The point was this chip would override any of the patient's normal brain reasoning. I didn't understand any of it, but I went along with their plan. When you saw me talking with Brian after the second operation, I was training his brain to accept my voice as his ultimate command."

Reggie paused. He looked at Cliff to see if he had any questions before he went on with his story.

"It's getting more interesting as you go along, but I know most of what you are telling me. The FBI has been aware of his activities for some time now, but they can't prove anything. Is he willing to tell the FBI what you told me this morning?"

"He didn't share that with me. Everything I'm telling you stays between us, okay? If so, I'll continue on with the most important news I came here to tell you. If not, we'll end this right now."

"Get on with it. You have my word."

"Your brother didn't murder those two CIA operatives. Doctor Ulsheeh controlled his mind, and he ordered Brian to shoot them. He admitted that to me this morning."

20

"Well, well, well, the truth is finally out. Reggie, I can't tell you how much this means to me. I knew all along Brian was not capable of doing such a horrible thing because it wasn't his nature to do so, and for you to hear it directly from Doctor Ulsheeh's lips will clear Brian completely of his part in the murders. Reggie, this news means everything to me, and now we must go to CIA Headquarters to record your statement. Otherwise, it won't mean a thing coming from me. I have been living with this dark cloud over my head for some time now, and it has just about done me in. Excuse me— I need to call my sister to tell her this good news."

Cliff vigorously punched in her number. Ted answered.

"Hello. This is Ted."

"I need to talk with Marianne. It's important."

"Everything you do these days is important. She's resting right now."

"Give her the damn phone, will you. I know this will help her feel better."

"Okay, I hope you're right. She is not doing well right now. Here she is."

"Marianne, I just got proof Brian didn't murder those two CIA men. Isn't that the best of news?"

"Yes it is Cliff. You made me feel better already. I knew prayer would find him innocent. Has he been released from prison?"

"I'm sure he hasn't been, but that will be my next project. Let's savor the moment for the time being." Cliff closed his cell with a light heart.

He looked at Reggie and smiled. "I can't wait to tell everyone about this good news. First thing, we need to go down to the CIA Headquarters in Langley, and record what you told me."

"I promised Doctor Ulsheeh I wouldn't tell anyone except you. He said you were still his attorney and you wouldn't be able to tell another soul."

"You can't mean what you are saying—or is it, you won't? This evidence straight from Doctor Ulsheeh will clear my brother of what he is accused of doing, and it might be a reason to free him from that Iranian prison. Come on Reggie, put your ethics in a suitcase and throw it into the ocean. You need to tell the CIA what Doctor Ulsheeh confessed to you, or what you told me doesn't mean a thing. I have been shouting his innocence from the roof tops since day one."

"Sorry, my word is my bond. As a doctor my word means everything to me." Reggie rose to leave.

Cliff's cell vibrated. He ignored it.

"Wait! You can't leave like this. We have to settle this thing right here and now!"

"Cliff, it's settled, I gave my word to Doctor Ulsheeh. I cannot do as you asked."

"Let's not leave it like that! My brother's whole future depends on someone coming forward with the truth. Reggie, it must be you!"

Cliff's cell vibrated once again. He ignored it. Cliff grabbed Reggie by both arms and looked him straight in the eye.

"Please Reggie, share this news with the CIA. You did the right thing coming here to tell me, and you risked your life in doing so. Tell me, do you believe your life is in danger because of what Doctor Ulsheeh told you?"

"It could be. I have no way of telling."

Cliff's cell vibrated again. He looked at the name on the screen. It was Teddy.

"Reggie, I have to take this. Don't leave, please."

Cliff flipped open his phone while his eyes followed Reggie to the door of his outer office.

"Hi Teddy, what up?"

"We've been at the airport for some time. I thought you were going to meet us."

"Is that today? I'm sorry, something has come up."

"Sonny Boy, this is Molly. You're not very reliable, are you? We'll find other transportation. Answer your cell in the future when it rings. Goodbye!"

Cliff didn't get a chance to answer her. He looked up, and Reggie was walking through the outer door of his office. *What next,* he mumbled as he slumped back in his chair. A moment later two pops resounded—sounds he'd never heard before. He rushed to the hallway to find Reggie lying on the floor with blood coming from his mouth and chest. He looked at the elevator to see the door closing. He turned him over, and blood streamed from his mouth onto Cliff's shirt. He cradled Reggie in his lap and tried to stop the blood from gushing from his chest. He pressed harder, but it gushed between his fingers.

"Reggie, stay with me," Cliff pleaded. Reggie's eyes widened and then closed. He was gone. Cliff fought back the tears as he opened his cell to call 9-1-1. A dazed Cliff sat on the floor holding Reggie while waiting for help to arrive. Reggie had given up his life to carry the news to him.

Cliff recalled the night before. If he hadn't drunk so much Reggie would have told him about Brian then and maybe this wouldn't have happened. A feeling of remorse grew deep down in his gut. Reggie was dead because of his drunkenness, and now his story about Brian's innocence went with him.

A stray thought entered his mind. *Could I be next?* He mumbled out loud. After all, he was the only one who shared Reggie's secret, but if that was so, why didn't the killers kill him at the same time they shot Reggie? His question was left unanswered. Cliff felt totally alone waiting for help to arrive.

The paramedics arrived. They lifted Cliff from the floor and helped him to his office chair, and then they went back to tend to

Reggie. Moments passed, but Cliff had no idea of the time. He looked up and saw an official-looking burly stranger before him.

"My name is Detective Donavan. Clear your head, and tell me what happened here while it's still fresh in your mind."

Cliff looked up at the burly Detective. His eyes still crowded with tears, he gathered himself to answer.

"There isn't much to tell. I was on my cell when Reggie left my office. I heard two pops that sounded like firecrackers, and I ran out to the hallway. Reggie was lying on the floor bleeding, and I called 9-1-1. I turned him over to see if I could help him, but he died in my arms."

"I see you have blood all over you. You're not hurt are you?"

"No, I'm okay. You have to find out who did this to Reggie."

"It's our job to find out. You need to answer some questions for me. Tell me everything you saw and heard."

"I'm pretty well shaken up. I can't think straight. Leave me alone for a few minutes."

"That's understandable. I'll have a look around while you think about it, okay?"

Detective Donavan went back out into the hallway. Cliff thought about what he saw and heard in those precious moments before Reggie was shot. He put his head in his hands while he played back through the whole time. Detective Donavan came back in and sat across the desk from him.

"Did you hear any shuffling of feet? Did you hear anyone say something before or after you heard the shots? Did you hear more than one person in the hall? Did you hear any other noises?"

Cliff didn't answer him. Donavan turned and spoke with Detective Freddie, "Check the stairway. Walk all the way down in case someone left a gun or something on the stairs. We're not getting much from the witness."

The stairway door creaked. Moments passed, and everything became quiet again. Then Cliff spoke out.

"Detective Donavan, I heard the stairway door creak just before or just after I heard the shots. Shortly thereafter I heard the elevator door close."

"If that's so, tell me, did you see the person who did this? Was he tall or short, did he have long hair, was he white or minority, and how was he dressed?"

"It all happened in such a hurry, I don't remember it all."

"Tell me, do you know a reason why Reggie would be shot here in your office? Also, tell me the reason for his visit."

"It's all so complicated. Reggie is an intern at the hospital, and he has been assisting Doctor Ulsheeh with his operations."

"That's unimportant at this stage of my investigation. I'm attempting to find out something about the person that shot Reggie. Do you know anyone that might have a motive to kill Reggie? Are there any cameras in the hallway or the elevator?"

"My answer is no, no, no to all of your questions. This is a law office, and people wouldn't take kindly to being photographed coming or going from my office."

"Do you have any firearms in your office?"

"This is a law office. I don't have a need to have a firearm on the premises. I need you to find the killers, and not stand around asking me questions."

"Am I getting an attitude here?"

"No, I'm just telling you how I feel."

"If you had nothing to do with this murder, then I expect more cooperation from you than what I'm hearing. It appears you are not telling me the whole story. Come on, help me out, will you? Is the victim a friend of yours, or was he a client?"

"He wasn't a client, he was a friend. We went to high school together. He came to tell me something about my brother, something I can't tell you until I talk with Larry Ross. It's rather complicated."

"Uncomplicate it for me. Who is Larry Ross? I have above average intelligence."

"It's an ongoing case I'm speaking about. A case the FBI recently turned over to the CIA. I suggest you get in touch with Larry Ross at Langley in Washington D.C. I can't tell you anything more."

"Cuff him, Freddie. We have an uncooperative witness to a murder here. We'll finish this questioning downtown."

Before leaving his office Detective Donavan searched the office. Cliff held his breath when he opened the top right hand drawer of his desk. It was then he remembered his father's pistol. Detective Donavan looked up at Cliff and displayed the Lugar from the drawer. He held the gun to Cliff's nose.

"Explain this in ten words or less, will you?"

"It was my Father's World War II trophy. He gave it to me for protection. I don't know whether it works or not. It's just for show in case something unusual would happen. It hasn't been fired for years."

"That's more than ten words, but I'll accept your answer. I can tell it hasn't been fired for some time."

Detective Donavan continued to search his office. He pulled books from the bookshelf onto the floor.

"Stop, will you? I'm not hiding anything. I don't understand what you are looking for?"

"You've given me nothing but gibberish about the FBI and CIA. but you can't tell me anything. Believe me, if I take you downtown you'll have something to tell me."

He continued pulling books off the shelves while throwing them on the floor.

"Stop! What are you looking for? You are wrecking my office. What could you possibly be looking for?"

"Answers. I'm looking for answers as to why this man was murdered in your office, and you weren't."

The shelves were bare and the books lay piled on the floor. He turned to his client files.

"I need the keys to the file cabinet. Hand them over."

"There is nothing in there to do with this case, believe me."

"Freddie, record his refusal to cooperate. We'll open it later."

He went into the bathroom, and came out with a syringe in a plastic bag.

"Okay, tell me about this?"

Cliff stared at the syringe. He'd never seen it before. He couldn't answer the Detective's question. He shrugged his shoulders, and gave him a blank look.

"Can't talk, or don't you want to implicate yourself or one of your clients, is that it? This case is getting more interesting by the minute. Freddie, take him to headquarters while I finish up here."

Detective Donavan unloaded the Lugar and put it in his waistband, then turned to continue searching Cliff's office. His office lay in complete ruin. The elevator door opened. Molly and Teddy's eyes widened as they exited the elevator. Cliff was speechless.

Detective Freddie held Cliff's handcuffs and said to Molly and Teddy, "Stay where you are. This is a murder scene. A murder has been committed here."

They set down their luggage, and the elevator door closed behind them. The hallway was taped off and books lay on the floor near the outer office doorway. Detective Donavan appeared.

"What do we have here, Detective Freddie?"

"They arrived on the elevator. I thought you would want to interview them."

"Good. Are you clients or friends of Cliff Mercer?"

"Friends. What going on here?"

"It's a murder scene—I ask the questions, not you."

"Who was murdered?"

"There you go again. I ask the questions, and you answer when I tell you, remember? Let's start from the very beginning again, shall we? I repeat, are you clients or friends of Cliff Mercer?"

"Friends. We are Cliff's friends. We just arrived from overseas. Here's our airlines tickets if you don't believe us."

Detective Freddie handed them to Detective Donavan, and he looked at them. "I see you just arrived. You're free to go. Sorry for the inconvenience."

"I'm not satisfied. I want to know what's going on here. Who was murdered, and why is our friend in handcuffs?" Molly replied.

"Leave it there. Remember, I ask the questions, you answer them, or would you rather go to Headquarters with Cliff."

"Don't get tough with me. I'm used to police bullying."

"Molly, leave it. I'll explain later." Cliff pleaded. Teddy and Molly picked up their bags to leave.

"Hold it." Detective Donavan spoke to Teddy, "Is that bulge in your waistband a gun?"

Teddy's face flushed. "Yes."

"Do you have a permit to carry a concealed weapon?"

"I do, but I don't have it on me."

"Stand still—Freddie, remove the gun from his waist."

Freddie left Cliff's side and removed the gun from Teddy's waistband and handed it to Detective Donavan. He checked the chamber, and found it was loaded.

"Ma'am, I need to search your purse. Please hand it to me."

"There is a small caliber gun in it. I carry it for protection, and I don't have a permit. You can't arrest me for that because I declared it before you opened my purse."

"Someone with legal knowledge? That's all I need—a smart answering woman with a page out of a law book. Everything you've said is true, but I can impound it and take you down to Headquarters to find what you are all about."

"I don't care to be pushed around by someone that's enamored with his badge. I've been around long enough to recognize ego on display when I see it."

"Who let you out of a wheelchair, old woman?"

"Molly, that's enough. You're making things a lot worst for us." Teddy pleaded.

"Yes lady, you've said enough. Freddie, call for additional transportation. I'm tired of these people giving me half-truths, and someone who believes she is above the law. We need to find out who these two really are."

"If you are going to arrest us I will need a receipt for my bags. It's not that I don't trust you two, but I've run into characters like you before," Molly suggested.

"You don't know when to keep that mouth of yours closed, do you? Freddie, take her out of my sight. I can only take so much of her wise cracks."

Cliff sighed. "Sorry guys. I guess this isn't our day."

"Don't worry about it. Teddy and I have been in tighter spots than this one." Molly surprised him with a wink. This was just another game for her.

Cliff opened his cell to make a call.

"Don't do that. Freddie, take his phone. You'll get a chance to make a call when I'm done interrogating you. If you are an attorney, as you appear to be— you should know the routine."

"I don't understand any of this. I called 9-1-1 to report this murder, and I stayed here until you arrived. I have nothing to hide. I did not do this to my friend, and these friends just arrived from overseas."

"Oh! You want to talk now. You know nothing of what happened here, and you give me a story about me asking the FBI and the CIA if I want any answers. Your story doesn't resonate with me. I've been dealing with low-lifes like you for a long time. You make up stories as you think them up. Freddie, put wrist bands on those two, and check why our transportation hasn't arrived."

21

They all arrived at police headquarters. The two detectives separated Cliff, Molly, and Teddy for questioning. Detective Donavan led Cliff down the hall to an empty room with a table and four chairs and told him to sit. The detective paced the room for a protracted time before he sat down directly across the table from Cliff. His cold eyes met Cliff's for an extended period before he said anything.

"I'm a respected attorney here in town."

"Cliff Mercer, I'm aware who you are. All of your answers have been sketchy, you lied about having possession of a weapon, and you gave me that story about the FBI and the CIA, and you didn't have an answer about the syringe in your bathroom. Do you use drugs?"

"I've never used drugs in my whole life. I don't know where that syringe came from. I've never been arrested in my life."

"Let's just say you have never been caught. Just because you're an attorney with an office doesn't cut it with me, and it doesn't give you a free pass to break the law. I don't know what it is with you attorneys—you think you are God Almighty and you can outsmart us detectives with your glib talk. You're in trouble and I hold your future in these two hands. If I charge you with first-degree murder it could ruin you future. Understand—do you understand!"

"I can hold you on two minor charges for the time being while I work on this murder charge. You're putty in my hands right now. I have enough evidence to hold you until I get the evidence to have the District Attorney charge you with capital murder. Furthermore, if you had answered my questions and cooperated with me at your office, then I wouldn't have trashed your place the way I did. Also, I understand you are a defense attorney and you practice criminal law right here in town. I'm surprised we haven't come across each other because I am summoned to court for a number of cases to give testimony. If you cooperate with me right now, I'll keep the options open about your future."

Cliff paused, disturbed by the canned talk the detective was using on him—talk he'd heard used many times by other detectives in the past while questioning his clients.

"You have nothing on me. You want me to talk—well talk I will. You have no evidence on me—no smoking gun, no reason for me to kill my friend, you have no evidence at all. You wrecked my office with the paltry excuse you were looking for evidence. I could ask for an attorney to represent me right now, and you would have to release me right away, but I don't need to do that. Detective Donavan, you are all bluff. Also, you arrested my close friends knowing they weren't anywhere near when this murder occurred. You have nothing on me, and you have nothing on my friends."

"Know it all, do you? Playing detective now, doesn't that beat all. The wheel of justice moves slowly and right now it is turning in my direction. All your wise talk won't convince me of your innocence. It is my job to separate the half-truths from the real- truths, and then I make a decision as to what to do. I would like to get the correct story from you now— right from the very beginning. I don't know how you three are involved, but I intend to find out. Let's get on with my questions, shall we? The sooner I can get some decent answers from you, the sooner I can make up my mind about your future."

There was a knock on the door. Detective Donavan rose to answer it, obviously agitated by the interruption. Cliff sat quietly while the detective talked with someone on the other side of the door. Detective Donavan returned to his seat and agitation shone from his every pore while he mumbled obscene phrases.

"You can go now, along with your friends."

"What's happening, can you tell me?"

"The CIA doesn't want me to question you or your friends any further. I get extremely irate when the Feds stick their nose into our business and ask me to butt out. My chief says hands off when he gets a call from the Feds. My guess is, it is all about the money they funnel to us. That's all I can tell you for the time being. One more thing—perhaps you can answer one question for me, and then you can leave. Was the murdered victim involved in this CIA case too?"

"Yes, he was. I have a question for you—why did you throw all of my books on the floor the way you did? It seems to me you could have removed a few, and then looked behind them."

"For your information, I have free run at what I please. I need to have some fun sometimes. Don't repeat that to anyone, will you?"

"Doing something like that exposes your intellect. Is it all right if I leave now, or is it time for me to call my attorney?"

"Sure, wise guy, you can leave, but stay in town. Consider it a request, not an order."

Cliff walked to the entrance of the police headquarters. It felt good to be released. He walked outside and stood waiting. The fresh air smelled so good. Teddy came out to greet him.

"You missed the whole circus. Molly had them on the ropes for a while before the word came down from the CIA. Can I stay with you for a couple of days because my brother-in-law is staying in my apartment—promise, I don't snore or anything as grievous as that." Teddy laughed.

"Of course you can—maybe we can get to know each other. Where did Molly go?"

"She left with the CIA Agent. She volunteered to go with him, and she told me to get some rest."

"That's good. I was hoping she and the CIA could find some common ground. On the way to my place maybe you can fill me in on what happened in Iran."

"There isn't much to tell. When I got over to Iran and found her, Molly was still recovering from her injuries. She didn't want me to do anything until she was a tad better."

Cliff called Marianne to pick them up. He knew it would agitate Ted, but he delighted in creating a rift between them. Marianne pulled up and they got into her car.

"Marianne, this is Teddy. He is an associate of Molly's."

"Do you always carry that much luggage?" Marianne asked.

Teddy laughed. "Oh no, two of those suitcases belong to Molly—only one of them is mine. Hers and mine are full of dirty clothes because the laundry service in Iran is terrible. We just arrived this morning."

"Tell me, were you able to see and talk with Brian?"

"Didn't I tell you? We located him in prison. Molly needed to come back to take care of her injuries. If you don't mind I can't answer any more of your questions just now."

"Marianne, I have some sad news for you. Doctor Marsh was shot and killed just outside my office a few hours ago. I don't know anything more, but that's why we were at the police station without a car."

Marianne dropped them off at the family home and drove away without saying another word. Cliff didn't know if she was miffed because of the short-snipped answers she received from Teddy or if the case was escalating beyond what she could stand.

Cliff showed Teddy where he could sleep and went to the refrigerator for a beer. No beer, then he remembered —he drank the last one. He sat in his father's recliner and thought about what Doctor Marsh had told him. The whole episode took a toll on him. He questioned why Doctor Marsh was killed. Trying to put the disturbing thoughts aside and out of his mind, Cliff finally went to bed.

Cliff woke in the middle of the night and as he returned from the bathroom he heard a noise from downstairs. He found his housecoat in the dark, picked up his flashlight and the bat from his closet, and slowly made his way down the stairway. A light was on in the kitchen. He approached the open kitchen door.

"Teddy, what are you doing up at this time of night?"

"It's 9 o'clock in Iran right now. My body hasn't adjusted to the time change yet. By the way, I heard you coming down the stairs. Put that bat down before you hit someone with it. I made some coffee. Do you want some?"

"Sure, why not, it's my coffee."

"What's with this 'it's my coffee?' You are mad at the world right now, aren't you? Believe me, it won't get you anywhere. I went down that road when I first started with the British Intelligence, but soon found out I couldn't change the past. After that, I spent my time on positive thinking and doing what I could to change the future and not dwell on the past."

"You're right. My world was so tame before all of this happened to Brian. I'm not used to what is taking place right now, but perhaps with your help I could do better."

"Good, you got my point. I marvel at how cool Molly keeps herself. She is a master at the game we play. It's time to level with you. Molly told me to be your bodyguard until the CIA can provide one for you. I took a short nap, but I have been up ever since. Molly is of the opinion Doctor Ulsheeh is in some kind of hot water and it may spill onto you. We understand no one except you knows what Doctor Marsh told you about Doctor Ulsheeh's activities, and if that is so, then your life may be jeopardy. Molly believes something interrupted the persons who shot Doctor Marsh, and it is possible you could have been their next target."

"Well, truthfully, my safety has entered my mind, however I feel safe when I'm in this house. Believe me, it was quite a shock when Doctor Marsh was shot in my outer office. He told me someone tried to run him off the road earlier, but he managed to survive, and I guess when that failed, they decided to get rid of him another way."

"Your house is the most likely place the people who shot Doctor Marsh would seek you out. By now the murderers must know you are out of jail and where you would likely go. Believe me, Molly knows what she is doing."

"This is too painful for me to talk about. Let's talk about Brian, shall we? You haven't leveled with me since you and Molly returned. I realize other things have happened, but it is time to tell me about what's going on over there."

211

"There's not much to tell. When I reached Molly she was hurting pretty badly. She has no idea who attacked her, but she put some heavy hits on her intruder. There are a lot of random burglaries over there, and that may have been one. She doesn't believe the Iranian intelligence is on to her."

"Her arm was in a sling, but she didn't look like she was hurting too badly."

"She is a tough cookie. I believe her shoulder is still out of place. That's why we returned when we did. Molly located Brian in a prison in the upper regions of Iran before I arrived. That's where they keep their special prisoners. According to our sources they are preparing him to go to their military compound to work on their laser projects. We believe he has convinced the hierarchy he wants to work with them. It's good news in a way, because he might be a step closer to locating the other scientists working on similar projects."

"Are you sure he hasn't been harmed in any way?"

"I couldn't say, but chances are he can take care of himself. He has done a good job of taking care of himself so far, and Molly believes he is smart enough to do the job he volunteered to do. That's all I can tell you for now. Molly should be here in the morning and she can fill you in on what she plans to do when we return to Iran."

"Tell me, how long have you and Molly been working together?"

"It's close to thirty years now, but it seems like yesterday. We were both quite young back then, and we were magnetically drawn together. At that time I was impressed with her unlimited energy and she saw something in me she liked. In all of those years she hasn't slowed a bit, but I have grown weary of the action. When we first met she was working for the CIA and I was working for British Intelligence. At the time, I was being detained and questioned nonstop in a Russian prison for well over a month, eating nothing but potatoes and drinking their stale coffee. One day Molly was arrested and placed in a cell down the cellblock from me. I could hear her singing and calling the guards flirty names. She had them laughing and I think she was bribing them with promises she didn't intend to keep. Within a week she negotiated her release and mine too, which I considered a miracle. Those Russians were tough to deal with, but Molly had her way with them. To this day I don't know how she pulled it off, but when I attempted to find her afterward she was long gone. She didn't wait around to collect my thanks. I went back to England, and I didn't know where she went. She is like that—constantly on the go, nonstop. She doesn't give up, and she doesn't wait around to accept thanks when she deserves it. I didn't run into her again until years later. She was in a bind and I got her out of it. Years later I heard she was killed, but there were no details backing it up, so I lost track of her for another spell. Later I heard she was alive and had left the CIA and was working on her own. Out of the blue she called me a couple years ago and we've been working together ever since."

"I imagine you've seen and done a lot in your time."

"My years with the British Intelligence were good, and I learned a lot about the spy business, but working with Molly has been a pure delight. She is constantly stirring the pot and it makes things happen. I don't know how she became interested in your brother's case, but you're lucky to have her working for you. Go on back to bed—I'll stay downstairs to look out for the bad guys for a while."

Cliff went back to bed, mulling over the thought he might be next on the killers list. His mind searched for some reason as to what was happening to his former quiet world, and what had changed so much to allow his life to unravel the way that it had? And why was Molly so concerned about him being at the wrong end of a gun? She must know something he didn't, or she was using that special reasoning power she claimed she had at her disposal. She had Teddy stay to protect him, which he didn't think was necessary, but regardless of what he thought, his mind was put at rest. He could count on Teddy to protect him if evil ever struck.

It was the middle of the night and he hadn't slept well. He turned and tossed throughout the night. He woke, went to the bathroom, and then smelled bacon cooking. He glanced at the clock—2:00 am. *Couldn't be*, he muttered, that Teddy was cooking again. He made his way to the kitchen, wondering if his imagination was playing tricks on him or what? He opened the kitchen door.

Molly and Teddy were fixing breakfast. They had made themselves right at home.

"Hello Molly. Welcome home. How did your visit with Larry Ross go?"

"It went well. I used to work for Larry's former boss. When I arrived he had my complete file on his desk. He appears to be a good listener, and we got along fine. He has a plan for Teddy and me to implement for him, and we will be leaving here in a day or two. In fact, the CIA will pay all of our expenses for the time being. You're off the hook for further expense money requests from me. I'm sure you are glad to hear that."

"You are the bearer of good news. Teddy told me you've located Brian, and you feel he is safe for the time being. Does Larry's plan include getting Brian out of Iran very soon, or is it still in the plan to rescue all of the scientists before he does?"

"It's difficult for me to answer that question. You see, I don't know how things will work out once we're back in Iran. However, I believe he has a solid plan with a good beginning. His plan appeared well thought through. I judge a person by how they view the overall situation instead of just short-term thinking. As for me, I work on a problem daily and react on what happens that day. You should be well aware of my routine by now. Working with the CIA will allow me more room to roam in Iran, and will allow me monies to further my investigation. My 30 years with the CIA taught me to spend money when needed and not worry about it. In the meantime, I am concerned about your safety. Larry Ross promised he would send a bodyguard over in a day or two, and as soon as he is in place, and I feel okay with the situation, Teddy and I will leave for Iran. Have you got a bed I can crash in for a few hours?"

"Of course. It's the first bedroom on your right. There are clean towels in the closet. I'll have some of that breakfast now."

Molly left and Teddy filled a plate of eggs and bacon for Cliff, poured another cup of coffee for himself and sat down. It appeared he wanted to talk.

"I feel so confident when Molly is in charge. She has so much faith in what she does, and nothing deters her. However, something is bothering me about our return to Iran. I can't put my finger on it, and I can't talk with Molly about it, but I need to share my feelings. It is the dire feeling that one or both of us will not come back. If she had the slightest hint I have lost confidence in her ability to keep us both safe, she would go without me, and believe me, I couldn't have that happen."

Molly appeared in the doorway with a gun in her right hand. "I couldn't sleep. You guys weren't talking about me, were you?"

"Molly, go to bed. Put that gun away. Cliff and I were just talking about things in general. Now go back to bed and get some good sleep."

Molly gave a hollow laugh, turned, and went back up the stairs.

Moments later the outside kitchen door crashed open. A large, hooded man dressed in black appeared in the doorway with his gun raised. Fire instantly came out the end of his gun. A volley of shots sprayed the kitchen. Teddy pushed Cliff under the table, then stood up and shot back. The gunman fled as Teddy's gun kept firing. And then, Teddy fell on the table and then slid to the floor. Within seconds Molly appeared from the stairway with her gun raised. She ran to the outside door and returned to Teddy's side. Cliff stayed frozen in place.

"Cliff, call 9-1-1," Molly said as she knelt beside Teddy.

A stunned Cliff opened his cell and punched in 9-1-1. Molly held Teddy in her lap and pressed the wound on his chest. Gushes of blood appeared around her hand. She talked to Teddy in a slow even tone. Cliff couldn't understand what she was saying.

There was a heavy thrashing at the front door. Cliff yelled as loud as he could, "Back here, hurry, my friend needs immediate attention."

The two paramedics arrived and lifted Teddy onto a stretcher. One pulled Teddy's shirt off while the other checked his pulse and put an oxygen mask on his face. Molly, covered with blood, stood by watching as the paramedics kept working on Teddy.

The paramedic asked, "Are you hurt?"

"Don't worry about me, tend to Teddy." Molly replied.

Cliff looked toward the front door. The shadow of a huge bulk of a man stood in the doorway. He walked toward Cliff.

He stopped in front of Cliff and looked around the kitchen. Meanwhile the two paramedics were working on Teddy as he lay on the stretcher in front of Molly. She stood as still as a statue watching the paramedics work on Teddy.

"Mr. Mercer, what do you make of this?" Detective Donavan inquired.

Cliff looked up at him with an icy stare. He didn't know how to respond to the Detective's question. Donavan turned to look at Teddy lying still on the floor. He asked the paramedic something, but Cliff couldn't understand what he said. It was then Cliff realized Teddy was dead. The paramedic covered Teddy with a blanket. Molly stood by, her face pale and expressionless. Her eyes were a bright fiery red. The paramedics urged her to go to the living room, but she refused. The Detective took the gun from Molly's limp hand, and picked up Teddy's gun from the floor. He walked into the living room and sat next to Cliff.

"Tell me what went on here?"

"Teddy jumped in front of me when a hooded man fired in our direction. There was nothing I could do. It all happened in a split second."

Detective Freddie came in from outside and whispered something into Detective Donavan's ear. Molly continued to stand next to Teddy. Donavan walked over to Molly.

"For what it's worth, your man got the shooter pretty good. There is a trail of blood leading to the street. Our forces will cover the local hospitals. I know it isn't my case, but right now you need our help."

Molly didn't reply. It was obvious Teddy's getting shot took the wind out of her sails. She sat next to Teddy's still body with her hand on his chest and her head bowed like she was saying a prayer or was saying something to him. Cliff and Detective Donavan watched her in total silence. A minute passed, then two. The paramedics wanted to move the corpse, but they stood silently by out of respect for Molly. The coroner arrived and instructed the two paramedics to lift Molly away from the body. She fought off their efforts, but finally gave in. They led her to the living room and sat her next to Cliff. He held her hand, but he didn't know how to console her. Teddy's death had affected her deeply.

"It's cruel to say at this time, but I've noticed Teddy has slowed a bit. He would have shot first twenty years ago. He and I covered each other's backs for more years than you can count. You lose a partner like Teddy and it is like losing part of yourself," Molly quietly eked out.

Cliff felt her pain, but didn't know what to say in Teddy's defense. Silence seemed to be best at this time. Teddy returned fire instantaneously, but Molly was in no mood to hear an explanation from Cliff.

Cliff continued to hold her hand. He noticed her hand became rigid, much like the rest of her body. *Was it her way to keep from crying*, Cliff questioned himself. Two men from the coroner's office took Teddy with them.

Cliff went back to the kitchen to get her a glass of water. The kitchen was in a terrible mess, but he made his way around the stains of blood remaining on the floor. He offered the water to Molly, but she didn't move.

"Molly, drink this, you need to keep up your strength. I know you're hurting, but you can't make yourself sick over what has happened."

22

After hours of sitting with Molly, Cliff rose and stretched. He had sat in the same position for many hours trying to comfort her. The sun had risen and its rays were now streaming through the windows. The time had passed and Cliff felt empty, but during the whole time Molly hadn't moved a muscle. She needed to find a way to get past this tragedy and go back to Iran to rescue his brother, but Cliff had no answers about how to help her.

He walked into the kitchen and surveyed the shambles of what happened the night before. Detective Donavan and his crew took a summary of what happened, the coroner left with Teddy, and a chair was thrust against the broken kitchen door. Teddy's blood had dried on the floor and the table and chairs were pushed aside to make room for the response team. Cliff didn't know where to start with a cleanup effort. He heard his cell play 'Yankee Doodle' like it did after extended vibrating attempts. He couldn't find his phone. He followed the music and found it next to his father's recliner. It was Marianne.

"Cliff, why haven't you answered your phone?"

He didn't answer her at first. Marianne asked again. Cliff answered, "Sis, something terrible has happened. Can you come over to Dad's house to help me?"

"Cliff, are you serious, do you want me over there to clean up your mess? You and Teddy treated me like hell when I picked you up from jail. You involve me when you want me to do something for you, and you shut me out when something important comes up. I'm not coming over there unless you tell me what's going on."

"Sis, come over, I need you now. Please Sis, come over now."

"Something has happened to Brian hasn't it? Something you couldn't tell me in the car, and it's something you can't tell me on the phone. Is that it?"

"No Sis, it happened here, last night, it happened right here in Dad's kitchen. I need you to come over here to help me."

"Happened there? What happened? Make sense, will you? Are you hurt?"

"Enough! I'm not hurt. Sis, I can't explain it all on the phone. I need you to come over to help me. I'll tell you all about it when I see you, okay?"

"Okay, you don't have to make a mystery out of it. I'll be over there as soon as I can."

Cliff leaned back in the kitchen chair. The kitchen was in too much of a mess to make coffee, let alone think about breakfast. He decided to go upstairs to shower before Marianne arrived. He started up the stairs and thought about Molly in the living room. He returned to the living room to see if she was okay. He peered around the corner so he wouldn't disturb her—and she was gone. He hadn't heard her leave. He would shower, get cleaned up, and call her to see if she was all right. He was finishing getting dressed when he heard Marianne downstairs.

"Cliff, come down here. This kitchen is a mess, the back door is busted, and what is this big stain on the floor? It looks like blood."

"Be right down. I am getting dressed."

On his way down the stairs Cliff decided how to tell Marianne what happened the night before. She was sitting in Dad's recliner.

"Sis, give me a hug. We had a terrible night here last night."

"By the looks of the kitchen I'd say a lot happened."

Cliff's cell vibrated. "I need to answer this, just a minute."

"This is Detective Donavan. Your shooter died on the operating table several hours ago. I tried my best to talk with him but he kept going in and out of consciousness. He was the guy because he was still dressed in that dark outfit like you described. It seems like your friend got him good. I've turned all my information over to the CIA. Stay out of my radar, will you? I don't want something to happen to you." He laughed.

Cliff laid down his cell and described in full detail what had happened to Teddy the night before.

"Cliff, you must be there for Molly. You had better call her. There is something I don't understand. Why would someone want to kill you?"

"Doctor Ulsheeh admitted to Doctor Marsh he put a chip into Brian's brain when he operated on him because the Iranian Secret Service threatened to harm his family in Iran if he didn't do exactly what they asked of him. He planted the chip in Brian's brain so they could control his future in Iran, and gain control of his knowledge about the laser program he was working on. By Doctor Ulsheeh admitting his part in their conspiracy, the Iranian Secret Service is afraid the whole story will get uncovered. Help me clean up the kitchen so I can make some coffee, then I'll call Molly."

Cliff finished his second cup of coffee and felt a lot better. By then Marianne finished cleaning up the kitchen.

"Sis, what would I do without you? We're the only ones left in the family and our need to keep close is more important than ever. Ted and I don't get along that great, but I'll work on that. Most of the troubles between us come from me, but I promise, I'll do my best to make things right between Ted and me. Since Brian has been gone things haven't gone well for our family, something we both have to work on to make it better. We'll have to accept the possibility that Brian may not return home for years or maybe ever, but whether he makes it back or not, we'll have each other, so whatever happens, let's work together to move on with our own lives, shall we?"

The doorbell rang before Marianne could say anything. It had been an emotional time between them, a closeness that they needed to talk about, and a together time for them both. Annoyed by the interruption, Cliff went to answer the door. He opened it to find a bulk of a man standing in front of him.

"Cliff Mercer, my name is Hank Morrison. I've been assigned by Larry Ross to be your bodyguard."

He held out one hand to shake Cliff's hand, and he displayed his CIA badge in the other. Cliff leaned against the door and looked up at his face. He was young and physically well built, and confidence shone from his face.

"Hi, come in will you, this my sister Marianne. We were just cleaning up from the fracas that happened last night. Do you want something like water or coffee?"

"I'm good. We need to talk alone. I mean right now."

Cliff gave Marianne one of those get lost looks, and she picked up on it right away. She hugged Cliff and left. The door closed behind her.

"I'll be as brief as possible. I am not much of a talker and we'll spend many quiet hours together. I'll try not to interfere with your regular routines, whatever they are, and I'll try to give you private times as much as possible. However, to properly do my job, you will need to follow my instructions to the letter. I will not tolerate it if you try to break away from my coverage of you. Do you understand?"

"I appreciate the fact Larry Ross sent you here to be my bodyguard, but I'm not sure I need you."

"After two murders within forty-eight hours—believe me, you need me." He scanned the neighborhood, pulled the drapes closed, and walked into the kitchen.

"Let's get started. We need to keep these drapes closed all of the time. I would prefer you stay out of the living room and kitchen as much as possible. They are outside entrances, and they are susceptible to a quick entrance. Take me upstairs."

Hank walked through both bedrooms, checked the windows, and said, "When I get that back door fixed I'll board up this window over the roof. It is too easy for someone to enter that window from the roof."

"You leave nothing to chance, do you?"

"I've had this type of duty many times, and the people I've guarded in the past complain I stay too close to them. Also, I am a marksman and anyone that I feel approaches you in a threatening way will deal with me first. It is my job to make you feel safe 24/7. You'll have to make the best of a bad thing, okay? Oh! Mr. Ross said he would call you in a couple hours to verify my being on the job, and to answer any of your questions."

"I'm feeling safer already. I appreciate you being here for me. I'm easy to get along with, and I'll try hard not to display my bad temper or habits." Cliff laughed.

"You need to replace this door with a solid wooden door, and I need to secure that bedroom window. Do you have a repairman, or should I make a few calls for an estimate and immediate repair? I can handle this without a sweat."

"Handle it, will you. My mind is still on what happened here last night."

While Agent Morrison was getting estimates for the door and the window closure, Cliff called Molly. She didn't answer. He decided to try again later that morning. His cell vibrated.

"Cliff Mercer, this is the funeral home. Molly Moonshine asked me to call you about the burial of Teddy Marshall. It will be at the Greenwood Cemetery at 2:00pm today. Please come to the office and we'll provide transportation to the gravesite."

Cliff slowly closed his cell while thinking it would be a difficult day for Molly and him. He thought about what he might want to say before they covered the casket with dirt.

He arrived at the burial site and saw two people sitting near the casket. There was Molly, but who was the other man? The cart he and Hank were riding came in to a stop a few feet from the casket. Hank, his bodyguard, stood twenty feet from the casket under a low hanging tree with his back to the tree. Cliff got out and walked toward Molly. She appeared exceptionally thin, her shoulders drooped, and she was dressed in black with a black veil covering her face. He sat on the other side of her because a man was sitting on her right side. He reached for her hand in a gesturing way. She gave it to him. Cliff felt a lump in his throat knowing the burial would be difficult for Molly and for him too.

"Cliff, I'm pleased you are here. This is Colon Musgrave, a representative from Teddy's British Foreign Service. Teddy gave them the best years of his life."

Cliff nodded in his direction, and he nodded back. All three sat in silence until a clergyman approached. He approached Molly and extended his hand to her, and she held out her hand to him.

"Molly, I am sorry for your loss. If you are ready to begin I will start with a short prayer."

Molly nodded, and the clergyman began reading from his Bible as Molly recited the passages with him from memory. After the prayer was finished she rose and walked to the casket with Colon Musgrave supporting her. She blessed herself with a sign of the cross and began.

"Teddy, my friend, I didn't mean for this to happen. It is times like this when the unexpected happens, I mean, I was confident you would handle whatever came up, but God intervened, didn't he? When I asked you to guard Cliff, I expected something to happen, but I expected you to come through it without harm like you have done so many times in the past. Cliff told me you pushed him to the floor and took the bullet in his place. If it is any comfort — the man who shot you is also dead. You answered your call to duty. When I called you back into service to help me bring Brian safely back you answered my call and was ready to do what I ask of you. When I asked, I knew you couldn't refuse my request—my Teddy, please forgive me for doing so. We have been working in the service of our countries for many a decade fighting the bad guys. We were not only friends, but we were able to cover each other's backs during many confrontations with our enemies. In all of the time we worked together you never questioned my thinking or erratic actions." She paused, lifted her veil, and leaned closer to the top of the casket. "Teddy, I wish they were burying me here today instead of me burying you. Teddy, I won't say goodbye, because you will live forever in my heart."

It appeared Molly was about to collapse, but the clergyman on one side and Colon on the other side kept her from falling as they helped her back to her seat. Colon rose with a sword in one hand and a case with a medal and ribbon in the other. He gently placed the sword on top of the casket then placed the medal right beside it. His eyes roamed throughout the cemetery, and then came to rest on a hillside in the east where a lone bagpiper stood silently by. He extended his sword to the bagpiper, then turned and extended his hand to Molly to join him beside the casket. The bagpiper started playing. The sounds of the bagpipe floated from the far hill toward the casket in an eerie way. Colon started his eulogy.

"Teddy Marshall, by the order of the Almighty Queen of England I present you with this sword and this medal in recognition of your service in the Foreign Service. I carry this sword directly from our beloved Queen with orders to elevate you to knighthood in her Majesty's home guard. I present you with this sword and this medal given freely by our Queen and the government of the United Kingdom. The Queen personally asked me to make sure you were buried with this medal and this sword so you could continue to battle our enemies into eternity."

He stood next to the casket and recited a Gaelic quotation. The Funeral Director rose and opened the casket, and Colon placed both items on Teddy's corpse. A tear formed in the corner of Cliff's eyes. On the further hill the lone bagpiper played a farewell song to Sir Teddy Marshall. When it was silent again Cliff could hear Molly sobbing. The Funeral Director looked to Cliff to see if he wanted to say something. The service had been simple, but it had been beautifully put together. There was nothing more Cliff could add.

Molly put her hand on Cliff's. "Thanks for being here, please leave now. I will remain until Teddy is secure under the ground. You see, Teddy and I took care of each other for many years, and I must be here to send him off to his next battles."

Cliff raised her veil and kissed her on the cheek. It was wet with tears. It was some distance, but he decided to walk back to his car. His bodyguard joined him. The ceremony was incredibly simple, but it had touched his heart in a most meaningful way. Teddy had given his life so Cliff could continue his life.

23

Cliff returned home to find the carpenter hard at work replacing the kitchen door. He went up to his bedroom and lay on the bed to get some quiet time. *What next,* he asked himself. His bodyguard stood watch outside his doorway. His safe world had evaporated and his future was laced with uncertainty.

His cell vibrated. "Cliff, it's Larry Ross— we need to talk. I'm on my way to you at this very moment. Stay where you are— I'll be there in fifteen minutes."

Surely he's not going to ask something more of me, Cliff imagined. He turned on the radio to catch up on the latest news, and to get his mind on other things. In a few minutes Hank knocked on his door.

"Mr. Mercer, Mr. Ross is here, shall I let him in?"

"Yes, by all means."

Cliff got up swiftly and sat in the chair next to his bed. Larry Ross approached him with his hand extended.

"Cliff, I know you have been through a lot in the last 48 hours, but we have to move ahead. With the case exploding like it has in this country with the two recent murders I have brought the FBI back into the case. It is my job to get Brian and the other scientists out of Iran and back to the United States, and it will be the FBI's job to protect you in the future. For the time being I have assigned Hank for their use in protecting you. I honestly believe you are in immediate danger. I suggest you work closely with Hank to keep your life safe. He is the best bodyguard I have. Believe me, I know about things like this, and you must take my word for it."

"I know you are a busy man with a lot of other cases, but you need to know how important it is to get my brother out of Iran."

"I'm well aware of your overwhelming desire to get Brian returned. There is one thing you must remember—it was Brian's choice to go there to bring the other scientists back with him. In the coming weeks Molly will be working on my plan to bring them all back. I'm asking you not to contact Molly or interfere with my plans in any way. Are you perfectly clear with my request?"

"I find it hard to believe you are counting on one old woman to rescue them all. You need to send her some help. I won't interfere, but Molly needs additional help."

"Your concerns are noted, but after my review of her previous CIA record and talking with her, I believe she can get it done on her own. It's kind of funny, but she said, 'Give me plenty of money and stay out of my way.' She convinced me that she is capable of completing the job and bringing them all back safely. Now for you— I want you to get back to your regular life like nothing has happened. Someone may attempt to take you out, but Hank is one of our best bodyguards, and I'm sure he would protect you with his life."

"That's all fine and dandy, but I don't think I could live with the knowledge two people died defending me."

"Cliff, you have no other choice. We need to draw out whoever is behind all of this, and you are our guinea pig, so to speak."

"I don't feel like being your guinea pig. How do you like that?"

"A little humor, I like that. Having a bodyguard won't put you in any additional danger, and it will keep you much safer around the clock. Let Molly and me do our job getting Brian home, and all I'm asking is that you resume your law practice like nothing has happened."

"I don't understand why I have become the center of attention."

"You of all people should have the answer to that. Doctor Marsh lost his life telling you about Doctor Ulsheeh's confession to him. The Iranian Secret Service is hell-bent on continuing their quest to get more noted scientists to work for them and Doctor Ulsheeh appears to be weakening in his resolve to follow their orders. I suspect sooner than later he will come over to our side and give us the necessary information to run the Iranian Secret Service out of our country."

"Okay, I'll go along with your plans, but it is with the utmost reservation. I need to know what's happening to Molly in Iran in a reasonable time frame, and what progress you are making with getting my brother safely back home."

"I can't make any promises I can't keep, but I'll do my best to keep you in the loop on what progress we are making. When I am dealing with events overseas I need to make the snap decisions that are needed at the time. Many things change within the hour and I can't keep you informed about every little thing. If something major happens, then I will tell you about it."

"I believe you. One thing—can you tell me where Doctor Ulsheeh is at this time?"

"He is presently under protective custody. I can't tell you much more, but you can rest assured he will not be contacting you."

"I understand, but don't keep me in the dark too long."

"Okay, I'm pleased we have an understanding. Hank will be joined by an FBI agent to cover you 24/7. He will be here shortly after I leave. I implore you not to try to ditch my guys in an effort to have some personal privacy. If you do, it will put your life in jeopardy, and it may even cost you your life."

Larry left, and Cliff returned to his bed once again. Larry's plan excluded him from everything. How could he live with that thought? He couldn't just flush thoughts of Brian's safety from his mind so easily. How could he get on with his law practice and pretend nothing happened? The questions kept unfolding without answers as he thought through what his future would be like. A restless night and an early morning wakeup left Cliff drained. He must find a way to recapture his previous life. He dressed, ate a bowl of cereal, picked up his briefcase, and walked toward the garage.

"Where do you think you are going?" The voice came from a stranger sitting in his Dad's recliner.

"What's it to you. Who are you, anyway?"

"I'm Hank's relief. You were sleeping last night when I came on duty. If you leave the house we must discuss where you are going so I can prepare the way. By the way, my name is Special Agent Bryant Tuttle of the FBI."

"Hello, Bryant Tuttle. I guess I slipped into my old routine without thinking. I'm going to my office. I've got to get used to dealing with you and Hank."

"Okay, I need to check your car for any explosive devices before we go into the garage. Stay in the kitchen while I check it out."

"You leave nothing to chance, do you?"

"When you're working for Larry Ross you can't make mistakes." He laughed and went to the garage.

Cliff heard the car starting and he started out the back door. He didn't see Bryant coming up in front of him and then he was being shoved back inside.

"I told you to stay inside. You follow my instructions or we stay in the house all of the time. Do you understand?"

"I'm sorry. What can I say? I didn't think. That's all."

"Follow my instructions to the letter in the future, and we'll get along just fine. I'm here to protect you. Surely you realize you are someone's target."

Cliff didn't have a rebuttal answer. He felt rather sheepish for his series of blunders in such a short time. There was little talk on the way to his office.

They arrived at the office. When Cliff opened the door he realized he hadn't cleaned up the mess he left it in. He and Bryant worked for hours replacing the books on the shelves. He sat down in his chair near the window to get a breath.

"Don't sit there. It's too dangerous. We'll have to move your desk to the outer office and away from the windows."

"God, what next. Okay, I know you must have your way. For your information, my desk has been in the same place for years. I don't like changes."

Cliff's cell vibrated. "Cliff, it's Detective Donavan. I received tests back on the syringe I picked up from your bathroom. It contained 100% cocaine. I would like you to think back on who used your bathroom last."

He thought, and then remembered it was Teddy. He paused…

"Well, cat's got your tongue?"

"I can't recall. I'm busy putting all of the books back in their rightful place. Can we forget about that syringe for the time being?"

"Considering all that has happened to you in the last 48 hours I guess I could let it go. Let me know if you come up with a name, will you?"

Cliff closed his cell, knowing it was Teddy who probably left the cocaine syringe in his bathroom. Meanwhile Bryant closed the drapes and Cliff settled into his new space in the outer office.

He picked up his briefcase, opened it, and began reviewing his law practice. He'd lost almost half of his clients since Brian was in his accident. He made a dozen calls filled with apologies for his absence from his work. For the first time in weeks he was feeling good about himself.

In the meantime Bryant got a chair and sat between the stairway and the elevator. He heard someone talking. Bryant appeared in the doorway.

"There is a lady here that wants to talk with you."

It was Anne.

"Hello, stranger. Got a bodyguard now. What else is new? It has been a while hasn't it? I talked with Marianne and she thought you might be here."

"Here I am. Can I have a hug? Yeah, I have been through a lot, but I'm back to my normal routine. It's good to see you. Can you stay for a while, maybe help me clean up this mess?"

"I see you have rearranged your office. I like it, besides I'm a great believer in change. I'm on my way to work, but truthfully, I've been stopping by here every morning hoping to see you, and this morning you were here. Did you lose my cell number?"

"I really don't have an excuse. I have missed you too. I'm trying to get my life put back together, still working on it, and this is my first day back. I'm pleased you are still interested in me."

"Of course I am, you big loaf. Let's get together for dinner tonight or Saturday, what do you say?"

"Saturday would be good. I'll make the arrangements and be in touch."

"I got to go. You know me— I hate to be late, especially for work. Give me a hug."

Anne left and Cliff felt better—another piece of his former life was returning. Anne had been in his life since high school. His cell vibrated.

"Cliff, it's Larry Ross. Are you sitting down?"

"If you have any news for me, spit it out. After what I've been through I can accept almost anything."

"Doctor Ulsheeh has committed suicide."

Cliff slumped down in his chair. He was speechless, and didn't know how to answer him.

"Hello, are you there?"

"Give me a second, will you? I thought you had him in protective custody."

"He wouldn't allow us inside his home. I had five agents around his home to stop him from leaving and to prevent anyone from entering. He kept demanding his civil rights, and we didn't have any concrete evidence to lock him up."

Cliff closed his cell. He had nothing more to say. Another link to Brian's future was gone. He felt sick inside, almost to the point of throwing up. Thoughts flashed through his mind about how the doctor put a chip in his brother's brain— and everything had escalated from that point on. He heard a ruckus in the hallway, and when he looked out he saw an old time client in a tussle with Bryant.

"Bryant, he is okay. Mr. Willow is a client of mine."

Bryant let go of his coat sleeve. An agitated client entered his office.

"What's happening here? I don't like to be searched without an explanation of some kind."

"I'm sorry. It's a long story. I'll have a talk with him. It won't happen again, believe me. Can I get you some water or something?"

"No, I'm good. Have you been on an extended vacation or something? I've been calling your office without an answer from you."

"I'm here now—what can I do to help you?"

"It's the same old story. The dispute I've had with Leon Badger is back on. He has started building on my easement again. I'm here to have you stop him in his tracks from encroaching on an inch of my land. As you know, we've been to court three times on this same issue, and we've won all three times, thanks to you."

"I'll go to work on it right away. I'll put a cease order on his construction activity and we'll take him to court again."

"He is so damn stubborn, every time he takes a fancy to do these foolish things it costs me money."

Mr. Willow left. Cliff felt good again about what this day had brought. First it was Anne, and now a client needed his services. They were good thoughts, but Cliff's mind returned to Doctor Ulsheeh. He was a brilliant surgeon, a good family man, and he relished being a citizen of this country. He enjoyed his family, so why he would commit suicide was a question that kept returning to his mind. Cliff's cell vibrated.

"Cliff, it's Ross again. We found a suicide note. Doctor Ulsheeh made a complete confession. He's written what happened in Iran when Brian shot the two CIA operatives. It will expunge any charges against Brian. That should make your day."

"It does. It appears things are moving along very quickly, aren't they?"

"Enjoy the news. I'll talk with you again when I have more news. Molly is safely back in Iran and is working to get Brian free."

Cliff closed his cell. It was now up to Molly to bring Brian home, and everything would be right again. He and Anne went to dinner on Saturday night while Hank sat at the table next to theirs. Things were awkward at times with Hank sitting so close, but during the evening he and Anne found a way to break the ice that had formed between them.

Weeks passed with no word from Larry Ross. Cliff was slowly winning back the clients he had lost, and during that time he'd won two court appearances.

Hank and Bryant continued their watch over Cliff. They had found a workable solution so in time Cliff hardly noticed they were there. He, Marianne, and her family had dinner together and Cliff did his best to make up with Ted. He'd been working on their father's estate and it was almost complete. Since Brian was out of the country a judge ruled the estate couldn't be completed until Brian returned home or was declared dead.

More time passed, and Cliff had received no word from Larry Ross. He became totally focused on his work as an attorney. It was the nights as he lay in bed, before he fell asleep, that he thought of Brian and Molly. It had been a while, quite a while, since he'd heard anything from Ross. He knew Marianne was praying for them, but there was nothing he could do to help them.

It had been a month since Molly returned to Iran, and still no word from anyone. He would shelf his thoughts about her by digging deeper into his work. Suddenly, an uncanny feeling came over him. Someone was in his room. He didn't know whether to turn on the light or not. Hank had never entered his bedroom, so it couldn't be him. He slipped out of his bed onto the floor, figuring he could roll under the bed quickly.

"Are you awake?"

It was Hank speaking.

"Yes. What are you doing in my room?"

"The same car has circled the block three times. I've called it in, but I haven't received any backup. Stay where you are. Here he comes again."

Shots rang out, and with it, the sound of shattering glass. It sounded like the downstairs was being demolished. As quickly as it started, it ended in utter silence.

Cliff heard Hank leaving his room, and saw the hall light come on. "Stay where you are until I check this out." Hank yelled.

24

Cliff lay on the floor next to his bed, unsure what was happening, but he could see Hank's feet in the hallway. Soon Hank's feet were joined with other pairs of feet.

"You can come out now, it's safe." Hank said.

Cliff came out into the hallway, and there were three other agents with Hank.

"Larry said something was due to happen, and he was right again. The living room is a complete mess. We have a tail on the car with the gunman who did this, and it should be a matter of hours before we have them in custody," another agent was telling Hank.

"Cliff, let's have a look. Do you want to join me?"

"Let me put on my bathrobe, and then I can join you."

They walked down the stairway together and entered the living room. The windows were broken, the drapes completely ripped apart, the furniture shredded, and splinters of wood from the walls and ceiling were strewn all over the floor. Cliff couldn't believe the destruction. His father's recliner was totally shredded.

"Now you know why I didn't allow you to stay in the living room area."

Cliff didn't answer. It was plain to see someone wanted him dead, and it was now apparent why Larry wanted him guarded so closely. He didn't go to work that day or the next, but stayed mostly in his bedroom or the kitchen. A day passed...

"Do you have a clue who did this to my Dad's home?" He asked Hank.

"No, they got away. I don't know what to expect now that Doctor Ulsheeh is dead," Hank replied.

Another week passed. There was no word from Larry Ross or Molly. Cliff's bodyguards suggested he not visit with Marianne or Anne because his visit might cause harm to them. Cliff felt alone, holed up in his house for over a week. He was getting fewer and fewer calls on his cell. It was like the outside world had evaporated, and he was forgotten. The empty hours wore on. Another week passed...no change. His cell vibrated.

"Cliff, I have some news for you. Molly has freed Brian and the three scientists from the military compound where they were being held, and they are making their way out of Iran. They are thirty miles from the border. It is 1:00am there, and they are fleeing in total darkness. I will keep you updated as soon as I have further news." Larry signed off.

A day passed.... no word from Larry. Cliff could not take his mind off of Brian and Molly and what dangers they must be facing. His cell never left his hand. He opened his briefcase in the hope he could concentrate on something else, but nothing worked.

"Cliff, I'm going off duty now. Tomorrow I will be able to take you back to your office. Another agent by the name of Stuart Ashley will be replacing Bryant. He'll be here in a couple of minutes," Hank explained.

"Introduce him to me before you leave, will you?"

"I can't. I have to take my daughter to school. You will only be alone for a few minutes. Please don't tell Larry on me, okay?" He laughed. "I'll leave the outer kitchen door unlocked for him. If you stay in your bedroom you will be okay."

Cliff thought. *This is the first time I've been alone in weeks.* In a way it felt good, but in another, he considered himself unsafe that something would happen. He heard the back kitchen door open.

"Hello, Stuart, I'm up here." Cliff called out.

There was no answer. Cliff heard the lock on the kitchen door snap shut, leaving him with an uneasy feeling. He got his pistol from the end table drawer, and went to the bathroom and locked himself in, not knowing why he was being so cautious, but maybe it was because Stuart didn't answer him.

He turned on the shower to mask any of his movements in the bathroom, and lay down in the bottom of the tub. He saw the knob on the bathroom door turn.

"Hello, it's Stuart. Are you in the shower?"

Cliff didn't answer. Why? He couldn't—his reply stuck in his throat. He wasn't sure it was Stuart. He punched in Hank's number and waited…he didn't answer. "I need you now." He whispered into his cell.

Shots pierced the door, bouncing around the small bathroom like ping pong balls. He crouched in the tub curled up like a fetus, with bullets hitting the tub and walls. Another volley of shots rang out. Again it sprayed the whole bathroom, shattering the mirror and sinks. Moments passed — then, deadly silence. He heard someone call out his name from downstairs. His cell vibrated.

"Cliff, it's Hank. I'm on my way to you. Are you okay?"

"Hurry up, will you. I'm in the bathroom."

Five minutes passed.

"Cliff, open the door, it's Hank, and I have Stuart with me."

Cliff climbed out of the tub shaking from head to toe and opened the door for Hank and another person standing next to him.

"I'm sorry as hell. Stuart was supposed to be here, but he was late."

"I'm sorry too. I could have been killed. You are supposed to be here for me. Larry said you are the best he had, but I'm beginning to doubt that!"

"I had no idea Stuart would be late. Are you hurt or anything?"

"Not hurt, but pretty well shaken up. Is this Stuart?"

Larry Ross walked in.

"What's going on here?"

"A shooter got into the house and went after Cliff in the bathroom."

"Who's got an answer for something like this to happen?"

"No excuse." Hank replied. "I left Cliff alone for fifteen minutes because I needed to take my daughter to school. The gunman must have known I was gone. I can't tell you how or why."

"Go downstairs, I'll deal with you two later. I want to talk with Cliff alone."

"Cliff, I'm sorry as hell this happened. I have my best men on your watch, and they let you down. I'll take care of them later. Are you hurt at all?"

"No, I'm all right, I'm shook up and pissed your guys weren't here for me. Why are you here?"

"I'm upset with them too. I have to assume the gunman was watching the house and saw Hank leave with no replacement arriving— he made his move. It is something that shouldn't have happened."

"I don't know what to say. Hank's been here all of this time, and nothing has happened."

"In our business I don't leave anything to chance. It is all white or all black, nothing in between. Let's move on. I've heard from Molly. She is trying to get all four of the scientists to the Turkish border, but she's having trouble doing it. She's within fifteen miles of the border, and traveling in the dark has been extremely difficult because Jeffery was wounded during the escape. She has enough water and food for the trip, but they have had to carry Jeffery most of the way, which has slowed them down a lot. I now have men just across the border waiting to help them, but I've given them instructions not to cross the border. It would create suspicion where Molly and the scientists will cross."

"If they're in trouble, you've got to go in to help them."

"My hands are tied. The President said we couldn't go in. We've got to trust Molly and Brian to get them out. If they get within a mile of the border, I'll send my people in to help them cross, but that's the best I can do. It should be sunrise in Iran in a couple of hours, which will make their journey more dangerous. I have to leave, but I'll keep you informed."

Cliff lay back on his bed. It had been quite a morning. He decided to wait before calling Marianne because he didn't want to raise her hopes and then dash them with bad news if it happened. He turned on the radio, hoping it would occupy his mind while he held his cell in his hand waiting for the call from Larry. Cliff's cell vibrated. He looked at the screen: it was Larry. He took a deep breath before answering it.

"Cliff, I have some news for you. You won't be pleased with it, but I'm being upfront with you."

"Tell me what you have to say, and quit beating around the bush."

"Two of the scientists made it to the border—Donald Sutherland and Claude Windsor. They ran into an ambush just before sunrise, and Molly told them to make a run for it. She and Brian were going to stay with Jeffery Wilbur, and try to bring him across the border after dark tonight."

"That sounds like something Molly and Brian would do. Thanks for keeping me informed."

"By the way, I've got one Agent inside your house guarding you, one outside the residence, and one in a car down the block. I've corrected what happened, and it won't happen again."

Cliff ended the call without a reply. Larry Ross had been upfront with him from day one. He called Marianne and told her to pray for Brian because he was trying to make his escape. Cliff was hungry, but he couldn't make himself eat until he heard from Larry Ross again. Surely Brian, Molly and Jeffery Wilbur would make it to the border. Hours passed with no word from Larry.

The time seemed to drag by. His cell vibrated.

"Cliff, it's Larry. There was heavy gunfire near the Iranian border. We think Molly, Brian, and Jeffery are close to the border, but there is no way to tell. I'll call back as soon as I have more news."

The hours dragged by with no message from Larry. Cliff was beside himself. The waiting became unbearable. His cell vibrated. He took a deep breath before he answered it.

"Good news— Molly, Brian, and Jeffery Wilbur have been wounded, but they're all across the border. I'll let you talk with Brian as soon as I can."

Cliff sighed. Brian's absence had been a real challenge for him and Marianne. He lay back on the bed and said a short prayer. He thought about Molly and the work she had done to free them all. Indeed she was a wonder. Even after losing Teddy she had enough courage to finish the job they had started.

Days passed without a word... When would he hear from Brian? It had been so long since they last talked. He could think about nothing else. His cell vibrated.

"Cliff, it's Larry. Brian, Molly, and Jeffery are being flown to a military hospital in Germany. They have all been critically wounded. I've considered having you flown to Germany, but I've put it on hold for the time being. Hang tight— we're doing everything possible to bring him back to you. That's all the news I have for you now."

"*What next.*" Cliff sighed. Maybe it would be too much to expect him to come back like he had left. He didn't want to worry Marianne so he didn't call her. Instead he went to the kitchen to make a sandwich.

"Make one for me," Hank said. "I don't know if I will have a job after this assignment is over. I never got a chance to tell you how sorry I am for not being there for you."

"It's history, and I survived. Forget it—I have. I pile on the peanut butter and jelly really heavy, I hope you like it that way."

"I'm starved. Any way you make it is fine with me." They both laughed. The heavy tension that plagued them both for days appeared to be history.

Cliff was pleased, but down deep he was concerned about Brian. He would have to put everything on hold until Brian was back home. The only thing he could do was wait for Larry Ross's call. He turned on the television, but turned it off in a short while. He tried to read, but couldn't concentrate, so he went to sit in his Dad's recliner, but it was shattered. He returned to the kitchen. His cell vibrated.

"Cliff, good news. Brian, Molly, and Jeffery will be coming back to the States. I have made arrangements for Hank to take you to the airport. You two will be here to see them come off the plane. I'll give all the details to Hank. Well Cliff, it's finally happening."

Cliff couldn't answer. He closed his cell and sat in silence for a time. All that happened was too unbelievable. Brian was coming back home to him and Marianne. These past months had been a living hell for him and Marianne. He thought about Brian—could he be too badly wounded to be able to go back to his work? So many thoughts cascaded through his mind. A day passed, then two…no word from Larry about when Brian and Molly would be flying home.

25

"Cliff, it's Larry, pack your bags. I have a flight for you in a couple of hours. Hank will take you to the military airport. Brian, Molly, and Jeffery will come into Andrews Air Force Base, and I'll have you there to greet them."

"Thanks, Larry. That's the best of news. I'll be ready and waiting."

A calm fell over Cliff. Brian was coming home after all that happened, and he and Marianne could have their brother back, and the family could return to their normal lives again. It was like a dream, a dream he once considered an impossibility had became true. He went to the bedroom, packed a few clothes, splashed some water on his face, and looked in the mirror. He saw a face gaunt from stress and uncertainty. The thought of Brian coming home was more than he could have imagined.

Hank loaded Cliff's only bag in the back seat and drove to the airport. A military jet was ready for them, and once they were on board it took off. On the way Cliff thought of how great it would be to get back to his old routine. Maybe he and Brian could spend a few days at the cabin and mend their lives together again. He fell asleep, and when he woke it was time to land. It was time to put those exhaustive days filled with anxiety and doubt behind him, and enjoy the coming days with a brother he thought he would never see again.

Larry met them at the airport. His face expressed concern.

"What now? You have one of my father's troubled looks?"

"Cliff, I don't want you to expect too much. What I'm trying to say is, Brian and Molly have been severely wounded, and it will take a while for them to recover."

Cliff didn't respond, not knowing what Larry was trying to prepare him for. The past many months had been filled with one disappointment after another, and he didn't want to hear about the next one.

They arrived close to a very large plane, and the whole tail section opened up. Cliff and Larry walked as close to the opening as they could without being in the way of the handling crew. Cliff could see a number of people inside preparing to carry the patients out. Two ambulances pulled up, and another three waited close by. Cliff started to shake involuntarily. He didn't know what to expect. He needed Marianne next to him, but he grabbed onto Larry's arm. A soldier came over and asked them to move back.

"We've eight patients to remove, and you can't crowd the medics. It would be better for you to go to Walter Reed and see whomever you are meeting at the hospital," the medic explained.

Cliff didn't move. Larry tugged at his sweater to move back, but Cliff wouldn't move.

"We better do what they asked. I know you're anxious, but we must do what we're told."

"No, I'm staying. I want Brian and Molly to know I'm here. They can't come all this way and not know someone like me cares enough about them to be here when they arrive back in the States. You go if you want to, I'm staying."

It started to rain. The ambulances moved closer to the opening of the plane. Cliff edged forward too. He was determined to see Brian, and for Brian to see him the minute they brought him from the plane. Two more stretchers came out and were put into ambulances. It was then Cliff recognized Brian as they carried him from the plane. He rushed up to his side, while Larry stood back. The soldier moved forward trying to block him, but he was already by Brian's side.

"Brian, it's me, Cliff." Brian didn't respond. A medic walked up to him. "We medicate our patients for the flight—you'll have to go to the hospital to see him when he wakes up. I suggest you leave now."

Cliff didn't move. The soldier took his arm to move him back. Cliff shook off the soldier.

"I need to see Molly. I don't care if she is asleep."

Two more stretchers came out, but Molly was not on one of them. Another ambulance arrived. The last patient was carried out with a woman nurse by her side. It was Molly, and Cliff edged closer to touch her. A heavy blanket covered her, but he stroked her hair as she passed by. She didn't move. The bearers moved her quickly into the ambulance. The ambulance pulled away, leaving Cliff standing in the rain. Another patient on crutches walked slowly out of the plane opening. Larry whispered into Cliff's ear. "That's Jeffery Wilbur."

Cliff edged closer to meet him.

"Hi, I'm Brian's brother. I understand he and Molly helped you escape."

"I'll be eternally grateful for what they did for me. If they hadn't carried me to the border they wouldn't have been wounded, and I wouldn't be here now."

Cliff patted him on the back and said, "Welcome home."

"Cliff. Let's go. They're home, just like I promised," Larry said. "I need to leave now, but Hank will be here to help you. I've made accommodations for you two at a hotel close to Walter Reed Hospital where Brian and Molly will be."

Cliff was too emotional to respond. He expected them to walk off the plane, but it didn't happen that way. His spirit crushed, he barely made it to the car. Hank helped him inside. They arrived at the hotel.

"Cliff, clean up, and I'll meet you in the dining room in an hour," Hank said.

Cliff threw himself onto the bed. He was totally mentally and physically exhausted, and soon fell asleep. Several hours passed before he woke. He pulled the drapes back, only to see it was still raining. He looked at the room phone — a light was flashing indicating a message. He walked into the bathroom and took a shower. He dressed, and then turned to the phone. The message was from Hank wanting him to call. Instead, he called Marianne. She was not available, and he didn't want to leave her a message because he needed to talk directly with her. He sat on the edge of the bed deciding what he should do next. The phone rang.

"Cliff, it's Hank, you didn't call me back. I'm coming up with food, and then I will take you to the hospital. Unlock your door please."

He jumped up. That's exactly what he wanted to do. He was inwardly pleased. He didn't know how long he'd slept, but now he felt well rested. Surely Brian and Molly would be awake by now, he thought.

Hank entered with a tray of food. He set the tray down and returned to the door to lock it. He poured Cliff a cup of coffee and told him to eat. While eating they heard someone outside the door. Hank removed his firearm from his holster and approached the door. Cliff stopped eating. Hank swiftly pulled the door open. A maid stood in front of him.

"What do you want," Hank said in a commanding voice. "Can't you read the do not disturb sign?" the maid backed away without uttering a word when she saw the weapon Hank had in his hand. He closed the door, locked it, and turned to Cliff.

"You never know. Finish up and we'll leave. It's a short drive and we'll be there in less than fifteen minutes."

They entered the hospital and were directed to the sixth floor. Hank walked over to the nurses' center and asked about Brian and Molly.

"You'll have to talk with the doctor first. Go into the waiting room, and I'll call you."

An hour went by, and then two. Both Cliff and Hank were getting edgy and restless. Finally a doctor approached them.

"Hi, I'm Doctor Eggard. I have been assigned to Brian Mercer's case, and I understand you are his brother. I'm sure you are anxious to see him, but we need to talk first. In case you didn't know, Brian was shot three times—once in the torso, once in the shoulder, and once in the chest area. The bullets in the torso and shoulder were removed in Germany and are healing nicely, but the bullet that entered the chest lodged in the spine. It's a miracle his spine wasn't severed, but we have him strapped down so he can't move and do harm to himself. In examining all of the data, it will take a noted specialist to remove it. Brian has no feeling in his legs—however, if we can remove the bullet from the spine area, there is a good possibility he could walk again. I have heavily sedated him to prevent him from moving around and possibly pushing the bullet further into the spinal cord. That said, I'm attempting to locate Doctor Tyler, whom I feel will be the most qualified surgeon to operate on him. I suggest you not see him today because he is heavily sedated. If you would leave your cell number with the nurses' station, I'll update you when I am able to contact Doctor Tyler." He got up and left without waiting for a response from Cliff.

He sat dejected with the news, and compassion for his brother's ongoing problems welled into his throat. Hank detected Cliff's sentiments, and left to inquire about Molly. Cliff decided to call Marianne.

Her cell rang and rang and finally she answered it. "Cliff, where are you? I've been calling, and you didn't answer."

"I'm at Walter Reed Hospital. Brian is back in the United States, but he is badly hurt. There is a bullet lodged against his spine and he can't move his legs. The doctor is waiting to contact another doctor who could operate on him. You better pray hard for Brian."

"Oh Cliff, what next? I have been praying for him nonstop forever. When are you coming home?"

"I haven't decided. I guess Molly was pretty badly hurt too. I'm going to try to see her next. I'll let you know as soon as I know about the both of them."

Cliff closed his cell as Hank walked in the door.

"Molly is being operated on at this very minute. We need to go down to the third floor and wait again." Hank said.

Cliff didn't want to leave Brian behind, but Hank was insistent on his coming with him. He showed Cliff to the waiting area, and Hank went to the nurses' station to inquire about Molly's surgery. Hours passed, and Hank went to the nurses' station a number of times, but came back with no news. Finally a doctor approached them.

"Hi, I'm Doctor Busby. I have been operating on Ms. Moonshine for the last two hours. It was a difficult operation, and I wasn't able to help her. You see, the bullet fractured her femur just where it connects to the hip. With the damage to her femur close to her hip, I can't install the hip replacement without a modification to the hip replacement hardware. I need to go to the artificial hip manufacturer and perhaps they could come up with a modification for me. Because Molly is rather elderly I chose not to repair her fracture until I can do the hip replacement. For the time being she will have to spend some time, perhaps months, in a wheelchair until I can get that modification made to my satisfaction. You may go in and see her in an hour or so, but please don't discuss anything I just told you with her. I will talk with her at a later date."

The news was not good and Cliff knew Molly would not be pleased with the news about her future. The nurse came by and told Cliff he could go in to see Molly. He entered, expecting to see a grouchy old lady, but instead she was busy on her computer.

She looked up and said, "I brought Brian back to you just like I promised to do. We both got a little banged up at the end because we had to carry Jeffery the whole way—otherwise we would have come back unscratched."

"I can't imagine what thirty miles traveling in the dark was like. How did you keep your bearings and know where you were going?"

"I navigated by the stars. There was no trouble doing that, but Donald and Claude weren't strong enough to help Brian and me carry Jeffery, who slowed us considerably."

"I can't say enough to thank you, especially after Teddy got killed, and you went back alone."

"Don't bother, Sonny Boy. Surely I can call you Sonny Boy now? It makes me uncomfortable when someone I know gets too mushy. I did my job as I was expected to do and that's that. Case closed."

"You can call me anything you want. I'm so pleased you and Brian made it back. Did the doctor talk to you after the operation?"

"Yeah, he said he had a little problem, but he said he would work on it, and get me fixed up so I can go home and create some mischief. I'm okay with that if it doesn't take him too long, I'll go home and come back when he is ready for me."

She barely finished her sentence when she closed her eyes and slumped over. Cliff called for the nurse. The nurse arrived, followed by a doctor. She called for additional help. Molly was taken out on a gurney followed by several nurses and attendants.

Cliff returned to the waiting room not knowing what happened. An hour passed, then two. A nurse came in and told him that Molly would be in intensive care for the rest of the day and that night.

"Can you tell me what happened?"

"It happens sometimes after an operation. A blood clot broke loose and settled in her lungs. It can be fatal, but the doctors got it cleared. We'll watch her very closely for 24 hours in case more clots form. It was good you were there when it happened."

"Cliff, we have the rooms for another day and then we must leave. Tell me, is that alright with you?" Hank asked.

"I can't answer you just now. I'm not sure what I want to do. It does appear rather bleak, doesn't it? Let me sleep on it, and I'll let you know in the morning."

After a number of hours alone in his room, Cliff decided to go down to the bar and have a drink. Perhaps it would help him unwind. It had been one of the toughest days of his life. Larry walked in and sat beside him.

"What are you doing here?"

"Hank called me and told me you had a tough day and you were here trying to ease your pain. What are your plans?"

"Plans? I wish I had one. I can't help either Brian or Molly right now, so I thinking about going back home."

"Something has come up that we must talk out. Special Agent Boller called me this morning, and he brought up something I hadn't thought about. Brian still has the chip in his brain. Now that Doctor

Ulsheeh is deceased, I don't know if another Iranian would have the power to tell him what to do. From what I know, Brian gave away a number of important formulas after Doctor Ulsheeh left Iran, so I'm leaning toward the possibility others can control him. I'm sure they know where he is right now. I suggest you talk with him about getting it removed while he is waiting for the specialist to remove the bullet from his spine. Do you think you could talk with him about having it removed while he is waiting for the other doctor?"

"A decision like that would be up to Brian. I would be glad to discuss it with him, but I can't help him make that decision."

"Good, I talked with Doctor Eggard about it, and he said you could see him in the morning."

Larry left. It was then he saw Hank in the corner of the bar. Cliff had two more drinks.

"Have you been there all evening?"

"It's my job. If you're ready to go to the room we can leave now."

He lay on the bed thinking about what Larry had said. The more he thought about it, the more he realized Brian needed to get the chip removed from his brain, and the sooner the better. He had a restless night pondering what would happen with Brian the next day. He finally fell fast asleep about 3:00 am.

26

"Cliff, wake up, it's Hank. Something is happening at the hospital. Larry called me and wanted us to meet him there as soon as possible."

"What? How did you get in here? What the hell time is it? What is it Larry wants?"

"Cliff, get up. Here are your clothes. Get dressed. Larry needs us right away at the hospital."

"What's happening?"

"I don't know, but Larry called saying for me to bring you to the hospital ASAP. Get dressed, will you?"

"Okay, okay. I'm up, and I'm getting dressed."

Hank rushed him out of the door and down to their car. A motorcycle policeman was there to escort them to the hospital.

"What do you think happened at the hospital?" Cliff asked on the way to the hospital.

"I don't know, but it must be something big to give us a police escort and everything. Did you notice the policeman changed the lights from red to green."

They reached the nurses' station and found Larry surrounded with a number of soldiers with guns.

"Cliff, this is Colonel Colleen. He's in charge here. He will tell you what is happening and why I called you here."

"Okay, Colonel, does this have something to do with Brian?"

"You bet it does. His nurse went in to check on him a little over an hour ago. He told her there was a backpack filled with explosives under his bed and a detonator was taped to his wrist, and he demanded to talk with the person in charge of the hospital. I called you instead. Since Larry is charged with Brian being in the hospital, I got in touch with him, and he suggested you might be able to talk him out of doing anything irrational. If you think you could delay it, the extra time would give us time to move all of the patients out of this wing."

"Show me the way, I'll give it a try. There's a chance he will listen to me, but he may not."

"There's something else. We need you to cut the wire to the detonator. Cut the red wire at the base of the detonator, and move the wire aside so it can't touch the end of the other end— otherwise it could detonate. Do you think you could handle that?"

"If my hand isn't shaking too badly, I think I can. I'll do my best to do everything you ask."

"Good, one more thing. I need twenty minutes to move all the patients out of this wing. Do you think you could stall him that long?"

"You are loading me up with a lot to do. If you're done, show me the way."

"Oh, and one more thing—push the call button if you've disarmed the explosives. Brian's room is 671. It's just down the hall. Knock before you enter and identify yourself. A couple of my men tried entering the door, and he threatened to set off the explosives."

"Get me some good coffee with a straw in it. He loves a good cup of coffee."

The nurse left and came back with two cups—one for him and one for Brian.

Cliff reached the door, took a deep breath, and called out Brian's name before entering.

"Brian, I brought you some coffee. We need to talk."

"Cliff, is that you? You brought some coffee."

Brian lifted his head when Cliff entered. Cliff held up a cup of coffee for him.

"Well, I'll be damned if it isn't my kid brother. What do you have there?"

"I brought you some good strong coffee." He removed the lid so his brother could smell it. "I came to visit for a while. It has a straw in it so you can drink it. I met you at the plane, but they had you all drugged up."

"They have me strapped to the bed. I can't move anything but my head and arms. Do you know what's going on?"

Cliff held the coffee closer so Brian could smell it, and then he moved it over so he could taste it.

"What's that in your hand?" Cliff asked.

"It's a detonator. I woke up and it was strapped to my wrist and hand. A man was standing in the shadows near the bathroom door and he gave me instructions. I'm supposed to detonate this backpack if they don't have me in the parking lot by 7:00am. What time is it now?"

"It's 6:45 now. How can you let them control you like that?"

"Beats the hell out of me, but they can. When he strapped this thing onto my wrist he told me what to do and when I'm supposed to do it."

"But I thought only Doctor Ulsheeh could do that."

"Me too, but while I was in Iran they got me to give them a number of formulas I didn't want to give them."

"Brian, what can I do to help you? That's why I'm here, you know."

"What time is it? Give me another sip of that coffee, will you?"

"It's 6:50 now. Why do they want you in the parking lot?"

"They want me back in Iran to finish my project. I need to follow their orders—otherwise they will blow up the whole Middle East with a nuclear bomb, and I can't let that happen. Tell those loggerheads out there I will blow up this whole damn hospital unless they follow my instructions."

"Brian, how do you come up with all of these weird things?

"Bro, you should know what it's all about. They control me with this thing in my brain. These are ruthless people I am dealing with, and I can't help myself. I don't want you to get hurt, so it's best if you would leave now, and not look back."

"Have another swig of this coffee before it gets cold."

Cliff leaned over Brian holding the coffee in one hand and the cutting pliers in the other. He held the cup so Brian couldn't see what he was doing. He cut the wire, threw the coffee aside and pulled the red wire end away from the one he cut.

"What the hell are you doing, Bro?"

"I just disarmed your explosives. I'm trying to save you from yourself. Those Iranians are mostly threats and seldom back their play. We Americans have called their bluff many times in the last twenty years. That's why they are so desperate to steal our secrets. I don't understand why you came out with Molly if you wanted to stay in Iran."

"I promised Special Agent Boller I'd bring the scientists out, and Molly has a convincing way of getting anyone to do what she asks. By the way, how is she?"

Cliff pushed the call button to summon Colonel Colleen and Larry. Then he answered Brian.

"She took a bullet to her hip area and the doctors are having a hard time getting it fixed, but they haven't dented her spirit."

Immediately two men from the bomb squad entered the room and took the backpack out of the room, then untied the device from Brian's hand.

"Let's finish our coffee before the room fills up with people, shall we?" Brian and Cliff laughed together. It was the first time they felt at ease together since all of this nonsense began.

"What's with this strapping me to the bed?"

"There is a bullet lodged near your spine. They are waiting for a spine doctor to remove it, and until then, you'll have to keep still."

"Get me Dad and Marianne on the phone. I want to talk with them—it's been a while."

"Brian, there is something you need to know—Dad passed away some time ago. There was no way I could get in touch with you."

"That's a heavy blow. I hope he didn't suffer too much before he passed. Also, did he leave a note for me or anything?"

"He had a heart attack. He was ready to go because things were getting unmanageable. Marianne arranged a nice funeral, and I buried him right next to Mom."

Larry approached the bed.

"Brian, this is Larry Ross of the CIA. I have been working with him to get you released." Cliff said.

"I guess I've been causing you a lot of problems lately, haven't I?"

Larry laughed. "Yes, you've kept me on my toes; however, it's Molly that's responsible for getting you and the scientists out of Iran."

"She's amazing, isn't she? I still don't know how she found her way through the wilderness in the dark."

"Brian, we've arrested the person that strapped the bomb onto you, but there is something more important I need to discuss with you."

"You're all business. What is it?"

"Donald Sutherland and Jeffery Wilbur are dead. Within the last twenty-four hours they both had massive brain hemorrhages, which we think was set off by the Iranians. Claude Windsor went to a ranch in Montana and we haven't been able to get in touch with him. I'm asking you if you are up to immediate brain surgery to remove the chip Doctor Ulsheeh put in your brain—otherwise you may be subject to the same disaster."

"What next? When I first went to Iran I thought there was a good chance I'd not make it back home. Two of the three guys Molly and I rescued are now dead. It seems like everything we did for them has been lost. Sure, if it will help science, why not? Maybe I can get my life back again."

"Good, we'll leave now and send in the prep team. The operating team is ready for you."

Cliff leaned down and kissed Brian on the forehead.

"Good luck Bro, I'll be waiting for you."

Cliff left the room with a tear in the corner of his eye. His brother had been through so much since his accident. He thought about Brian and his father having a good talk on his birthday night. He went to the waiting room and collapsed on the sofa. It had been a stressful two hours since Hank woke him up in the hotel. Colonel Colleen walked into the waiting room.

"I would like to have you on my team. You performed rather well in there. I wanted to shake your hand because you saved a number of lives this morning. The bomb squad said there was enough explosives in that backpack to destroy this whole wing."

The Colonel reached down and shook Cliff's hand and left a Ranger insignia badge in it.

"What is this?"

"I consider you a Ranger and part of my team. You carried out my orders to the letter—you earned it today." He turned and left.

"Cliff, do you want a cup of coffee?" Hank asked.

"No, I think I'll just rest for a while. Isn't your job with me mostly done?"

"Larry has the say on that. Anyway, I'll stick around for a while. When I'm around you there's never a dull moment."

Cliff laid back and soon fell asleep. It would be a day he would never forget.

27

"Cliff, wake up. You have been sleeping for three hours. Brian is back in intensive care, and you won't be able to see him until tomorrow. Also, Molly was here, and she is being discharged tomorrow. She wants to see you before she leaves. We can go see her when you are ready," Hank said.

"I sure slept. It seems I left myself go. Okay, let's go see Molly now."

They entered Molly's room, and she was busy on her computer.

"What are you doing on that computer?"

"I'm looking for an apartment to rent, and then I'll look for another job."

"You won't have to look for a place to stay. You can stay with me in my father's house. I've decided to buy it and live there. It would be hard for me to live alone in such a big house. I'd love to have you stay with me, and maybe you could share some of your adventure stories with me. You won't need a key to get in because I know you'll find a way."

"Cliff, you're funny. I don't know what to say. I'll be in this wheelchair for a couple of months at least, and then I hope they have a fix so I can start walking again. Okay, you have a houseguest. I promise not to call you Sonny Boy ever again." They both laughed. "Give me a hug, will you?" They both shed a tear.

Molly left the next day for California, and Cliff stayed for another week until Brian completed his brain and spine operations. Then

Cliff brought Brian back home to California. It took Brian another two months before he could walk again. He, Molly, and Cliff stayed in his father's house.

Marianne and Ted threw a welcome home party for them. Everyone came— Anne, Larry Ross, Hank Morrison, Detective Donavan, Special Agents Henry Boller and Agent Salture, Neal Umber. Cliff invited Jo Ann Roxley, the young reporter, to write about it in the local paper.

Cliff, Brian, and Marianne went to the cemetery to visit their parents' gravesite. Being together again was more than Cliff ever envisioned. They talked and laughed about their childhood days and the fracas they caused their parents. Yes, their parents were gone, but the three of them could again be together and live a normal life once more. The hours spent at the cemetery with his brother and sister lifted Cliff's spirits. Good days and a good future lay ahead for the Mercer family. And their family now included a new member— Molly Moonshine.

They all joined Molly when she went to visit Teddy's grave, or was it, Sir Teddy Marshall's gravesite. On occasion Molly shared a few stories about how she and Teddy came out ahead of the bad guys. Brian suggested she write a book about her adventures, but she declined by saying, 'I enjoy reliving those memories myself, and I'm not willing to share them with anyone except family.'

It was time to put the past and all of the stress and trauma far behind them.

Lightning Source UK Ltd.
Milton Keynes UK
UKOW01f2012291016
286372UK00001B/42/P